A little matchmaking mischief…

She's the girl of his dreams, but she belongs to another man. Still, that doesn't stop rock star Brian Ellis from standing by Suzi's side when she needs him most. Or offering her a strong shoulder to lean on when her relationship crashes and burns. But will Brian get burned by the beautiful writer when Suzi goes back to the man she believes she loves?

Suzi has always had a crush on Brian, which doesn't mean she's ready to risk everything for the sake of a fling. Yet the more time she spends with him, helping the sexy single dad with his kids, she knows there's more between them than simmering sensual tension. An invitation to join him in the sweet mountain town of Potterville, West Virginia, may be too tempting to resist. But how can Suzi give her heart when she's already promised herself to another?

Books by Christa Maurice

Drawn to the Rhythm Series
Satellite of Love
Heaven Beside You
Waiting For A Girl Like You
Let Me Be the One

Arden FD Series
Three Alarm Tenant
Struck By Lightning
Spark of Desire

Weaver's Circle Series
Secrets Everybody Knows
Long Memory

One Ring to Rule
Melody Unchained

Published by Kensington Publishing Corporation

Let Me Be the One

A Drawn to the Rhythm Novel

Christa Maurice

LYRICAL PRESS
Kensington Publishing Corp.
www.kensingtonbooks.com

First Electronic Edition: December 2015
eISBN-13: 978-1-61650-556-1
eISBN-10: 1-61650-556-7

First Print Edition: December 2015
ISBN-13: 978-1-61650-970-5
ISBN-10: 1-61650-556-7

Printed in the United States of America

Chapter 1

Suzi wiped sweat off her forehead as she searched the crowd. One would think industry parties would be more fun when the industry was rock and roll. Instead, it felt like everyone was posturing for everyone else. Or maybe she was just too hot and too ill to deal with anything today. Dodging around Nikki Sixx, she spotted Toby chatting with a couple of guys from BroRide, so she headed toward him. She needed to find Logan and go home before she finished her miscarriage. Maybe it wasn't a miscarriage this time. Maybe it was just cramps. Maybe…maybe that spot in the sky was a pig flying overhead.

"Toby, where's Logan?"

"No clue."

Suzi pursed her lips. He answered far too fast. Glancing at the BroRide guys, she rephrased her question. "When was the last time you saw him?"

Toby shrugged. "I dunno."

She closed her eyes. Tears formed along her lashes. This morning she told Logan she wasn't feeling well and she didn't want to hang out long. If he hadn't insisted, she wouldn't have come at all. Of course, it might have helped if she'd told him *why* she didn't want to come.

If Brian were in town, she wouldn't be in this position at all. He'd have taken her back to the hotel or back to his house the minute she'd asked, which would have been as soon as they got here two hours ago. Better, she could have called him last night, and he'd have offered to let her hang out at his place instead of coming to this stupid party at all. Logan would have been okay with that. Logan was always fine with her spending time with Brian.

"Suzi, are you okay?" Duke asked. He put his hand on her shoulder. "You look pale."

"I don't feel well."

"I'll give you a ride home." Toby hooked his arm through hers.

She resisted, pulling away. Toby was nice, and she didn't want to upset him, but she wanted Logan. Her baby's father. "I'd rather find Logan and go home with him."

"Randy Mirandy!" Brett grabbed her from behind and lifted her off the ground. After the last tour, Suzi was prepared for Brett to do about anything, including bite her neck, which he did when he set her back down. She liked him, though. As much as everyone warned her he was a womanizer, he'd always been merely friendly with her.

"Brett, have you seen Logan?" she asked.

"Ten minutes ago he was over by the bar with that hobag Gillian."

Suzi thought she heard Toby, Duke, and Jerry scolding Brett for his advanced case of foot-in-mouth, but their words came from a long distance, as though she was hearing them through a tunnel. The hobag in question was very familiar. Too familiar. She'd gotten herself hooked into the tour through Duke and had worked her way through the opening band and both headline acts. When the tour ended, she had settled in with Brett. Suzi had been so proud of Logan for resisting. She used to think he was the only one who had. Until now.

"Hey, where you going?" Brett asked as she pushed her way around him.

"You know where she's going, you dick," Toby snarled. "Suzi, come on back. We'll get you into the shade, get you a drink. Duke, go find Logan."

Suzi stumbled into someone and her sorry was answered with "not a problem, love." They knew. Every one of them. How far back did it go? How long had they been covering for him? Someone tried to grab her arm, but she shook him off.

Logan stood about ten feet from the bar with his back to her. Around his shoulder, she could see Gillian's bleach-blond hair. He looked great from behind. Shaggy brown hair. Tight ass encased in black jeans with white stitching up the sides. Black shirt with the sleeves cut off to display his tattoos. The rose vines tangling up the left arm. The panther crawling down the right. Which was bent at the elbow.

Because Gillian had his fingers in her mouth.

Suzi's jaw locked, silencing the scream that bubbled up inside her throat. Her legs still worked, though. She spun around and sprinted away, ping-ponging off people and pursued by pounding feet.

"Suzi, stop." Brett seized her shoulders, halting her so fast her feet went out from under her. He pulled her against his chest. "What's the matter?"

Icy pain shot down her thighs. "Logan."

Brett glanced over his shoulder. "Let's get out of here."

* * * *

"Suzi broke up with Logan." Marc squinted at the laptop screen. He had it balanced on his legs, which he had stretched across the hotel hallway.

"What do you mean Suzi broke up with Logan?" Jason asked. He sauntered over and peered at the computer. "Our Suzi?"

"Our Suzi."

Brian leaned out the door of his room. His fingers twitched. What had that idiot done to make her leave him? Where was she? Was she okay?

"Jesus, she didn't just break up with him. She ran out of a party." Jason squatted to get a better view of the screen. "Look at her go."

"What are you watching?" Brian asked.

"YouTube video," Marc said.

"What happened?" Bear walked from down the hall and peered over Marc's other shoulder.

Brian bit the inside of his cheek. They made it easy for him to get info without having to ask.

"According to this, she came running out of the American Music Awards party, got into Brett Cherney's car, and took off."

"Brett Cherney." Brian's teeth clicked as he snapped his mouth shut. Still. Brett Cherney? Suzi—Randy Mirandy—had always been faithful to Logan, no matter how bad he screwed up. Now she was with Brett Cherney who had his furniture cleaned weekly because of bodily fluid?

"Didn't Savitar just finish that tour with BroRide?" Jason asked.

Bear shrugged. "A couple of months ago."

"I'm sure she spent a couple weeks on the road with them. You don't think she and Cherney...?" Jason's lip wrinkled.

"Suzi?" Bear asked. "Nah. Give her credit for a little taste."

Marc tapped at his laptop keyboard and studied the screen. "Man, this must have been ugly. Logan's beating on the car as they're driving away. Whoa. Now he's fighting with Toby and Duke from BroRide."

"Start that again," Bear said.

"Poor Suzi." Jason shook his head.

"You say that like you're sure it was Logan," Marc said.

"Hmm." Jason held out his hands like scales. "Suzi cheating on Logan. Logan screwing up with Suzi." He dropped one hand to the floor and cocked an eyebrow at Marc.

"Just because it's unlikely doesn't mean it's impossible. Maybe she wised up," Marc said.

Brian retreated into his room and pulled out his phone. He didn't want to watch a video of Logan freaking out because he finally found the straw that broke Suzi's heart. And here Brian was on the other side of the world while she was alone. Worse than alone. With Brett Cherney.

To: SuziQ@SuzetteMirandaBazian.com
Subject: Call me.
Suzi,
We're in Japan on tour, but if you need me, just call. You've got the number, don't you? Call the office if you don't. I have a house sitting empty right now. Sandy will give you a set of keys and the security system code. Or I can fly you here if you'd rather, but we're only going to be here about three more days. Or whatever you want. Just let me know. I'm so sorry. Let me know what you need. The other guys are worried about you too.
Brian

He hit send and checked the time. It was the middle of the night in California. Hopefully, she was asleep. He didn't want to think about her sleepless and in pain. He also didn't want to think about her sleepless and with Cherney. Pulling up YouTube, he found the video of her on the front page. It had been posted less than twelve hours ago and already had a couple million hits. At the beginning of the video, she darted out the entrance. Cherney grabbed her by the arms, and she almost went down. The camera jogged as it zoomed in. She was wearing a crimson T-shirt and a black miniskirt but had lost her shoes someplace. Once the zoom settled, he could see her face was pale. Cherney whispered something in her ear, and she clutched him. Cherney picked her up and carried her off camera. The video ended, and the next suggestion was Logan, so he clicked it. This one showed Logan pounding on the trunk of Cherney's car as it peeled out of the parking lot. Duke and Toby had a couple of choice words with Logan that the camera didn't pick up.

Didn't it fucking figure Logan would screw up when Brian wasn't even in the right hemisphere?

* * * *

Shit. *Shit!* Logan threw his phone across the room. Her voicemail was full. With messages from him. He'd driven past Cherney's, but there wasn't anyone home. He'd also tried every one of her old haunts and a couple of Cherney's. No real good reason she'd be in a strip club, but if

Cherney managed to get her drunk…shit, if Cherney managed to get her drunk….

Logan rubbed his hand through his hair. What the fuck had he been thinking? Suzi told him she didn't feel good. He'd only planned to make an appearance. Somebody from one of those bullshit pop bands was telling her how much he liked her books. She was being polite and gracious like she always was. Gillian wanted him to walk with her to the bar. Walk her to the bar? What kind of moron fell for that shit? Logan turned, catching sight of himself in the mirror over the dresser. That kind of moron. He'd avoided that slut for sixteen months on tour just to fuck up once he got home. She wasn't even that hot, but everybody said she was amazing in bed.

Which was just another good reason to stay the fuck away from her. Everyone had gotten some of that. Suzi—Suzi loved him.

Suzi *had* loved him.

He walked across the room and grabbed the phone to dial her number again. The voicemail was still full. Not answering her phone. Not checking her messages. What about her email? Would she check her email?

His phone chimed. He answered without looking. "Suzi?"

"No, fuckhead," Greg snarled. "We looked fucking everywhere. She's gone. Nobody at Cherney's. She isn't at any of her hangouts or any of his or any of the other places we stopped at in between. Jude has called every bookstore in Southern California, and she isn't in any of them. Duke said Brett isn't answering his phone, either. He's probably fucking her brains out right now. You're a dick, you know that?"

Logan bowed his head. He'd rather Greg just came over and pounded on him for a while. Snapping his phone closed, he walked to the mirror. In the reflection, he traced the thin, spidery letters around his neck. Three months after he met her, just before they recorded *Succubus* with Jason and Brian, he'd had her pen name tattooed around his neck like a collar. Suzette Miranda Bazian. She'd been so pleased.

He got it because he wanted her, and everyone else, to know he belonged to her. Her fidelity he'd never doubted. When Touchstone decided to record in England while he was stuck on tour a couple of years ago, he'd been thrilled that they'd invited her to visit. She could go hang out with those guys for a few weeks and drag them to all those weird castles. Even when she told him about the Trivial Pursuit drinking game, he hadn't been worried. That had more to do with trusting the guys in Touchstone than Suzi, though. When she was drunk, she was…

Jesus, what if Cherney got her drunk?

Shit, so what? It didn't matter what she did on her lost weekend as long as she came back.

He crossed the room to the table by the window. He should have just left her at the hotel this morning, or better yet, he should have left her back home in Rochester. Then if he'd wandered off to the bar with Gillian, it wouldn't have mattered. He wouldn't have brought Gillian home.

What Suzi didn't see didn't count.

Oh hell yes, it counted. He wasn't smart enough to get away with cheating on her. She'd figure it out. She was way too good for him. Way too good.

Her laptop sat on the table beside her computer bag. On the other side was the legal pad she used to make notes on her work in progress. Didn't matter where she went, she took her office with her. Any second she might walk in, sit down, and start creating more nightmares.

Please let her walk in, sit down, and start creating more nightmares.

He fired up her computer and opened his email account.

To:SuziQ@SuzetteMirandaBazian.com
Subject: I am really fucking sorry.
Suzi please please please. Just listen. I'm a fuck up. I know that. Give me a chance. I need you. I want you. I love you. Please come home. I don't know what I was thinking. I got stupid. Nothing nothing nothing matters but you. Just please come home.

Chapter 2

Five years ago

Logan parked on the circle in front of the house. Suzi peered out the car window, smoothing down her skirt. She was overdressed. Not for the house. For the crowd. The large ranch house had a vaulted entryway with a second story window. Through the window shone a star-shaped light. Was that supposed to be symbolic?

At least with the house, she fit in perfectly. This could be the set for a nighttime soap opera. The meeting Touchstone part? Not so much. They had been famous when she was little. In high school, the other kids had made fun of her for liking such an old band.

Logan opened the car door and held out his hand, leaving her no other option but to get out. Trapped between equal chances to be overdressed and underdressed, she had opted for a black velvet skirt, a purple mock turtleneck, and black heels, a tried and true first-meet outfit. She had on an unstructured white sweater against the evening chill. Hopefully, nobody would try to take it away inside so she could wrap it around herself like a security blanket. She clutched the bottle of wine in front of her.

Charity slithered out of the car parked behind them. She threw her head back, shaking her long blond hair into position, and started for the door. Greg hooked his arm through hers, glancing over his shoulder at them. Suzi wasn't sure if the look was *hurry up* or *help me*. She voted *help me* because after three months around Charity, that was her own desire.

"You okay?" Logan asked, closing her door.

As good as I can be when I'm in over my head and swimming against the current. She nodded and hoped she could get through the evening without puking on her shoes. The high heels were supposed to make her feel more confident. Instead, she felt like that eight-year-old girl who'd danced around her living room to "Lucky Charmer" with her mother.

At least they didn't make her look like a whore. Charity had overdressed, too, but in the other direction in a fire engine red minidress and matching heels. When Suzi questioned her about the choice, she'd said it was a rock and roll party. Suzi was certain the email had said dinner, not orgy. She hoped she was right. If not, she was going to do more than puke on her shoes.

A car door slammed behind them, and Suzi glanced back. Toby and John had followed in their own cars. She shook her head. Arrival by motorcade was a Los Angeles thing she'd never get used to. Last semester she'd crammed nine friends in her car for a McDonald's run because she was the only one on campus with wheels.

Greg rang the bell, and the door opened. Suzi's vision blurred for a second before she could focus on the man who'd answered. Jason Callisto, guitarist for Touchstone, her favorite band ever.

Jason beamed. In person, his hair was black as sin, and he'd had it trimmed shorter and shaggier than he'd been wearing two years ago. Maybe this was his version of the mommy cut. He and his new wife had just had a baby girl. How old was she? Nine months?

"Good, you made it. You must be Greg." Jason shook Greg's hand. "And this must be your girlfriend."

"I'm Charity!" Charity said, bouncing. "I'm so excited to meet you. I've been a fan of yours forever."

"Thank you. And you're Logan." He held out his hand to Logan.

"Nice to meet you." Logan shook his hand and eased Suzi forward. "This is—"

"*This* is Suzette Miranda Bazian," Jason said.

Suzi watched her hand disappear into Jason's and hoped she wouldn't keel over backward. If she did, Toby was behind her. He'd probably catch her. Jason Callisto knew her name. Her whole name. "It's a pleasure to meet you, Mr. Callisto. Suzette Miranda Bazian is my pen name. Please call me Suzi."

"And you can call me Jason."

She forced a smile. Her mother would just die. "Thank you." She held out the bottle. Charity had told her it was stupid to bring wine, but Suzi's training insisted on a hostess gift, and now she felt dorky. "We brought some wine. I didn't know what we were having, so it's a blush." Hopefully, the plural pronoun would spread the blame.

Jason took the bottle. "Excellent. We'll have to have it with dinner. Come on inside."

Through the foyer, an archway led into a sunken living room. Photoreal paintings hung along the walls, depicting the same mountain valley, sometimes being attacked by dragons or aliens, and once being observed by Bigfoot eating a banana.

"The rest of the party is here," Jason announced, stepping down into the living room. "They brought wine."

Suzi wished she'd stayed in the car. In the trunk.

A curvy redhead stepped forward, holding out her hand to Logan. Dressed in dark-wash jeans, a loose yellow cotton top, and wearing a large yellow sapphire on a chain around her neck, she appeared pleasant and comfortable. "How nice to meet you. I'm Cass, Jason's wife." Jason's wife had the most welcoming smile. If only Suzi could feel something other than sheer panic.

"Now let me see. You're Greg, Logan, Toby, and John."

The guys all shook her hand and tried not to stare. Jason's wife had a brilliance about her. No wonder he'd fallen in love with her.

"And you must be Suzette Miranda Bazian." Cass shook Suzi's hand. Turning to Charity, she frowned. "I'm afraid I don't know your name. I'm terrible with names."

"Charity. It's so nice to meet you."

"Charity." Cass made the name sound outrageous, as if it should have an apostrophe in the middle, or an exclamation point like an African language. "It's nice to meet you. This is Brian Ellis, Touchstone's bassist, and his wife Bonnie." Cass gestured to the other couple in the room.

Bonnie stepped forward first to shake their hands. She was a tall blonde, sleek and beautiful enough to make Suzi want to crawl into a dusty old book. Brian didn't say much of anything, but he didn't need to. He was Brian freaking Ellis. Gorgeous, funny, friendly, cheerful. According to reports on the band's forum, he was even quite gallant at fan meet-ups. His blond hair had a tinge of gold to it in person. Not much, just a touch, and that might have been from the lighting. He wore jeans and a blue button-up shirt, untucked. Bonnie wore black tailored trousers, heels, and a white cowl neck sweater. Every pose she struck appeared practiced. Cass perched on one of the plush burgundy couches, but at the very edge, as if she were interested in the conversation.

Logan sat down on the opposite end of that couch, so Suzi settled beside him. Suzi wished she could take his hand or slip one of hers between his legs, but that might look weird. Instead, she chose to fold her hands on her lap. Maybe it was prim, but it was her best option. Brian sunk into a chair with his long legs crossed in front of him. Bonnie curved seductively into the corner of the opposite couch. Toby sat down next to Bonnie and immediately paled, as though he wished he hadn't. Greg sat next to him with Charity pinned into the corner. Charity arched, throwing her arm along the back of the couch so she could toy with Greg's hair.

"Would anyone like a drink?" Jason asked. Cass jumped up to help him.

After making something for everyone who'd asked, he turned and fixed his gaze on Suzi who had managed to duck him thus far. "Nothing for you, Suzette?" Her name sounded awkward coming from him, more like a form of address than a name.

"I'm sorry, I don't drink, and please, call me Suzi." Her face heated. It sounded so superior and condescending. Or nerdy.

"Tonic water?" Cass suggested. "Cup of coffee? It's a little chilly tonight."

Logan shifted beside her. He probably thought she was being difficult. Suzi would have loved a cup of tea, but that required heating water and messing with tea bags, making her more difficult. They might not even have tea in the house. Five minutes into meeting Touchstone and she was already a disaster. "Tonic water would be fine."

Jason delivered the drink and then sat down beside her.

Suzi clutched the glass as her mouth dried up. She wanted to drink, but she was afraid her shaking hands would spill it. Of course, that would provide her with an excuse to go home and change. Earlier she'd rejected an outfit of dark wash jeans and a green sweater that would have fit in better. Except spilling her drink all over herself would be embarrassing too.

"I just loved your last album," Charity gushed. "'Take It' is one of my favorite songs ever."

"That's off *Chaos*," Suzi corrected softly, focused on her tonic water.

"What's that?" Jason asked, leaning forward.

Suzi cleared her throat and tried to avoid staring into his dark, dark eyes. "I was just reminding Charity that 'Take It' was off *Chaos*."

"I know that," Charity snapped.

Suzi took a sip from her glass and gave Greg a hairy eyeball, pleading mentally for him to say something before Charity opened her mouth again. Unfortunately, he was giving Suzi the same look, and so were Toby and John, leaving her no choice. "I thought *Bayonet Ball* was a really interesting album overall. 'Love Lies Weeping' had a lovely lyrical—com—plex—ity."

Toby, John, and Greg were now staring at her as if she'd grown a horn in the middle of her forehead. She would have smacked herself in the face, but that would have been a lot more noticeable. And she might have impaled her hand on the horn.

"Thank you," Jason said. "That means a lot coming from you."

Suzi peered at him to see if he was joking. If he was, he hid it well. How could he not be? She'd just called his Grammy-winning, platinum album "interesting." Dork, dork, dork.

"We've read your books, of course," Jason told her.

Of course. "I hope they kept you up." As soon as the words were out of her mouth, she wanted to cringe. That had been her automatic response since she'd started getting published until Logan commented that her books kept him *up* in all kinds of ways. Could Jason tell how close she was to hypovolemic shock? All the blood in her body must have rushed to her face.

"Well, I'll go see how dinner is coming." Cass stood, breaking the spell.

"Do you need any help?" Suzi asked.

"No, I've got it." Cass picked up the wine bottle on her way out.

"So Jason, did you get a chance to listen to the demos?" Logan asked.

Suzi leaned against him. He was so getting some tonight for rescuing her. He was going to get some anyway, but she'd have to make it extra rewarding.

"We did. How do you guys like to work in the studio?" Jason asked.

Suzi sipped from her glass, trying to appear interested in the details of recording an album. She hated tonic, but unless she wanted to start drinking, she had to get used to it. She didn't imagine Jason would be too pleased to make her a Shirley Temple, even if she were able to ask for it.

* * * *

"That was fantastic. This is going to be so cool," Greg effused from the phone Logan had hooked onto the dashboard.

Logan glanced at Suzi. Greg's enthusiasm wasn't catching. She was staring out the window. His beautiful, bright Suzi had retreated into a shell before they'd left home, and he'd only seen glimmers of her all night. "Jason has some really good ideas, but he's gonna be a pain in the ass to work with."

"Exactly."

"I'm going shopping with Bonnie Ellis tomorrow," Charity sang.

"This is going to be the big breakthrough, man," Greg said. "This is going to be huge."

"I know." Logan caught Suzi's eye. Maybe she was jealous that Charity nailed a meet-up with Brian Ellis's wife. Suzi didn't like shopping, and Bonnie Ellis had been kind of a bitch all night, but that didn't mean Suzi wasn't down about it. "You got along well with Cass," he said to her.

"She's very nice," Suzi mumbled.

"I can't believe you told Jason you hoped you kept him up." Greg snorted. "I thought I was going to die laughing."

"Jesus Suzi, that was so dirty," Charity howled.

"I didn't mean it that way." Suzi twisted sideways in her seat. "I meant up as in with nightmares."

"But the way you write…" Greg whistled. "Sometimes you keep me *up*. Hey!" A thump had preceded his protest.

"You are gonna be so fucking famous," Charity said. "And then we are going to live in a huge house like that, and I am going to fuck you on every square foot of it." There were kissy noises on the other end of the line. Logan hoped someone was watching the road.

Suzi turned forward, staring out the windshield. "I didn't mean it that way."

"I know, Suzi." Reaching over, he lifted her hand to his lips. She didn't seem happy. Why wasn't she happy? Meeting two-fifths of Touchstone should have made her whole year. When he met her, she'd had a Touchstone poster hanging on the wall of her dorm room above the poster of his band. "It's going to be great. They read your books."

"Yeah. That's good. They didn't say if they liked them."

"He said your compliment meant something because they'd read your books. I think they liked them." The porno sound effects through the phone intensified. Not the soundtrack he needed for this conversation. "Hey, you die in a car crash now, and I'm gonna kill you."

"Fuck you," Greg said. Charity giggled.

"We're home. See you tomorrow." Logan disconnected the line. "Jesus, she's hammered. I'm glad we got out when we did. I think she was working up to hitting on Jason or Brian."

"Would she have?"

"When Charity's drunk enough she'll hit on anyone."

Suzi twisted her hands together in her lap. "I should have told Greg to stop her earlier."

Logan laughed. "Earlier, as in when she got dressed? I can't believe she went there like a total tramp. You looked fantastic, Suzi. You were the most beautiful woman in the place."

"Do you think I annoyed them when I was talking about the album? I was trying to cut Charity off before she said something even dumber than talking about songs from the wrong album."

"You were fine."

"I told them their platinum album was *interesting*." Suzi groaned and covered her face. "Damned with faint praise. I love that album. 'Love Lies Bleeding' is so beautiful it makes my mother cry. Why couldn't I have said that? Lyrical complexity? I sounded like a professor."

"It was good. They weren't mad."

"Oh God, I just about propositioned Jason in front of his wife. You don't think——do you think I caused an argument between Jason and Cass?"

Well, at least she wasn't worried about missing an outing she didn't want to go on with a person she didn't like. He should have guessed she'd be more inventive with her stress. "I don't think so."

"But at dinner he said I was a pretty young thing, and she sounded annoyed." Her sweet face wrinkled with worry.

"I think he said that because you're pretty and you're a lot younger than he is." Logan shook his head. "He's like fifteen years older than you." Though Jason had been watching Suzi a lot... Had his register lowered when he said Suzi was pretty?

Jason could be thinking about trading Cassie in on a younger model, or rather, writer. How was Logan supposed to fight that? *Gee, Suzi, I know you're being wooed by the singer of one of the greatest rock bands in the world, and I'm sure you think he's sexy, but you should stay with me because I'm cute, too*? All Jason had to do was crook his pinky at her, and she'd be gone. What woman in her right mind would pass up the chance to live in that house? With that guy?

And Jason Callisto was what? The fifth guy he'd thought was trying to steal Suzi from him in the past three months? Sixth? Suzi was hot, but every guy in the world couldn't be after her.

Could they?

"I don't think they like me," Suzi muttered.

Logan pulled the car into the garage. It was tiny, so he had to concentrate, which gave him a minute to let that sink in. They didn't like her? How could they not? But if that's what she thought, good. It would make it easier to keep her. "It doesn't matter if they like you. I love you." He reached across the seat and pulled her into his arms. "I can't wait until finals are over, and you can come out to West Virginia with us. I can't stand to be without you." He kissed her, teasing open her mouth.

Suzi melted in his arms. She twisted toward him in the front seat of the car. "Make love to me," she whispered. "Right here. Right now. Let me show you how much I love you."

"Suzi, I know how much you love me every time you look at me." He pulled her skirt up over her hips, relishing the silken softness of her thighs. She'd worn thigh-high stockings to please him. Before they left, she'd treated him to a preview. All night long, the knowledge of those stockings had lingered in the back of his mind.

"You make me feel so good." Unbuttoning his shirt, she kissed his chest as she bared it. "Every time you touch me, it's magic." She pulled his shirt out of his pants, and the friction was tantalizing. "Do you like this?" she asked, swirling her tongue in his belly button.

"I love everything you do." He tangled his fingers in her hair. In the harsh light of the garage, it lay across his skin like suede.

Her fingers worked open his pants, pulling them down. He'd hoped to get inside the house before they got this far, but when she wanted him, she was unstoppable. As if he wanted her to stop. Her hot mouth closed over him, and he shuddered. Every time she touched him was a gift. Her lips and tongue stroked him. "Jesus, Suzi. You're the most amazing woman ever."

"Ever?" she asked, panting. She continued to stroke him with her hand. "What about all those other women?"

"There are no other women." Opening the car door and reclining the seat, he reached for her before she could go down on him again. "No. I want to be buried inside you when I come. I want to feel you wrapped around me." He pulled her shirt over her head and dragged her into his lap so he could reach the clasp of her bra.

She straddled him, sinking onto him. Her body clenched, wringing a groan out of him. He arched up to capture one of her hard nipples between his lips.

"Oh yes." She threw her head back, clutching the headrest for balance as she rode him. "You make me feel so good. I love you. You're the only man I'll ever love."

His climax smashed into him, carrying him along for a few endless moments until it left him beached. Suzi thrust twice more before she cried out and collapsed on him. She lay with her head in the crook of his neck, gasping. Logan stroked her hair. "I love you, Suzi Q," he murmured. "I'm glad you want to come with us to record."

"I'm sorry I'm mucking this up for you," she whispered. Her voice grated on the edge of tears. She hated to cry. If she was that close to tears, she was really upset. "I know how important it is."

"You're not fucking it up." He twisted her hair around his fingers.

"Jason and Brian and their wives all hate me. Jason thinks I'm a little girl."

"He doesn't think you're a little girl."

"He called me a pretty young thing. Isn't that going to make things difficult for you?"

"No. You don't have to hang out at the studio if you're uncomfortable." That would make it a lot harder for Jason to seduce Suzi away from him. Logan could already picture the other man with his deep, golden voice talking to Suzi, luring her away. He could see her in Jason's arms. As if already being married would stop Jason if he decided he wanted her. Jesus, Logan was an idiot for bringing her around the other man at all. The risk was insane. He needed to keep her away from Jason. "I guess they live on the side of a mountain out there. You'll have the great outdoors to explore when you're not writing. And that campground Jason's wife owns. I bet there's stuff to do around there. I bet there's historical things, too. Stuff you like. Civil War battlefields and museums in Washington." She was interested in history. Letting her travel around would keep her out of Jason's range and still make him a hero.

Suzi lifted her head. "You wouldn't mind?"

"No, not at all. Even if you had to stay away overnight." He buried his fingers in her hair. "Just not too many nights. I'd get lonely." He kissed her again, reveling in her hot, sweet mouth. All semester he'd worried that the professor she liked so much would steal her away from him, and he'd stupidly brought her into the territory of a much more threatening rival. Now he had to figure out how to hang onto her.

* * * *

"The guitarist's girlfriend was a high and mighty bitch, wasn't she?" Bonnie took off her earrings and dropped them into her jewelry box. "Did you see how she cut off their singer?"

Brian hung up his coat, wishing he had a good exit from this conversation. He needed time to process the encounter with Suzette Miranda Bazian, but Bonnie hadn't shut up since they left Jason's, working her way up to Ms. Bazian—Suzi. She'd insisted on Suzi. "He'd had four, and Jason had poured all but one of them. You know Jason pours heavy. Greg was probably over his limit."

"But to just grab the glass out of his hand?" Bonnie slammed the top of her jewelry box closed.

"It looked to me like she just took it." In fact, she had intercepted Greg at the bar, talked to him quietly for a minute with her hand on his arm, lifted the glass away from him, and filled it with ice water. Logan had glanced over to see what she was doing but hadn't said anything. None of the other guys had even noticed anything was up, which led him to believe it wasn't unusual.

"You notice she didn't try to cut off Charity." Bonnie raised an eyebrow at him as if that explained everything. Naturally, Bonnie remembered the name of the slutty, stupid one. Charity had gone well over her limit. Suzi had made no effort to stop her, though Brian had seen her pull Greg aside for a moment just before Greg tried. Based on Charity's conniption, he wasn't surprised Suzi hadn't tried herself. "And what about that crap about lyrical complexity? My God, she had her nose so far up Jason's ass with that one her whole head disappeared."

Had she been sucking up? She'd called the album "interesting." He'd thought, and he knew Jason had, too, that it was a backhanded compliment. Jason had gotten that hawk-eyed expression when she said it, but by the time she zeroed in on "Love Lies Weeping," he'd been puffed up and pleased again. Brian unbuttoned his shirt. She couldn't possibly know how much time he and Jason had suffered over those lyrics. Plus, she was a writer. She had to be capable of sucking up a lot better than that. Brian balled up his shirt and stuffed it into the hamper.

"I noticed how she refilled all the men's drinks after dinner, but she never offered to refill mine."

"You hardly touched yours."

"Well, she could have offered."

"She's not the maid. I don't know why you insisted on coming tonight. You didn't even want to be there."

"Please. It's not like we do anything else." As she folded her sweater into a drawer, Bonnie stood in front of the dresser mirror so he could see both sides of her underwear. Some kind of expensive French lace. Made him wonder what Suzette Miranda Bazian wore under her clothes. "You'd be happy to just sit around the house drinking coffee and playing piano all the time. You have to be the most stuffy, boring rock star alive."

Brian pulled on a T-shirt. Bonnie was officially on a tear. She'd ruined dinner for him, and now she wanted to make sure he spent the night miserable, too. He never should have told her how much he liked Ms. Bazian's books.

"Where are you going?" she demanded.

"Music room."

"When are you coming to bed?" she shouted down the hall.

He muttered something that might have been an answer and might have been a growl. He wasn't sure himself, but as long as it shut Bonnie up, it didn't matter. On the way downstairs, he went past the kids' rooms. Bubbie had managed to turn himself upside down on the bed and throw his blanket on the floor. Brian turned the boy around and draped the blanket over him. Then he paused to brush Bubbie's reddish hair off his face and wondered why he didn't enjoy being a father. He'd always assumed he wanted kids, and when they came, he'd be thrilled with them. So far, the kids just seemed like something else he fought with Bonnie about.

Tess blinked when he opened her door. "Hi Daddy."

"Hello, sweetheart."

"Did you and Mommy have fun tonight?"

"Yes," he lied. He didn't remember the last time he'd had fun with Bonnie. Maybe four years ago when Bubbie was conceived. "What did you do?"

"I played a game with Sophie."

Brian brushed his hand through Tess's long blond hair, waiting for the rush he was supposed to feel. It didn't come. Again. Jason was nuts about Andi. All his other friends who'd had kids thought the sun rose for them. Was something wrong with him? "You go back to sleep. You don't want to get me in trouble, do you?"

"Good night, Daddy." Tess closed her eyes.

Brian left the room, wishing he could close his eyes. When Marc had called months ago to say that Suzette Miranda Bazian was dating the guitar player in Savitar, he'd been excited. It was the first time he'd remembered feeling that tingle in years. His wedding day. That was the last time. Marrying a beautiful woman, having a family. He'd anticipated settling into a real adult life. So far, adult life didn't live up to the sales pitch. Marriage had been the biggest disappointment. Marriage and kids. Hollow pantomime. One more thing he had to deal with.

His music room was the best room in the house. Bonnie hadn't let him decorate anything else, but this room was all his. It always felt warm and welcoming. Rich, golden brown walls and crimson carpet. The furniture, in a darker shade of brown, was big and comfortable. He ran his hand over the fuzzy cloth before picking up a guitar, but instead of playing, he set it down and picked up his e-reader from the top of the piano. Lying under it, he had a picture of Logan and Ms. Bazian ripped from *People Magazine*.

When he just had a few pictures to go on, he'd thought she was cute. The photo on her website was posed and formal, but hot. Marc had told Brian he wanted her the first time he saw her picture. Reading her book hadn't diminished that impression. The *People* photo was even better. Her lush lips parted in surprise as she gazed up at Logan who stared possessively into the camera. She'd looked so sweet and touchable in pictures.

In person? Aloof, untouchable, almost arrogant, but at the same time soft and vulnerable. Before dinner she'd been giggling with Greg. Brian would, have given anything to be the focus of that attention. To have those lips whispering in his ear. He'd been tempted to drink too much to see if she would cut him off, but he doubted she would have. He studied the picture, imagining himself in Logan's place. Those bright eyes staring up at him. Tonight, she'd looked at Logan like that, too. Every time her gaze fell on him, her face softened into utter devotion. That's what Brian thought he was getting when he married Bonnie. That rich, lush affection. Maybe that came with a price, too. What was Logan paying?

The phone rang at his elbow. "Hello?"

"Well?" Marc demanded.

"She's coming out to WVA in a couple weeks. Why don't you come see for yourself?"

"Come on, what's she like? He did bring her, didn't he?"

"He brought her." Brian set aside his guitar. "She's kinda…" Amazing? Ethereal? Bewitching? "Ordinary in person."

"Come on, come on. Don't give me that shit. She's got wings or fangs. She doesn't drink…vine." Marc gave his best Bela Lugosi and failed, as usual.

"Well, she doesn't drink. She sounds like the Queen of England when she talks."

"She does?" Marc sounded horrified. "How?"

"She said she thought *Bayonet Ball* was interesting overall, but 'Love Lies Bleeding' had lovely lyrical complexity." Brian winced at his own bad imitation of her elegant tone.

"Ugh. I feel like she patted me on the head and told me I was a good boy." Marc paused. "'Lovely lyrical complexity'?"

"Those were her exact words." Brian tumbled the phrase around in his mind. Lovely lyrical complexity. He recalled her tone as she'd said it. The light, musical quality of her voice. "She was looking at Jason's books, too."

"What books?"

"The books in the living room."

"The ones the decorator stuck there?"

"Yeah." After she'd refilled everyone's drinks, except Bonnie's, she'd wandered to the far side of the room and started leafing through one of the books. Logan had gone over and had a little chat with her. The expression on her face as he touched her cheek made Brian wish he had a camera. Before they went into the dining room to have dinner, Brian had checked to see what she was reading. Keats.

"I've never looked at them. What's he even got?"

"Old stuff like you'd read for school. She had one open."

"So she's a fruit bat intellectual? I'm not sure I want to bother with the side trip to meet her."

"I don't know yet. She's damn sexy in person, and she wasn't even working it."

"I thought you said she was ordinary."

"Ordinary in a sexy way."

"What was she wearing?"

"Just a skirt, a shirt, and some heels. Greg's girlfriend came in all tarted up, but Ms. Bazian looked very glamorous. Enough to piss off Bonnie."

"Bonnie was there? Why?"

"I don't know. Probably to make me miserable. She just wasn't what I expected at all."

"Bonnie?"

"Ms. Bazian. She wants us to call her Suzi. Her real name is Susan Begovich."

"So it's not Suzette Miranda Bazian?"

"No, that's just the name she writes under."

"Oh. But she's hot? For an ordinary girl."

Hot? Tiny and thin with straight brown hair to the middle of her back, deep set exotic eyes, a voice like late summer peaches. "She's hot. I hope she hangs around the studio just for the eye candy." Brian smiled, considering the way she'd filled out her little blouse and skirt. "Legs to there and a lovely swing to her hips."

"Well, maybe we'll have to put tape over her mouth and have her walk for us."

Brian laughed. It was a nice thought to dwell on, but he couldn't imagine her doing it. She'd say, 'Why would I do that?'" in her cultured tone, and that would be the end of it.

"Tell me, were you actually able to talk to her?"

"What do you mean?" Brian wondered if there was a way out of this. Jason had been riding him at dinner about his inability to talk to her. Did he need to listen to Marc, too?

"You didn't. You went all tongue-tied and shy." Marc clucked. "It's so cute."

"Fuck off." Cute. That's what Greg had said over dinner when they were whispering to each other. He'd kissed her cheek and told her she was "so cute." She'd grinned at him and transformed from this untouchable goddess into a delectable woman. Then she'd ruined it by turning to him and giving him a smile straight from lofty Olympus.

"I was trying not to piss off my wife."

"Right. Should I call Jason so he can tell me the truth now?"

"Fuck off."

Marc laughed and hung up. Brian put the phone down and turned on his e-reader. He'd only read everything she'd ever published seven or eight times. What was one more?

And what was he going to do when she arrived at the studio in a few weeks? Stay tongue-tied and shy, or learn how to speak English? He hadn't been this nervous about talking to someone since he met Mick Jagger.

The phone rang again and Brian grabbed it. "Hello?"

"She propositioned me." Jason laughed. Cassie was laughing in the background.

"What?"

"She propositioned me. Remember when we were talking about her books before dinner and she said she hoped they kept me up? Get it? Kept me up?" The phone clattered on the floor. Jason must have dropped it.

Brian chewed his thumbnail. *I hope they kept you up?*

"She went scarlet as soon as she said it," Jason said. "I thought she was having a heart attack. Logan froze, too. Like he knew what she'd meant instead of what she'd said. Cassie figured it out right away. That's why she went to the kitchen. She had to go out back so we wouldn't hear her laughing."

I hope they kept you up. A bubble came up Brian's throat. It took him a second to recognize it as laughter. He lolled his head on the back of the couch and let it roll through him. She'd propositioned Jason right there on the couch in front of his wife and her boyfriend, by accident.

"You think she's shy?" Jason asked.

"How could a woman who writes what she writes be shy?" Brian recalled a couple of scenes from her books and enjoyed a pleasant flush of heat. He'd never read a writer who could be so sexy and terrifying at the same time.

"She doesn't do it in front of an audience. Did you hear her when she refilled our drinks before dinner? She was so soft spoken."

She had gone around to everyone in the room first. Only the light touch of her fingers when she'd rested her hand on his shoulder to catch his attention let him know that she'd finally come to him. Her voice had been soft, but he'd assumed it was because she didn't want to interrupt the conversation.

"And she wasn't exactly dressed to be the center of attention, either."

"I thought she looked nice."

"She did look nice. She just didn't look like she was for sale."

Brian pursed his lips. No, not for sale. Not even available.

"You know what I mean. I was afraid she was going to show up dressed like the other girl and ruin all the ideas I'd had about her."

"You had ideas about her?" Jason was supposed to be blissfully married, not fantasizing about the little writer. Then again, he wasn't supposed to be having fantasies about the little writer, either, and what was he going to be doing as soon as he got off the phone?

"Like you didn't."

"You're a happily married man."

"A happily married man with a wife and a child who are going through some sleep problems, not a dead man. Just remember this is all your fault." Through the line Brian heard Cassie swat him.

"I didn't get Cassie pregnant."

"No, but you talked me into this recording gig. I don't need to be producing other bands."

"But think about how much fun it'll be." Fun. Yeah.

Chapter 3

Present

Suzi tried to focus out the window when Brett pulled into the entryway. She'd been asleep too much of the trip, but sleep was the only refuge she had. This wasn't Brett's house. It wasn't anybody's house. The rambling adobe structure could have been carved out of the desert. A valet in a crisp red and black uniform walked over to open her door as she scanned the surroundings. Not in LA anymore. How long had they been on the road? Somewhere between twenty minutes and six hours.

"I always thought Logan was a total territorial dickhead when it came to you. And the way he was about the groupies. Like he was better than the rest of us. Which he kinda was. But still. That doesn't mean he gets to rub our noses in it." Brett's voice was rough, as if he hadn't stopped talking the entire trip.

The valet opened her door. Suzi kept her mouth shut while they went through the check-in process. No one seemed at all surprised that they had no luggage. The lack of luggage, and Brett's apparent frequent flyer status, got them into a room in record time. The room was Southwestern themed. Water from the hot tub on the balcony cascaded into an infinity pool overlooking the desert.

Suzi stood in front of the mirror over the dresser. The people at the desk were pros. No one had batted an eyelash despite the fact that she looked like she'd escaped from an Alice Cooper road show. She should have invested in waterproof mascara. Did the hotel staff know?

Men screwed up, and women were supposed to forgive them. This wasn't her first miscarriage. It wouldn't be her last. She needed to toughen up already.

She wanted to curl into the fetal position and cry for a week, and she wanted Brian to hold her while she sobbed.

That wasn't an option.

"Why did you bring me here?" she asked.

"You know all those guys are gonna be looking for you. I figured you needed the time away. Nobody knows I come here." Brett wrapped his arms around her shoulders and kissed her forehead. "A little hot tub and a little weed, and you'll be feeling fine."

Weed. All her life she'd been avoiding stuff like that, and what had it gotten her? About now, she could see the allure of heroin. And what was she supposed to wear in the hot tub? Dumb question. She'd left the party with an infamous sex fiend. There were expectations. Plus, sex was great for getting rid of cramps. Might just be cramps.

In the bathroom, she washed her face. She didn't have anything to take off her make-up. The effort to call the desk and ask for something better than soap seemed like too much trouble. All her things were at Logan's hotel room or Logan's house. God, she'd even forgotten her cell in his car.

Wrapped in a thick terrycloth robe, she walked into the room. Brett stood on the balcony staring at the scenery. Thankfully, not naked. Yet. She sat down on the foot of the bed.

Brett heard her and strolled back into the room. "I love it here. It's so peaceful. It's a great place to get away from all that bullshit in town." He sat down beside her. "I'm tellin' ya. A little hot tub. A little swim. A little weed. You'll be back up to normal in no time."

She put her hands on his cheeks and kissed him. His lips parted under her assault, but instead of pulling her closer, he put his hands on her shoulders and pushed.

"Are you sure this is what you want?" he asked.

"No, but it's what you want, and at the moment, I could use the distraction."

"Don't think that I'm not totally game. You are the Holy Grail, but I don't want you doing anything unless you want to." He draped his arm around her like a big brother. "If you want, we can work on some good excuses. Relaxation. Revenge. We could get you drunk. A combination of all three. No one would blame you if you got drunk trying to relax and screwed me to get revenge on Logan."

A killing cramp sliced through her. Suzi doubled over, nearly tumbling off the bed. Brett grabbed her and laid her back on the mattress. Pulling her knees up, she wrapped her arms around them.

"Hey! What's the matter? Oh hell. You're not pregnant, are you? Please tell me you got some bad shrimp or something."

Another cramp cut through her.

"I'm calling an ambulance." Brett reached for the phone.

"No!" Suzi grabbed his arm, gouging her fingers into his flesh. "Don't."

"Why?"

"It doesn't matter. I've never been able to carry one to term." She hugged her knees to her chest. It had felt like this before, too. Only now the world was ending at the same time. Closing her eyes, she focused on the waves of pain emanating from her gut and spreading to the tips of her toes and the ends of her fingers. If she didn't move, she was going to get blood on the bed.

"You need a doctor." Brett pulled away from her.

"No! I don't want a doctor." She crawled off the end of the bed and started for the bathroom. She didn't want a doctor. She wanted her best pal, Brian.

"Where are you going?" Brett abandoned his phone quest to follow her. "Suzi."

"I'm going to need some pads."

Brett thrust out his lower jaw. "If you pass out, I'm calling a doctor."

"Fine." She pushed the door closed.

Chapter 4

Five years ago

Logan set Suzi's suitcase on the floor by the window. His hands were sweating, and his brain still rang with the nightmare he'd woken up from six hours ago. The one where Suzi was sitting on Jason's lap while Jason yelled at him for not being able to play. Logan flexed his fingers. They did work.

And she was not going to sleep with Jason Callisto.

Suzi turned around, her bright eyes warming him. She held out her arms, and he kicked the door closed before he laid her back on the unmade bed, kissing her. She tasted slick and hot. "Oh God, I love you. I dreamed about you every night." He dragged her sweatshirt over her head, tossing it across the room.

Suzi gasped. "You must have been having good dreams."

Logan licked under her breast knowing how much she loved it.

She arched under him, moaning. "Tell me, Logan. Tell me what you were dreaming."

The thought of her sitting in Jason Callisto's lap while the other man played with her hair kept his mouth busy licking down her stomach.

She squealed, writhing as he drove his tongue into the valley at the top of her thigh. "Logan, Logan, I dreamt of you. I dreamt I was sucking you. You were so thick and hot in my mouth, and I could hear you calling out my name. I love the way you taste."

His cock throbbed. He wanted to bury her under him and thrust into her. He yanked down her jeans. Her dark curls were already soaked. The scent of her engulfed him. In his dreams, she'd been naked. Her long white legs hanging over the arm of the chair, crossed at the ankles. She'd had a languorous gleam in her eyes. Sated, but still willing. He spread her open, searching for the perfect rosebud she hid there for him. Only for him. "Tell me more. Tell me what you like," he whispered.

She moaned. "I like this. I like the way your breath feels on me. All you have to do is look at me and I'm wild for you."

He licked her swollen clit.

"Oh!" The corners of the sheets popped off the bed as she pulled them.

He thrust his fingers into her, searching for that magic spot. She bucked against his hand. With his free hand, he shoved down his own jeans. At the airport, she'd been all for slipping into a bathroom for a quickie, but he hadn't wanted to treat her like some groupie slut. Where he had found the self-control, he didn't know.

"Please. I want to feel you inside. When you're inside me, on top of me, the world begins and ends with you. I want to be everything for you."

He climbed over her and paused for a minute to admire the flush on her face, her parted lips, and her glazed eyes. "Suzi," he groaned, driving into her. He pinned her hands above her head, thrusting into her. "I love you, babe. I love you so much. I want to be this close to you all the time. I want to be tangled up in you."

Her legs wrapped around his hips, pulling him as tight as she could. Her words were lost in a blur of moans. He clutched her hands, capturing her mouth in a deep, soul-stealing kiss until he felt her burst apart in his arms. That snapped his control. He growled, thrusting into her hard. She gasped, but ground her hips against his. Her muscles clenched, quivering and milking him for every ounce. "Oh Suzi," he moaned when he could talk again.

"Those must have been some amazing dreams." She ran her fingers through his hair.

Kissing her neck, he shivered with leftover passion. "I just missed you." Every second since he left her at the airport in LA until the moment he picked her up in Pittsburgh, he'd missed her.

"I hate to bring it up, but Greg said you have to go back to the studio, and if we keep laying here, you won't make it."

"Who cares?"

"You do." She lifted his head and kissed him. "And you know it. Come on." Suzi slithered out from under him and started pulling on her clothes, pausing only to throw his jeans at him.

For a couple of seconds, Logan just watched her. What did she like so much about him? If he could figure it out, he could do it more. He knew what he liked about her, and she did it all, all the time. She was smart and sexy and funny and sweet. Everything she did amazed him. Especially staying with him.

"Get up." She pulled a T-shirt over her head and put her hands on her hips. "I am not going to be the reason you didn't get any work done today."

Logan put on his jeans before he stood up to catch her in a tight embrace. Burying his face in her hair, he breathed deeply and prayed he could manage to hang onto her through this trip.

* * * *

"Thank gawd!" Charity threw her arms around Suzi. She'd stormed in the moment Logan left. "This place is so boring. There is nothing to do."

Suzi stared out the window to the valley below. The little town bustled with the height of tourist season. On the way up, she'd gotten a good view of Jason Callisto's house and the surroundings. Trees cloaked the mountain. His house sat in a small valley halfway up the slope. Behind the big house was a smaller building where the recording took place. A waterfall down the face of the mountain behind fed a pool in front of the house. The pool then fed a stream that dropped over the cliff on the valley side, not far from a set of stairs that led down to the guest cabin, which had a small pool beside it, too. The whole mountain was alive with butterflies and wildflowers. Who knew what other critters were hiding in the woods. According to the info Suzi had found on the website for the neighboring campground, there were regular sightseeing tours, craft classes, nature walks, and events.

Yeah, there was nothing to do here.

Suzi hefted her suitcase onto the bed to unpack. Might as well. She was going to be living in this guesthouse for the next three months. Guesthouse. Who had a guesthouse? Nice place, though. The front door opened to a communal living room with a fieldstone fireplace. Three bedrooms opened off the main room, and there was a door to a screened-in porch that ran across the whole back of the house and overlooked the valley. Toby was using the porch as his bedroom because he'd lost the coin toss.

Suzi wondered which rooms the members of Touchstone took when they were here. Did they have regular rooms? Suzi stared at the bed. Where did Brian sleep?

Why was she thinking about that? She'd just had sex with Logan fifteen minutes ago. Sex of the very satisfying, if quick, welcome-home variety. She shouldn't be thinking about where other men slept. And what they might sleep in.

Pajama pants? Boxers?

Nothing?

"...swear Brian never even leaves that building. I've only seen him like twice."

Suzi frowned at Charity. She should have been paying some attention to what the other woman was saying. "Brian's here?"

"Yep." Charity dropped onto the bed. "Brian and Bonnie are on a fast train to Splitsville." Charity had been promoting that theory since her shopping date with Bonnie months ago in LA, but if Brian was here without Bonnie...

"Bonnie isn't here with him?"

"No."

"What about their kids?"

"Home with mom until school lets out. I think the kids are going to be here for a few weeks, but Bonnie said she wouldn't be caught dead here. I don't blame her. Gawd, I hope they don't think we're in-house babysitters. I do not want to be taking care of somebody else's rugrats. Even if they are Brian Ellis's."

Charity might be on to something if Brian was here, Bonnie was there, and the kids were going between. Most of the time when Charity decided somebody was getting a divorce, it was wishful thinking, but this time Charity liked Bonnie Ellis and Brian couldn't be that bad.

Could he? All her life, Suzi had thought he was the most accessible member of the band. Warm smile, bright blue eyes, easy expression.

At dinner last month, he hadn't been so friendly. He'd been silent and distant throughout. During the meal he'd sat across the table from her, glaring. So far, in person, he was a total jerk no matter what his publicity claimed.

"I see the guys are working on their bottle collection." Suzi deposited the last pair of her shorts into the drawer and closed it. She'd glimpsed the row of empty liquor bottles along the front wall as Logan hurried her across the living room.

"Oh, yeah. Did Logan stop on the way home from the airport to stock up?"

"No. Was he supposed to?"

"Yeah, but I'm sure he had other things on his mind." Charity winked at her. Then she stood up and stretched. "I'll do it. It's not like I'm doing anything else. You want to ride along?"

"Sure. Just let me wash up." Suzi left Charity behind in the bedroom. Allowing Charity enough time to dig into Suzi's laptop to find out what she was working on. Charity didn't like to read much, but she loved to know what was going on.

The bathroom was spare and small and looked like four guys and one not-terribly-fussy woman had been living there for over a month. Washing her hands gingerly, Suzi knew what her first project was going to be, though she hadn't checked the kitchen yet. There might be a tie. She ought to head to the house to say hello to Cass since she was her hostess, too.

"I'm going to run up to the house to say hello to Cass," Suzi called. "I'll meet you in the driveway."

"'Kay!" Charity called from Suzi and Logan's bedroom. It shouldn't take her too long to find the current project. Suzi had left it on the desktop of her computer. Maybe Charity was reading it this time.

Suzi scooped her hair into pigtails as she trotted up the steps. Before she reached the front door, she heard raised voices. The voices stopped when she rang the bell. Jason yanked open the door, and Suzi stumbled backward.

"Hello Suzi. Did you need something?" His brow furrowed with serious anger, but his voice was even and calm.

"I was—I came to say hello to Cass." Suzi blinked as her brain jammed. All the manners her upbringing had indoctrinated in her failed with these people. She should have just gone with Charity on the booze run and skipped this.

"She's in the kitchen, but I wouldn't. She's tired," Jason said.

"Maybe later then. We're going into town if you need anything. Charity and I are." Charity and I *are*? Worse and worse.

Jason shook his head. "Thanks, but we're good. Nothing a good nap won't cure."

Suzi stepped back. "I'll let you get back to work then."

"If you need anything, just ask."

Suzi would rather become a mute.

* * * *

Logan studied his hands, trying to figure out why they didn't work. He managed to find the strings, but he couldn't press them down.

"Come on, Fitzpatrick. What are you waiting for? Quit fucking around."

He glared across the studio. Jason Callisto was sitting behind the soundboard with Suzi in his lap. She had her legs draped over one arm of the chair and her head curled on Jason's shoulder. "I'm having trouble with the guitar. Let Greg do his part first."

Jason toyed with Suzi's hair. "No way, kid. You're up. Now quit fucking around and play. You have work to do."

"Logan," Suzi whispered. Her teeth nipped his shoulder. "Wake up, sleepyhead. You have work to do."

Logan grabbed for her, but she jumped away from the bed, giving him a mock evil eye. She was still sweaty from her morning run, dressed in his Nirvana T-shirt and her black shorts.

"Shower quick. I've got eggs, bacon, and oatmeal."

"You went shopping?"

"When we went on the booze run yesterday, I stocked up."

"Suzi, that kitchen is—"

"I cleaned it. Come on."

Of course, she cleaned it. Logan hauled himself out of bed and located clothes. She hadn't even been here a whole day yet and she'd cleaned the kitchen and the bathroom and bought groceries. Not only was she hot, she was civilization in pigtails.

In the kitchen, she was cooking. Toby stood in the door observing and scratching his head.

"What's wrong with Cocoa Puffs?" he asked.

"I never said there was anything wrong with them. Even General Mills says they're only part of a balanced breakfast. Put plates on the table." Suzi pointed to a cupboard.

Logan slipped into the bathroom before Suzi assigned him a chore, too. By the time he dashed through a shower, the whole house smelled like breakfast and everyone was up. He shaved quickly before all the food was gone. As soon as Suzi moved in with him, his house had become ground zero for band meetings because they all knew the food would be good.

"My turn." Toby jumped away from the table with a piece of bacon in his hand.

Suzi walked out of the kitchen with a frying pan in her hands. The pigtails made her look about twelve. Good. He was pretty sure Jason wasn't a pedophile so he wouldn't be interested. The image of her sitting in Jason's lap had stained his brain. He grabbed her around the waist and kissed her.

"Good morning." She laughed.

Logan wolfed down breakfast while the other guys showered. By the time they were all done, Suzi had started to clean up with Charity's reluctant help. Logan kissed Suzi on the cheek before following the other guys out. They walked up the steps together. As commutes went, this one was fantastic.

"I didn't know Charity knew how to wash dishes," John said.

"She's got a professional to supervise her," Greg said, munching on toast. "You guys have fun last night?" he asked Logan.

"Did they!" Toby said. "Tonight I'm making popcorn and watching through the window."

Logan flipped him off and made a mental note to make sure the curtains were closed.

"Are you going to be less of a bastard now that she's here?" John asked.

Logan ignored the question.

"Kind of nice having her around, though." Toby rubbed his chin. "One day, and the bathroom is no longer breeding super germs, the kitchen is functional, and we had breakfast."

"You've got egg on your face." John poked Logan's chin.

Logan wiped his mouth. Living with Suzi had far more than the obvious perks. There had to be a way to make sure he kept getting those perks, even if he didn't deserve them.

* * * *

Brian sipped from his coffee cup, shuffling beside Jason to the studio. The West Virginia refuge wasn't working out as well as he'd hoped. Bonnie had passed pissed-off sometime during the last tour, so he knew his absence wasn't going to make her heart grow fonder, but his presence had only made things worse. Ms. Bazian—Suzi was here now. That was good news. Hopefully, she'd have some free time to talk to him about her books. That other girl who came with Savitar seemed to divide her time evenly between sunbathing and being in the way, but Suzi might be working on another book.

"It's not your fault," Jason said.

"Maybe."

"No maybe about it. Cassie's just tired. Andi's not sleeping again. She was so good about it for so long, and then she got sick, and I never hear her at night. I've had way too much practice sleeping on busses and planes to hear a baby crying at night. Even my own."

Brian glanced at Jason. What the hell was he talking about? Oh, the blow up this morning. "No, I know that. Don't worry about it. I remember this part of the drill. And I did think the dishwasher was full of clean dishes."

"Your girl is here."

"My girl?"

"Suzi. Suzette Miranda Bazian." He poured a heavy accent on the name. "You should try to talk to her. It's not like we all need to be in the studio all the time."

"I'm fine."

"You're fine. You've been analyzing the one time you met her for a month."

"I couldn't think of anything to say." Brian shrugged. He hadn't realized he'd been that obvious.

"How about 'I like your books.' Or 'I gave everyone I know e-readers with all your stories loaded onto them for Christmas last year.' Wait, I know." Jason elbowed him, making his coffee slosh. "Come here you sexy bitch and give me a kiss." He laughed.

Brian raised the coffee cup to throw at Jason and thought better of it. Cassie would be even less pleased about a husband with a concussion than the plate in the sink this morning. The image of Suzi puckering up popped into his mind, and it was going to be a long time before it went away. "That wouldn't go over well with my wife."

"A problem easily disposed of. I'll even pay half the settlement. As much as everybody else hates her, you might be able to take up a collection for the other half." Jason fished in his pocket for the studio keys. "In fact, you might end up with a profit on the deal. I think Tessa would give up a year's salary to the cause."

"What about the kids?"

"That's what the writer is for. You get custody of the kids, and she takes care of them." Jason pushed open the door. "Bonnie goes away, and none of us ever has to see her smug face again. Perfect solution."

The Savitar guys came up the stairs, joking and laughing with a lot more enthusiasm than they had greeted any morning yet. Brian had seen Suzi jogging down the mountain early this morning. Could she have made that much of a difference in one night? Would it wear off, or was it a permanent feature of having her around?

"Logan might object, too," he said

"So? It's her choice. How attached can she be to him? They haven't even been together a year yet."

Brian started the studio coffee pot. Most mornings, it took a few cups before they were up to working, though today might be different. He wasn't sure how he'd ended up in this mess with Bonnie. When he met her, he'd been crazy about her. Too crazy to notice that all she wanted was a wedding ring. He'd wanted to sow wild oats until they fermented, but stability, home, family had sounded so good in the fantasies she'd spun after those endless tours living out of dressing crates and suitcases. They had kids, but there was no sense of family. There was a house, but no home. Stability? Okay, he had stability, but it was more like cement shoes than bedroom slippers.

The door opened, and the guys tumbled in like a bunch of puppies. Brian remembered being like that. So excited about the prospect of making an album that none of them could stand to be out of the studio when the work was going on. Now, when Touchstone made an album, the whole band was hardly ever together. They went into the studio, did their bits, and left. With Jason having his own brand new studio in West Virginia, they'd probably be together less than ever.

"You guys all look on top of it this morning," Jason said.

"Our chief cook and bottle washer is in town." Greg grinned.

"Chief cook and bottle washer?" Jason asked. "Suzi cooks?"

"Cooks?" Greg drew a dramatic breath. "What Suzi does isn't cooking. It's magic. The stuff that comes out of her kitchen is what they serve in heaven when you've been really, really good. The food she describes in her books? She can make all of it from scratch from her head. And this asshole eats it every day." Greg bumped the back of Logan's knee, making him stumble.

"You're just pissed off because Charity can't operate a microwave," Logan muttered.

"Damn right, I am."

Jason arched an eyebrow at Brian before turning to Logan. "So Suzi's a good cook, too? She sounds like a wonder woman."

"Yeah." Logan glared at Jason. "So, we gonna get to work?"

Jason stiffened at the chill in Logan's tone. What had cranked Logan off so much was a mystery, but it wasn't doing anybody any good. Brian figured he had about ten seconds before Jason went to DEFCON 2.

"So you guys ready to jump right in? I'll get everything started up." Brian walked into the other room and started switching the equipment on. Logan had been grinning ear to ear until Jason had started asking questions about Suzi. Had they been fighting last night, too? It was all the rage these days.

The Savitar guys wandered into the room, followed by Jason. Whatever tension had blown up a minute ago was gone. Jason wasn't hanging onto things like he did before he met Cassie, and now that Suzi wasn't the topic of conversation, Logan had calmed down.

Logan and Jason were too much alike in the studio. They'd been butting heads since the first day, but this morning was different. This morning sounded less like a creative difference and more like fighting over a woman, which was weird since Jason wasn't on the market anymore.

Brian poured himself a cup of coffee and sat down at the table. Jason had managed to find the perfect woman by accident. *And what did I do? I attached myself to a woman who acts like I'm bothering her all the time and had two kids, so I can't leave unless I want to lose them.*

If he'd wanted to be a jerk, he'd have emailed Suzi last year when he first started reading her books. Then he could have gotten to her before Logan. He could have been that asshole who left his wife and kids for a much younger woman, and he'd be a lot happier now. Probably, so would they. Bonnie would have his money, or at least a good chunk of it, without the burden of being married to him. The kids wouldn't have to listen to their parents fight all the time. And Suzi? Could he make her happier than Logan did?

Too bad he wasn't going to get the chance to find out.

* * * *

A few days later, Suzi stood outside the studio door and took a deep breath. They weren't monsters. So what if they didn't like her? The disappointment wouldn't be crippling. She'd managed to avoid contact for two days, but she couldn't hide forever. Besides, John had sounded a little stuffy this morning, and she wanted to make sure he was feeling all right. Shifting her grip on the bottle in her left hand, she opened the door with her right.

Marvelous. Brian sat at the table in the little kitchenette nursing a cup of coffee. Was this what he was doing here all the time? Sitting around glowering? He looked up, and Suzi stiffened.

"Where're the guys?" she asked.

"Studio." Brian jabbed a thumb in the direction of the hall.

Jason walked out. "Oh, hey Suzi. What are you doing here?" He refilled his cup.

"Checking on John."

"They're in there fighting about chords. You might want to give them a minute. Are you working on anything?"

"Working?"

Jason raised an eyebrow at her. "Writing a new story? I thought I saw you with your laptop last night."

"Oh, yes—I—yes, I am." *Oh God. Dork alert.*

"What's it about?"

"An incubus." Suzi could feel the blood rushing to her face. He was going to ask what that was, and she was going to have to explain.

"What's that?"

Damn. They were both staring at her. She could not say the words "male sex demon" to them. "It's a kind of demon."

Jason nodded. "Cool."

Suzi fidgeted. Jason had moved on to stare out the window at the house, but Brian was still watching her. She carried the jar over to the counter and found a teacup. After heating up water in the cup, she stirred in a generous spoonful of orange goop from the jar.

"What's that?" Jason leaned over her shoulder, watching her.

Suzi tensed. "It's a reasonable facsimile of citron tea."

"A what?"

"It's close enough. I couldn't find actual citron tea so marmalade will have to do."

"That smells great. Can I have some?"

Suzi bit the inside of her lip. Jason was standing so close she could feel the heat of his body. "If you want." She reached up for more cups. Logan would want some, too. Too bad the cups weren't across the room, giving her an excuse to move. Jason continued leaning over her shoulder, watching her rotate cups of water through the microwave and adding a large spoonful of marmalade to each.

"Suzi, what are you doing here?" Logan demanded.

Suzi turned and gained a few inches from Jason. "John sounded a little off this morning so I went to town to get some tea."

Logan came over to check the cups, and Jason shifted back a step. "I'm glad you came in. I missed you." He kissed her temple.

"I missed you, too." She handed him a cup. "Drink up. I don't want you getting sick, too." She handed another cup to Jason and set one on the table in front of Brian. She should have asked him if he wanted it first, but she couldn't bear to get a grunt for an answer.

Jason took a deep breath of steam before taking a sip. "This is fantastic, isn't it Brian?"

"Yeah." Brian cradled the cup in his hands, letting the steam rise over his face.

Suzi carried the remaining cups down the hall to the others. Wan and breathing through his mouth, John was slouched against the wall. If he'd been this bad at breakfast, she wouldn't have let him leave the house. "John, you look awful."

"You are here. Logan said he thought he heard you," John said.

Greg took the cups out of her hands. He was a little pale, too. Whatever they had, it was going around.

Suzi checked John's temperature and felt the glands in his neck. Swollen, just as she'd suspected. He was in bad shape. "You should be in bed."

"You coming, too?"

"You should be in bed alone."

Jason walked in, followed by Brian and Logan. "All right boys. Back to work."

"John needs to go to bed," Suzi said.

"He's not dying, and we have work to do. You can work through it, can't you John?" Jason asked.

John gave him a thumbs up.

Suzi braced herself. Some battles were worth fighting, and this was one of them. "He could work through it, but he shouldn't. He's got some kind of nasty virus his body isn't prepared for. He needs rest."

"Honey, it's just a cold. It'll pass."

Suzi bristled at the patronizing tone in Jason's voice. "It'll pass sooner if he gets some rest. He can't do any good here, anyway. What he can do is pass his germs around so every one of you gets sick. And then you'll all be down for the duration."

"There's no need to baby him," Jason said. "Sometimes you just have to do the job."

"We don't all have to be here," Logan said, no doubt trying to avert disaster. "And we planned to record guitar, anyway."

Suzi held out her hand. "Come on, John."

"And who made you a doctor?" Jason asked.

Suzi opened her mouth to tell him who made her a doctor, but Brian strolled between them and said, "Don't be a bastard, Ebenezer. We can work around his part. Go back to bed, John. Be here all the earlier the next morning." Then he walked out of the room.

"I am not Scrooge." Jason stomped after him.

"What just happened?" Toby asked.

A Christmas Carol. Brian had just quoted Dickens in her defense. She might just have to fall in love with him for that. "Come on John, let's go." Suzi grabbed John's hand. She wanted to get him out of there while her luck held.

* * * *

Logan had started sweating bullets when he'd walked into the kitchen and saw Jason standing so close to Suzi. It had taken everything in his power not to yank her away. When they'd started fighting about John, he'd been relieved. Now, he wondered if it wasn't sexual tension. When you can't fuck, you fight. Did she want Jason? Did he want her? That was a dumb question. Everybody wanted Suzi. He could see the greed in their eyes the moment they met her. He scraped orange rind into the trash and rinsed his cup. The others were working, but he wanted to see Suzi. Was she still around, or had she run an errand? He'd never hear the end of it if he slipped out to go see her. They already said he was pussy hypnotized.

"Bit of a dynamo, isn't she?" Brian asked.

"A bit."

"She's really talented."

"Yeah." Talented, hot, sweet, innocent. Incredible. Way too good for him. If Jason wanted her, Logan should just get out of the way. Jason could do a lot more for her than he could, and she wouldn't have to deal with his psycho jealous fans.

But he didn't fucking want to. Small moon-shaped bruises on the backs of his hands. She'd latched onto him while they were making love last night and had been horrified when she realized she'd left marks. Suzi was the most magical thing that had ever happened to him. Forming the band, getting a contract, having a hit, touring—nothing compared.

"So she's working on another book."

Logan grinned. "Yeah." In addition to sweet, hot, and incredible, she was talented and industrious.

"What's it about?" Brian leaned on the table.

"A sex demon."

Brian laughed. "A sex demon?"

"Yeah." Logan grinned. Suzi was way too good for him. There had to be a way to keep her.

Chapter 5

Now

Greg stood with him at the car rental place. "That's your great plan? Go home and wait?"

"She's got to come home."

"No, she doesn't."

"All her stuff is there." Logan stuffed his hands in his pockets and hunched his shoulders. He still wished somebody would deck him. If he could've done it himself, he would have by now.

"I'm sure Brett will be happy to buy her new stuff."

Logan ground his teeth. "He can't replace everything."

"I'm sure he's doing a fantastic job replacing you."

"Fuck off."

Greg turned and glared at the door to the service area. Then he jerked back around. "I knew you were going to fuck this up. I knew it."

"Maybe you should have let me in on the secret."

"I did. She did everything for you. Everything. Did that just make it easier for you to walk all over her or something?"

"I can fix it. She didn't see what she thought she saw."

"Um, I saw some groupie sucking your fingers in the middle of a party. What was really happening?" Greg sneered. "Were you just checking her gums to see if her baby teeth were coming in straight? Was Gillian choking, and you were pulling a piece of gristle out of her windpipe? Do tell."

The door opened, and a tech walked in. "The car is in good shape. We found this under the passenger seat." He held out a phone covered in blood-red rhinestones.

"Well, now you know why she isn't answering your calls." Greg flung out his arms. "What a relief to know she isn't screening you."

Logan swung at Greg, but Greg ducked and swept Logan's legs. Logan landed hard on his ass. Before he recovered, Greg had grabbed him by the shirt and pulled him to his feet. For a second, he hoped Greg was going to give him the pummeling he deserved, but then the fury went out of Greg's eyes. He shook Logan, tossed him against the wall, and walked out.

"If you'll just sign here." The tech acted as though nothing had happened. Or as if his customers were always beating the shit out of one another. He handed Logan a clipboard with Suzi's phone balanced on it. The rhinestones were a joke. He'd put them on it for her so she wouldn't lose it.

She'd lost it, anyway.

She'd looked pale and waxy that morning as if she was gonna puke. But the whole point of coming out to California this week had been that stupid party so he could promote the new album. No pockets for her phone in her little denim miniskirt, and she hadn't carried a purse, so she must have left it in the car. If she didn't have her phone, then she didn't have any money or ID either.

She had to come back for that stuff.

Logan took his copy and walked out to Greg's car.

"And you still think she's going to come home." Greg started the engine.

"She doesn't have any ID or money. She has to."

"How is she going to fly back to Rochester without ID?"

"Then she'll go to your house and you'll—"

"Hold her prisoner until you come? Not bloody likely. I'm thinking if I find her first, I'm gonna help her get her shit back and keep you away from her."

"That's what friends are for," Logan muttered.

"And I'm beginning to think I'd rather be her friend than yours."

* * * *

"She's not answering her phone and her voicemail's full," Jason reported. "You email her?"

"I did yesterday, but she didn't answer." Brian picked up his bass. His brain no longer felt like a hopped-up hamster on an exercise wheel. Now, it felt like two hopped-up hamsters on the same exercise wheel. If he didn't hear from Suzi soon, a third one was downing a six pack of Red Bull in preparation to join the first two.

"Marc didn't get an answer either. Cassie's freaking. She wants to hire detectives to hunt her down."

"Cassie's a little overprotective." Private detectives. That wasn't a half bad idea.

"I told her to hold off until we get home. You think she's still with Cherney?"

Brian shrugged. He'd been trying not to think about that.

Bear strolled over, twirling a drumstick through his fingers. "I talked to Logan."

"What did he say?" Jason asked.

Brian stared at a seam in the stage. After the show tonight, they went home. With the sixteen-hour time difference, they'd be landing about four hours before they took off. Add in time to recover from jet lag, and it was going to be at least two days before he could seriously start searching for her. The kids. He got the kids when he went home, too. Bonnie would dump them with him at the airport if she could. Of course, the kids liked Suzi, so they'd be all for helping him search.

"He said some groupie stuck his fingers in her mouth and that's when Suzi walked up and saw it and it was just bad timing and there was nothing to it and he's sorry and do I know where she is because he's sure she'll contact one of us because she doesn't have any ID or her phone or anything on her," Bear said.

"In one breath?" Jason asked. "Poor guy."

"Yeah, I hate it when strange girls stick my fingers in their mouths." Brian rolled his eyes. "And that shit just happens to him all the time."

Bear and Jason both stared at him as if he'd slipped a gear. "How many times has Logan been caught in a tight spot like that?" Brian demanded.

Jason shrugged. "It happens."

"You know who she caught him with, don't you? Gillian Blue Sky."

"Gillian?" Bear dropped his drumstick. "You're kidding. Who told you that?"

"Yes Brian, who told you that?" Jason narrowed his eyes at Brian.

"I got an email from Duke." Of the thirty or so he'd sent out. Some of the people he'd tried hadn't been at the party. Hell, SendDown was touring Europe. They hadn't even heard and asked him for information.

"And?" Bear scooped up his stick. "Don't hold out."

"He just said Suzi wasn't feeling good and went hunting for Logan and found him with Gillian. I'm a little disappointed in his taste. Gillian's a skanky whore, and he had Suzi at home." *Had* being the operative word.

"True, but Bear would know more about that than I would." Jason smirked at Bear.

Bear pointed his drumstick at Jason. "That was a long time ago, and she wasn't as skanky then. I am a happily married man now, and I don't need those kind of petty distractions."

"Are we done here?" Brian scowled. Standing around yammering wasn't the best use of his time. He needed to get back online and check his email. There might have been new developments, or Suzi might have returned one of the half dozen emails he'd sent since the day before yesterday.

"I'm not surprised she ran out without ID or anything." Jason started strumming randomly. "She's known for that."

"Yeah, but she ran with Brett Cherney. If you want to talk about questionable taste." Bear made a wobbly hand gesture.

Brian walked away. If they weren't done with sound check, they could come find him. He had better things to do than stand around rehashing Suzi and Logan's break-up. None of his friends were thinking about Suzi with Brett Cherney, who was twenty-four, at the beginning of what appeared to be a long-running career, and carried a reputation for being wild. Brian didn't want to think about that.

Ditching his bass in the rack, Brian headed down to the dressing room, surprising the caterers in the act of setting up. They bowed, giggling. He bowed back. They bowed again. He decided it was a losing battle and grabbed his laptop off the coffee table. Suzi lived most of her life online. For her to be off for more than twenty-four hours was unthinkable.

But nothing was updated. Not Facebook. Not Twitter. Not her blog or her website. All of them had comments from her friends and fans asking where she was and if she was okay. Checking to make sure no one could see him, he logged onto the writing forum she belonged to. There was a thread at the top that already spanned several pages, but no one had heard anything. He logged off and erased the history. Following Suzi to her forum always made him feel like a stalker. Dipping into Savitar's forum, he found a discussion raging about her there, too. Not as nice as the one on her writing forum. The girls there were all singing "Ding Dong The Witch Is Dead" and making guesses about whether or not she'd died, gone into rehab, or been committed. Suzi deserved to be committed for leaving Logan, they had decided. He logged out before he posted something unfortunate. The Touchstone forum had a mention of her. They'd tossed around a few rumors, but most were nicer, less invested, and talked about her books and times she'd been sighted with the band. A couple had posted pictures of her with Touchstone, but he already had those squirreled away on his hard drive. They did reveal that Cherney hadn't been seen around either. Wherever Suzi had gone to ground, Cherney had gone with her.

Chapter 6

Five years ago

Logan shook his hand, trying to make it work. His fingers flapped like ribbons.

"Come on, Fitzpatrick. What are you waiting for? Quit fucking around."

He peered through the studio window. Jason was sitting at the soundboard and Suzi was naked on his lap. She had her legs draped over one arm of the chair, her head curled on Jason's shoulder, and was teasing her hand through Jason's chest hair.

"I'm having trouble with the guitar. Let Greg do his part first," Logan snapped. He shook his hand again, and his fingers tangled together.

"No way, buddy. You're up. Now quit fucking around and play. You have work to do." Jason lifted Suzi's face to his and kissed her. Suzi responded eagerly. She buried her hand in his hair.

Logan tore his gaze away from the spectacle to stare at his fingers. They'd knotted together. He looked back at the pair on the chair. Jason was sucking Suzi's pink nipples, his eyes closed in appreciation. Suzi had her head thrown back. Through the com, he could hear her moaning, "Oh Jason, you're so good. I had no idea."

* * * *

Logan balanced his beer on his knee and stared at the trees. Trees. What the fuck? He was a city boy. What was he doing here? Suzi loved it, though. Every morning for the past two weeks, she'd gone out for her run and spent her afternoons exploring the woods. Not much else for her to do, but she didn't seem to mind. She was still convinced Jason and Brian didn't like her, so she stayed away from the studio.

John and Toby had driven up to Pittsburgh for the night. Charity had flown back to LA. The backwoods charm didn't work for her. Cassie had taken the baby down to visit her parents overnight. Logan and Greg had seized the opportunity to hang out with their heroes.

Even if he was having nightmares about one of his heroes screwing his girlfriend.

"Where's your girl tonight?" Jason asked.

Woman-stealing bastard. "Out communing with the trees, probably."

"Trees?" Jason paused with his beer bottle halfway to his mouth.

"She likes to go walking in the woods. She grew up out in the sticks." A cornfield. That's what was across the street from her parents' house. That's all he remembered from the day he helped her pack her stuff so she could move to LA with him. Right after her father had told her if she left, she couldn't come home.

"She wrote that one about the woods," Brian said. "*Bats With Baby Faces*. Is she still working on the one about the sex demon? I keep seeing her with her computer."

"She finished it the other day. She said something about wanting to do a romance."

"Romance!" Brian made a face. "I think I'll skip that one."

"Unless it's going to be one of those dirty ones." Jason leaned across the table. "Those aren't all bad. And if she wrote it, it would be hot. She's a scorching lady. I wish I'd met her before you. I wouldn't have minded taking her for a turn."

"Cassie might object," Brian pointed out.

"Well obviously before Cassie." Jason leaned back in his chair, smiling. "She has a shotgun."

"And after Stella."

"Shut up."

Logan studied the tabletop. Would a wife really keep Jason away from Suzi if he decided he wanted her? Cassie might be flexible about that kind of stuff, and Jason sure as hell could do more for Suzi's career than Logan could. Jason could single-handedly finance one of those little indie film projects her friends wanted to make of her books.

"Wouldn't have happened." Greg announced. "She was a virgin when she met Logan."

Brian shook his head. "I've read her books. She couldn't have been."

"She was," Logan said. There had to be a way to get out of this conversation. With any other woman, he'd have bragged about taking her virginity and the sex life they'd had since. Suzi was making up for twenty years of virginity with zeal, but it felt wrong to brag about her.

"You should have seen his back that first morning. Looked like he'd been in a fight with a tiger." Greg took a deep draft of the dark European beer Jason stocked and immediately regretted it by the expression on his face. Logan regretted that Greg hadn't taken a drink before he'd opened his big mouth.

"She's really smart, too. And funny," Logan said. If they'd asked him to list the reasons he was with her, sex would have been near the bottom. Yeah, the sex was incredible, but so was everything else.

"Too bad she doesn't hang out much," Brian said. "I'd love to get to know her."

"In the biblical sense," Jason added. He pulled another bottle out of the cooler beside him. His fourth. "You would. Not me. My wife has a shotgun. Yours just has the Visa."

"No, I'd just like to talk to her. I love her books. They're like puzzles. I've read a couple of them three or four times and figured out new things every time."

Jason snorted. "You'll just get tongue-tied like you did when we met Paul McCartney."

"Yeah, because you've done such a great job talking to her," Brian snapped.

Greg raised one eyebrow at Logan. Logan was too busy reeling with the idea to respond. Savitar had been here for six weeks, awed to be working with their heroes. Since Suzi arrived two weeks ago, she'd been too nervous to talk to Jason and Brian much because she'd been a fan of them since she was a little kid. Logan had assumed the idol worship only went one way. But if they had her on the same level with Paul McCartney…

"Not to piss you off, Logan, but your girl is the only one I want to curl up with that my wife will let me, if you know what I mean." Jason winked and glanced away.

"Some of her books are hot," Brian said, staring at his bottle and beginning to blush. "Nothing dirty in 'em, but sometimes…wow."

"She wrote Logan a porno," Greg said.

Jason focused on Logan. Brian peered into his bottle, blushing harder.

"It was…nothing," Logan said helplessly. He didn't think Suzi would be happy to know he was talking about her like this. But Suzi was probably on the other side of the mountain. She didn't need to know.

"Nothing! Shit man, it was hot. It's the next book, isn't it? The one she just finished?" Greg seemed to have scented the advantage, too.

"So she's just as hot as she seems," Jason encouraged.

Logan remembered idolizing these guys when *Trigger Finger* came out. He'd wanted to be them. He'd tried to duplicate their stage clothes and worn their tour T-shirt until it fell apart. When Savitar's first album came out, he'd wanted to impress them. He still did. It was like being back in high school, trying to get in with the cool guys. If he couldn't do it with his music, then he sure could with his girlfriend. "In bed, Suzi is a demon. In bed, on the floor, against the wall. Anyplace we can get a little leverage." He grinned. Then he saw Greg's eyes flicker over his head.

Logan turned around to his worst nightmare. Suzi stood three feet behind his chair, frozen in mid-step, face pale against her dark hair. A smile still melting off her face. "Hey sugar," he croaked.

The words brought her back to life. She spun around and sprinted toward the woods. Logan lunged after her. If they thought he was whipped, then fine. He could handle being whipped by Suzi. A tree branch slashed him across the face.

For a small chick, she was fast. All that jogging was paying off. She was halfway up the trail before his eyes had adjusted to the darkness. He set off after her at a flat run, watching in amazement as she vaulted a downed tree. How did she move so fast? And where the hell did she plan to go? Jumping over the tree, he caught up to her. He grabbed her arm, only hoping to stop her, but she swung around and slapped him so hard his eyes watered.

"How dare you?" she snarled.

"Look, I was stupid. I didn't mean—"

"You were discussing our sex life with strangers."

"They're not really strangers, and I wasn't discussing—"

"How am I supposed to trust you now?"

She hadn't raised her voice, and she didn't sound as if she was about to cry. Relief accompanied that realization, but guilt followed the relief. He hated when women cried. "I'm sorry. I knew I shouldn't say anything, but I didn't think you'd ever know."

"And that makes it okay?"

"Well, no, but it's just the way guys talk."

Suzi bared her teeth, sucking a breath through them, making her face an unnaturally ugly mask. Then she closed her eyes. All the expression melted away. Somehow, that was worse than the fury. "I'm going home."

"You're leaving me?" Logan asked. She couldn't leave him. He needed her too much to let her go now.

"No, I'm going back to the guest house." She scowled at him. "Where else would I go?"

"Home to LA?"

"That's your house."

"But it's yours, too."

"Ms. Bazian!"

Logan turned to the voice. Jason was jogging along the path. A few paces behind him were Brian and Greg. He wanted them all to go away. He needed to talk to Suzi alone. There was something seriously weird happening in this conversation, and he needed to figure out what so he could fix it.

"It's my fault, Ms. Bazian," Jason said. "I am a total fucking jerk."

"It's all right," Suzi said coolly. "I shouldn't have shown up uninvited."

"But you're always welcome, Ms. Bazian," Brian said.

She put up a placating hand and backed up a step. "Please, call me Suzi."

"Come on back, Suzi. We'll get you a drink." Greg reached out as if to put his arm around her shoulders, but stopped short. Even he could sense the glacial chill surrounding her.

"Thank you, no. I'm going to take a walk. Good night." She turned and walked away.

"Sorry man," Jason muttered. "Thought I could make it better. Come on back. You can sleep at my house tonight."

"No. I think I better talk to her. Thanks." Logan touched his cheek, which was now stinging. Her nails had scratched when she slapped him. He started up the mountain after her. Up the mountain. She couldn't have picked a nice walk around. No. Up.

"Suzi…sugar, if I knew how much it was going to hurt you, I wouldn't have said anything." Liar. He'd known, and he'd said, anyway. He'd just thought he could get away with it. *Note to self: you can't get away with it, whatever it is.*

"It doesn't matter."

"Suzi." He caught up to her, but she veered off the path, crunching through fallen sticks and last year's leaves. "Sugar, please listen to me."

"It doesn't matter. You've already apologized and been forgiven."

"I don't feel forgiven."

She leaned against a tree. "Then maybe you have more guilt than I can forgive. I can't leave you. Isn't that enough?"

"What do you mean you can't leave me?"

"I'm here. I picked you. I abandoned everything for you. I have nowhere else to go."

"That doesn't make any sense."

"I moved out of my parents' house and stopped speaking to them because of you. I transferred to UCLA to be with you. I gave up everything I knew for you, and all you can do is brag to your friends about what a good lay I am."

"It was a mistake. You didn't hear the whole conversation." Hopefully.

"Suzi is a demon in bed. In bed, on the floor, anywhere we can get a little leverage."

"They wanted to know what you were like. They were asking me questions."

"So you told them I was a nymphomaniac?"

Logan scratched his head. This tack was not working. "They like you Suzi."

"I'm sure they do."

"No, I'm serious. They were talking about you like you're Paul McCartney. Brian's been trying to figure out what to say to you."

She frowned and dropped her gaze to the ground. "Don't tease me."

Logan stepped forward and cupped her cheek. She didn't deck him, so he thought he might have a chance. "I'm not."

"They always act so strange when I stop in. Brian Ellis hasn't said ten words to me the entire time."

"He said he's read your books three times."

She stared up through her lashes. "He has?"

"Or more. He mentioned the one about bats."

"*Bats With Baby Faces?*"

He eased closer, letting his body brush along hers. Sex always worked with her. If he could just keep her drugged with sex, he'd be able to hang onto her. "Yeah, *Bats With Baby Faces*. They really like you and I was—I was trying to impress them with the fact that you like me. You missed the part where I was telling them how smart and funny you are." Logan kissed the corner of her mouth. Telling her they liked her books meant she'd be more likely to hang around the studio. It was a risk he had to take. "I'm sorry. I just wanted to brag about my sugar a little. You're just so great. So smart and beautiful and hot."

Suzi turned into his lips. "You told them I was smart and funny?"

"They can see that you're beautiful."

She was going to forgive him. He was going to pull this one out of the fire. Logan slipped his hand under her shirt to cup her breast. "Come on, sugar. Let's go back to the cabin, and I'll show you how sorry I am. Unless you want me to show you right now."

"Right now?" Her eyes were hazy.

"Yes, right now." He licked her lips and unbuttoned her jeans with his free hand. His fingers strayed inside the waistband, touching the soft skin of her belly. "You are beautiful and smart and talented. Every man in the world wants to take you away from me."

"I only want you." Suzi laced her fingers through his hair as she kicked away her jeans.

Logan fumbled with his own zipper. Every time he was with her, everything went out the window. All he ever wanted to do was drown in her. "I'm supposed to be begging your forgiveness."

"I'll always forgive you, Logan." She hoisted herself up his body, shoving his jeans down with her feet.

"Always?" He buried himself inside her. She was hot and rich. Her mouth closed over his, stealing his breath. She would always forgive him. Always.

* * * *

Suzi clutched Logan's hand as they walked up the stairs and across the lawn to the studio. Greg trailed behind them like some kind of warped honor guard. According to Logan, Greg had done his fair share of defaming her the previous night, and she hadn't decided yet how to cope with that. The kitchen door opened, and Jason and Brian walked out, followed by the sound of a screaming baby. Jason was on the phone, but gave her a bright smile. "No, I understand. It's just, Cassie needs a break, and her mom and dad were up with her all night, too."

Brian changed direction and headed for them. "You're still here," he said. His blue eyes were brighter than she'd ever seen and his fingers were tapping out a nervous rhythm on his jeans leg. Ordinary Levi's, Buckcherry T-shirt. No showing off in his wardrobe, but the way the fabric stretched across his body drew her eyes.

He couldn't possibly have been that concerned about her and Logan's fight last night. She was just the girlfriend of the guitarist in an up-and-coming band. Unless he was as nice as she'd assumed from his press.

"Yes."

Jason hung up his phone and joined them.

"You looked mad last night," Brian said. "We thought you might catch the first flight out."

Suzi glanced at Logan. He'd been certain about that, too, but she still had no idea where he thought she was going to go. After they'd had sex, they'd gone back to the cabin, walking through the woods to avoid being seen. Then they'd spent all night clinging to one another. "No. Is something wrong?"

"Andi's sick again, and she's keeping Cassie up."

"Maybe I can help." Hopefully. Suzi crossed her fingers behind her back. "I'm good with babies." She'd been trying to find a way to chat with Cassie since she'd arrived but hadn't found the opportunity. Logan kept telling her not to worry about it. Cassie was in her hometown with her baby. She was busy. The one time Suzi had said hello, Cassie had been strapping Andi into a baby seat on her way out.

"Can't hurt to try," Jason said. "She's in the kitchen."

"I'll tag along," Brian said.

"You will?" Jason took a step backward. "I mean, have at it. More power to ya."

Logan kissed her cheek. "Have fun, babe."

Suzi headed to the house with Brian trailing behind her while the others headed toward the studio. As she reached up to knock at the door, Brian leaned around her and opened it. Cass sat at the table with her head in her hands listening to Andi wail. She glanced up as the door opened.

"I'm sorry. This is not a good time," Cass said. "I have my hands full."

"I came to see if I could help." Suzi stepped inside the door and stopped. Brian crowded behind her, causing an awkward flutter in her belly. Either he was following her or he wanted to spend more time with the unhappy baby.

"Unless you have some kind of magic spell to put babies to sleep, I doubt you can do anything."

Suzi walked over to the high chair and studied the baby. Andi was red faced and sweaty from crying. "Jason said she'd been sick."

"She was over it before we flew out here, but now her sleep schedule is screwed up again from the time change, and she hates to sleep, anyway." Cass sat with her chin resting in her palm. Brian had taken a seat opposite the high chair and sat with his long legs stretched out in front of him and his arms folded.

A challenge. One she had a fifty percent chance of losing. She never should have put herself in this position. She unstrapped the baby and checked her diaper. Clean.

"I just changed her," Cass said.

"I figured, but it never hurts to check the obvious, right?" Suzi set Andi on the floor in the hopes that she just wanted to be free range. That worked some of the time. Andi waddled around the room, still crying, but not stopping anywhere. Poor kid looked like she was lost at the county fair. Suzi picked her up and walked around the room humming tonelessly.

Andi started to scream louder. Suzi turned her around so she could see her mother. That reduced the screaming, but didn't stop it.

"Maybe I should just take her." Cassie started to stand.

"Let me try one more thing." Suzi pondered. She had a couple more tricks. Which one had the best chance of working? After sitting at the table with Andi on her knee facing her mother, Suzi leaned back on the chair and rested Andi against her. Andi reduced to sniffling.

"She's been inconsolable for days." Cass rubbed her hand through her red curls. "The only time she stops crying is when she's asleep. I don't know how Jason sleeps through it."

"Practice," Brian said. He still had no good reason to be here. Putting fussy babies to sleep was a neat trick, but it couldn't be that interesting. Not when there was music being made fifty feet away.

Andi's sniffles subsided to the occasional hitch in breathing.

"I'm sorry I haven't had a chance to talk to you," Cassie said. "I didn't mean to be rude. I've just been very busy."

"I understand." Suzi brushed Andi's dark hair off her face.

"I've read all your books. I can't believe how many you've published, in what? Two years? That's amazing."

"Most of them are novellas. It doesn't take nearly as long to write and edit a thirty thousand word manuscript as it does a ninety thousand word book."

"I guess not. You pack a lot of action into a little space, though. I always feel like I've read a full-length novel when I finish one of yours. Are you going to write any real books?"

Suzi blew her bangs off her forehead. Someday, she was going to get over being asked that question. Her books were real. They were just electronic. "I have an agent talking to traditional publishers about print rights."

"How interesting. I'd never heard of you until this last Christmas when Brian gave me an e-reader with all your books on it."

All? Suzi stole a glance at Brian, but he was wearing a poker face. "Are you enjoying the e-reader?"

"It's handy. A lot easier to lug around airports. I know Maureen is never without hers."

"Maureen?"

"Bear's wife. Oh my God, I think she's asleep."

Andi had begun to loll forward. Suzi adjusted her grip to keep hold of the baby who was now intent on slithering out of her grasp.

"Do you want me to take her? You look hot." Cass didn't hold out her hands and sounded a little resigned to taking the child. Suzi didn't blame her. Holding the baby was like hanging out in an oven, and poor Cass had already been roasting for a couple of days.

"Let's give her a minute to set hard." Suzi snuck a peek at Brian. He was watching her hold the baby with a blank expression that gave her no clue as to why he was hanging around. Logan said he'd been trying to talk to her. He might have decided this was his chance.

"Set hard?" Cass asked.

"That's what we used to say at the day care when we were trying to put a kid to sleep or they wouldn't wake up after naptime."

"I didn't realize you worked at a day care."

She grinned. "It's not exactly something I have in my bio on my website."

"No, I guess not." Cass put her elbows on the table and rested her face in her hands. "I'm so tired."

"It's hard when they don't want to sleep." Suzi cuddled Andi close. It had been a long time since she'd had a baby in her arms. She hadn't realized how much she missed it. "At the day care, they always said I had the sleep touch. They would put me in the infant room at naptime to put out the ones who didn't want to sleep. Then I had a couple of hours to sit and plot stories while the babies slept."

Cassie's head slipped sideways. Her eyes were closed and her breathing deep and even.

"She's asleep," Suzi said to Brian.

"I know. I'm impressed. That kid hasn't slept for more than ten minutes at a time for weeks."

"I mean Cass."

Brian leaned forward to get a good look at Cassie. "Wow, you do have the sleep touch."

"I guess we should have moved to the living room." Suzi studied Cass. She was going to wake up with an incredible crick in her neck.

"No problem." Brian shook Cassie's shoulder. Suzi cringed. She hadn't intended for him to wake Cassie up. The poor woman obviously needed her sleep. "Come on, Cassie, let's change venue."

"What?" Cass asked. "Were you saying something?"

"Why don't we go to the living room?" Suzi said before Brian could speak. "Then we can lay the baby down for a real nap."

"Good idea. I can't believe you got her to sleep." Cass stood up and swayed for a second. Brian stood behind her with his hands out as if he expected to have to catch her. Cass didn't even notice as she wove drunkenly toward the door.

Suzi had seen the living room through the window, but she'd never been inside. They had the same lush burgundy furniture here as they did at their house in LA, but the floors here were hardwood. The fireplace looked about the same, too. In the middle of the floor was a huge woven rug with a coffee table in the center, and to the left of the fireplace, a playpen where Suzi carried Andi. The baby was now deep asleep and lolled like a rag doll when Suzi laid her down.

Cass sat down on the couch. "Do you have any books coming out soon?" She yawned. "Excuse me."

"I have another one coming out next month." Suzi moved away from the baby reluctantly. Comfortable house, husband, baby. Was she even on that track? She'd never talked to Logan about kids. He was happy to provide the house, but marriage? Kids? He'd been anxious about leaving his shot glass collection behind when he came out here.

"What's it about?" Brian had settled into a chair near the floor to ceiling windows. His eyes were bright as he waited for her answer.

The last time she did a reading at a bookstore she'd been in less of a spotlight. "It's about a woman accused of murdering her boyfriends."

"That sounds interesting."

Interesting? It sounded awful, but this was why her publisher had a marketing team to make up hookier blurbs than she could. "It was fun to write."

"Logan said something about you writing a romance now," Brian said.

"When my editor read this one that's coming out, she said I should try romance, so I decided to give it a shot. It's different."

"How?" Brian shifted to the edge of his seat and leaned forward.

Suzi struggled to sum up the months of research she'd done on the new genre in a few pithy statements, but had about as much luck doing that as she'd had summing up her next release. "The focus is different. It's the same as the difference between the music you play and disco."

He nodded.

Suzi glanced at Cass. The other woman was asleep again, slumped sideways in the corner of the couch. No rescue from that direction. Being alone with Brian was giving her the shivers. Years of admiring his pictures collided with the awareness that he smelled heavenly, like leather and clove. The two-dimensional image becoming a three-dimensional man. That golden glint she'd noticed in his hair way back in LA was still there in the bright West Virginia sun. "You don't have to hang around here if you've got work to do." Suzi had yet to figure out what they did in the studio, but it seemed to take a lot of time and required the services of two grown men beyond the band. They went in first thing in the morning, had lunch delivered from town, and emerged at dusk, which at this time of year was getting later and later.

"They're fine without me." Brian was still sitting forward on his chair, studying her like a bug under glass.

"Well, do you want something to drink?" She stood. "I could use a glass of water."

He followed her to the kitchen, and she wondered if he expected her to steal the silver. "I liked the way you used the flowers in *This Lifetime*," he announced from the door.

"What?"

"The flowers in *This Lifetime*. Harold kept crushing flowers all through the book. It was like he was crushing Isabelle."

Suzi stared at him, amazed. That wasn't the observation of someone who just liked her stories. That was something a true fan would notice. "Thanks. Hardly anybody ever spots the symbolism."

Brian flushed. "It took me a couple of reads to get it, too. I'm sorry about last night. We had no right to ask prying questions like that."

Last night? Ugh. "It's all right. I guess I should have assumed there would be some locker room talk. After all, I am Randy Mirandy." Suzi clenched her teeth against her gag response to that nickname. She'd been enduring it for months, and it didn't seem to be going away. At least Sexy Suzi hadn't caught on. "So what do you guys do in the studio all day?"

"Record stuff, and then rerecord it, and then fight about which version was better."

"Fun."

"It's harder than it sounds. You know everything rides on making the right choices, and after a while, you aren't sure what that is." He started tracing a figure eight on the counter with the tip of his finger, watching his handiwork as if it meant something. Something bad. Suzi wanted to hug him and tell him it would be okay, which would be weird.

"Sounds a lot like editing," she said instead. "What is it you do at the studio?"

"Right now? Hang out. Not working on anything." Brian sat down at the table.

"Is that all you do? Just hang out with Jason?"

"No, not normally. There's just something going on now." Brian shrugged.

Suzi licked her lips as she filled a glass of water for him. He hardly talked to her, but he'd given her entire backlist to at least two people for Christmas, questioned Logan about her, and read her books enough to see the symbolism. "Savitar's recording. Do you think they're that good?"

He glanced at her. "They're good. Producing is Jason's thing. Mostly, I was hoping you'd be with them." The corner of his mouth curled. "Couldn't pass up the opportunity to meet my favorite writer."

"I'm honored." She set the glass on the table before she dropped it. Logan had not been lying when he said they liked her. That thought was going to take a little time to process. "But why are you here? Why aren't you at home with your family? Don't you want to spend time with your wife and kids?"

"You've met my wife. Would you want to spend time with her?"

Suzi studied his profile. His mouth had thinned and hardened at the mention of Bonnie. Poor guy. She needed to get to know him well enough that she could hug him and tell him it would be okay. Or make it okay herself.

Whoa. She had a boyfriend. A couple of months living with a musician and she was turning into a groupie, throwing herself at the nearest rock star. Suzi shivered. "I don't know. I only met her the one time."

"Trust me. She's like that all the time."

"Oh." Charity was right. Brian and his wife were splitting up. "I'm sorry you're having trouble."

He shrugged. "My own fault."

"What about your kids?"

"Tess is in school all day and Bub is in school in the morning and with the sitter in the afternoon. When I'm home, I see them for an hour or so every day. That's it. Not much of a family, is it?"

"Why don't you spend more time with them?"

"What would I do with them? Bring them around to hang out with the guys in the band? Besides, it would just confuse them. Kids need routine, and they have one. It's better not to screw it up."

Suzi considered saying something about child development and routines, but decided she wasn't on solid enough ground with Brian to start criticizing his parenting or his relationship with his bitchy wife. At least now she knew his press was right. He was a nice guy. "So I guess I'm not taking you away from anything important."

"Not at all. I'm not sure what I'm going to do with the kids when they come to visit in two weeks. Cassie's mother has been checking out stuff for them in town and at the campground, but they aren't going to want to do that all the time. I thought about taking them to Disney for a week just to eat some time. That would be more fun for them than sitting around here. You're the child-rearing genius. What do you think?"

"About taking them to Disney? They're six and four now, right?" Suzi bit her lip. She shouldn't know that. Only a stalker would know off hand how old his children were, but Brian didn't seem at all fazed.

"Yes."

"Then Disney would be good." Suzi sat down across the table from him. "But there's got to be lots for them to do here, too. I'm sure they'll want to spend time with you. Your wife isn't coming?"

"No. West Virginia is too boring for her."

That was exactly what Charity had announced before she went back to LA. Boring. "Maybe we can take them for hikes, or we could go out to Dolly Sods."

"What's that?"

"It's a local mountain top. The pictures I found online were beautiful, and it used to be a bombing range during World War Two. Lots of places for them to climb. I can find out how to get there from here if you like."

Brian smiled. "That would be great."

Chapter 7

Present

Brian sifted through the pile of scrap paper he'd been making notes on. As a system, it sucked. "Doesn't it seem a little strange that you haven't heard from her at all?"

"No," the woman on the other end of the line said. "I don't hear from her for months at a time. She doesn't have anything in the editing cycle right now. No releases coming. I figured she was having a personal thing, and I was leaving her alone."

"So, it's not unusual?" What kind of friends were these who didn't worry when Suzi went off the map for a month?

"No. It's not unusual."

Not friends. Her publisher. "Well, thanks anyway."

"If you need anything else, just email."

Just email. The phone call must have been a little odd. He'd had a hard enough time getting his hands on the number. Brian set the phone down in the charger and studied his mess of notes. When he'd gotten home from Japan, he'd only been able to spend an hour a day on his search, but since the kids went back to their mom, he'd had more time to pursue her. Not that more time yielded better results. The messy notes didn't help either, but it gave him something to do in his now-empty house.

Brian pulled a new legal pad out and started at the top.

She'd left the party with Cherney, but he was a total dead end. Cherney said he'd taken her to an ultra secret location and they'd stayed there for a couple of days while she ranged between hysterical and sick. Cherney claimed it was flu or bad PMS or something. When he brought her back, he'd helped her get a new copy of her ID, and she'd waved goodbye from the driver's seat of a white convertible rental that he'd paid for.

The BroRide management office gave much the same information when Brian asked Helen to call them. Helen was tight with their office manager, who had done the legwork on the new ID while Suzi was with Cherney at his undisclosed location. The new ID listed Cherney's house as her home address. That thought had Brian waking up in a cold sweat when he did manage to sleep. She might be planning to return to him when she finished her walkabout in her white convertible rental. She might have already returned and convinced Cherney to lie and say she wasn't there. Of all possibilities, that seemed like the least likely. Everyone swore Cherney was a horrible liar.

Greg said he hadn't heard one word from either Suzi or Logan. Logan had retreated to his house in upstate New York and headed straight down the neck of a bottle.

Which explained why both Logan's landline and cell went unanswered. According to the neighbors—Brian had gotten desperate enough to hunt down numbers for them three days ago—the house was shut up in the July heat with lights blazing at all hours and irregular visits from the local liquor store. One of the neighbors said she had stopped by with some food, but the way the house smelled, it was going to have to be fumigated before anyone could live there again.

John and Toby were just as useless, though they were planning to quit the band and start their own. When John had asked him if he thought they should bring Greg into the new band, Brian had pointed out they'd just be kicking Logan out. He didn't add that getting bounced from his band for being an idiot was the least Logan deserved.

The phone rang, and he grabbed it before it finished the first ring. "Hello?"

"What cha doin'?" Jason asked.

"Nothing." Brian turned over his notepad in case Jason had developed the ability to see through the phone. "What are you doing?"

"Dodging projectile vomit."

"Cool." Brian turned his notes back over. He hadn't checked her website lately, and last time he'd tried to email her, the message had bounced because her inbox was full. Maybe he could try that again.

"This one has aim. I think she'll be a jock."

"She's six weeks old. What's she going to play? Competitive napping?" He'd left himself a note at the bottom of the third page to start going through her dedications to see if he could track down any of those people and then forgot about it. He transferred the note to the legal pad and put a star beside it.

"When she gets older I meant. I'm not planning on pushing her into a career for at least eleven years."

"That's big of you."

"Marc said Suzi's email account is sending back messages because it's full."

"Still?"

"What do you mean still?"

Brian opened his mouth, but a good lie was not on his lips. *Be a little more transparent, why don't you?* "Wasn't it doing that before?"

"No."

"I thought it was."

"No, it wasn't. Didn't she have a ton of space for her email?"

"She did say her storage was huge because she didn't want fan mail to get sent back." Brian tapped his pen on the desk. She also went through it everyday to keep it cleared out because she couldn't stand to be out of touch.

"Aren't you even a little bit worried? She vanished out of that party a month ago and Logan's self-medicating."

"Has it been a month?" Thirty-two days. Brian glanced at the calendar. Yep, thirty-two days. A little more than a month. "She'll turn up."

"When did you get so heartless?"

"I'm not heartless. I just think she's a big girl, and she wants some time alone. She's probably thinking this whole love affair with a musician thing is overrated." Brian paused in the act of opening up the file on his computer that held all her books. Couldn't blame her. Logan might have done such a job on her she never wanted to see another musical instrument. He needed to go through those dedications. Not all of them could be musicians.

"She wouldn't do that. She loves us." Jason had just enough doubt in his voice to bump the idea higher on Brian's short list of major worries. What if she had decided to write off all musicians as a bad idea and moved on? She couldn't do that. Not without giving him a chance to plead his case.

Chapter 8

Five Years Ago

Brian walked down the stairs to the guest cabin. After a solid month of hanging out with Suzi and his kids, he figured he had exactly one good excuse left to talk to her. One last chance to capture that comfortable, family feeling he'd never had with Bonnie. Logan was a lucky guy to have that all the time. Brian found her standing at the edge of the slope by the stream, peering into the bushes. She was wearing what might have been the same pair of cutoffs she'd been wearing since she arrived, a pink T-shirt with the word *sweet* across the bust in rhinestones, and no shoes. Her hair was up in a ponytail. All of it made her look about sixteen and made him feel like a creepy old man. "What are you doing?" he asked.

"Wondering where this stream goes." She didn't look at him.

"Probably down the mountain."

"Probably, but how does it get there? Does it join with other streams or split into smaller ones? Are there waterfalls and pools? Or does it disappear underground to percolate to the surface as a spring someplace else?"

Brian observed the stream again and saw it for the first time. She kept doing that to him. Making him see things in totally new ways. Like his kids. This past month with Suzi and the kids, he'd felt less like a sperm donor and more like a dad for the first time. "I don't know."

"I don't either, but I think I'm going to find out. Wanna come along?"

"Sure."

"You'll want to leave the shoes behind or you'll ruin them. Trust me."

He did. Without question. Kicking off his shoes and rolling up his jeans, he stepped into the water after her.

"What did you really want?" She grasped a branch with both hands and used it to lower herself down a rock ledge.

"What?"

"You didn't come looking for me to go stream stomping. Did the kids get out okay?"

"Yeah, I put them on the plane this morning to go back to their mother. They wanted to stay here."

"Ha. They wanted to go fishing with Cassie's dad again. I think all they ever caught were s'mores. Watch it here. It's slippery." She held onto bushes on either side of the stream. "They had a good time, though. They've never gotten to be out in the woods like this before, have they?"

"No."

"Aren't you glad you didn't take them to Disney?"

"We can do that next time." Disney might actually be fun. He'd thought of it as a way to keep the kids distracted while they were forced together, but it would be cool to see Bub meeting Buzz Lightyear and Tess having tea with princesses. They could spend a day at Disneyland. Suzi might come along.

"That's what I'm thinking."

"I wanted to thank you for helping me out with them while they were here. You probably had writing you were supposed to do."

"Nope." Suzi waded into the middle of the stream. "Little fish." The tiny fish darted away from her, but when she held still, swam back to peck at her feet and ankles.

"Tess never got the hang of that." Brian crouched on the narrow bank. What would Jason think when he never reappeared at the studio? He was only supposed to be gone for a few minutes and this was developing into an all-afternoon adventure.

"She will when she's older. It takes patience and the ability to hold still for a long time." Suzi moved, and the fish scattered. Pushing through low branches, she waded down the stream.

Brian relaxed. For the last month, no, for the last several months leading up to leaving Bonnie and coming here, he'd felt like he was walking a tightrope between forty-story buildings. One misstep, and he would drop forever. He'd been dreading the visit with the kids because he knew they wouldn't understand. He'd been ashamed they had understood less than he'd thought. Suzi had insisted he try to explain, but he doubted it made sense to them yet. Right now, none of that mattered. He was in the middle of nowhere following a cute girl in cutoffs through a stream on a hot, sunny day. As long as the sun shone and the stream flowed downhill, everything was fine.

"Hey, look at—aaaahhhh!" One second, Suzi was leaning over something in the water and the next she was sitting in the middle of the stream. She stared up at him and started to laugh.

"What did you do?" Brian waded to her and tried to find a solid place to stand on the slippery slate of the streambed. He put out a hand to help her up, but she ignored it, sifting through the rocks with her fingers.

"I saw something. It was right here." She shifted onto her knees, still searching.

Brian peered into the water. He didn't see anything but rocks. "What are you looking for?"

"A rock."

"Suzi, there's a lot of rocks here." He reached down and picked one up as an example. "See?"

"This one was…" She peered at the rock he was holding. "That's it!"

Brian jumped when she shrieked and lost his footing. He landed next to her with a splash.

"Oh, no! You didn't drop it, did you?" Suzi howled. "You dork."

"Dork?" Brian waited to get pissed off. She'd called him a dork. Nobody outside his close circle of friends had called him a name in over a decade. Nobody but her. And why was that so perfect? Scanning the rocks, he spotted the one she wanted so bad. He grinned, scooping it up. "Am I still a dork?"

"Is that it? Gimme."

"Am I still a dork?"

She reached across him. "No, you've been upgraded to jerk. Gimme."

No way was she going to get her hands on that rock without climbing up the front of him. Brian licked his lips. He'd had women crawl on him before, but this was more fun. "Say please."

"Gimme, please."

This woman was devoted to some other guy. Teasing her might not be such a good idea, for either of them. Even though it felt good. Brian handed over the rock.

Suzi wiped the excess water off with her finger. "Look at this. Isn't it amazing?"

The black rock had the image of a fern stained onto the surface. For this she called him a dork?

"Look at the details. The lacy pattern of the leaf printed so perfectly." She put her hand on his forearm. Just a light touch.

"It looks like a stain on a rock."

"It's a fossil of something that lived millions of years ago." She turned her gaze up to meet his, and he started to understand the appeal of the rock. Anything that could get her this excited had to be magnificent. Even though he'd seen her get equally worked up about dragonflies and salamanders with the kids.

"Can you imagine what it must have been like here millions of years ago? When all of this was steamy jungle, and spiders the size of your head lived in holes in the ground waiting for prey. Dragonflies as big as helicopters flew over forests that stretched for thousands and thousands of miles. All of them hunting and eating and living and dying, never knowing that their time was short."

Her bright eyes stared through the leaves. The way she talked, he could almost see the trees and the giant bugs and the jungle steam, too. She turned back to him. Her lips parted, and her breath shortened. Her hand tensed on his arm.

Brian's groin tightened. She was so damned alive. He wanted to bottle that and take it home so he could nip at it when he felt down. He wanted to lean down and kiss her. She might wrap her arms around his neck and pull him tight. She might also scramble up the mountain to tell Logan, Jason, and everyone what a letch he was.

Yanking her hand away, she squeezed her eyes shut and shook herself. "I am getting way too big for my britches." Suzi stood up. She squeezed her shirt. "But apparently you can take parts of the stream home with you. What do you think? Should we forge ahead down the stream or turn around and go back up?" She tucked the rock into the rear pocket of her cutoffs.

Brian surveyed both directions. Up meant going back to the studio to listen to fighting and being asked his opinion when he didn't have one. Down meant a whole lot more time with Suzi. "I vote down. We already know what's behind us."

"Oh good, another adventurer. Onward and downward!"

Suzi led the way for a long time, occasionally stopping to examine a rock or show him something. Brian followed, running scenarios in his head about what might have happened if he'd kissed her back there. Most of them came out ugly. The best he could hope for was a little embarrassment. At worst, she would leave, and that was too high a price to pay.

She stopped. "Houston, we have a problem."

Brian stepped up beside her. The stream tumbled down a steep, jagged cliff face into a pool at the bottom. The rocks were wet but not submerged on either side. Beyond that, mud and the occasional stubborn tree edged the cliff. "We can get down that," Brian said.

"We can?"

"Sure, there's lots of handholds." He nodded to help himself feel more confident. "We've done harder ones."

"And when they find our lifeless bodies in a month because we fell and broke our legs and nobody knew where we were, can I say 'I told you so' then?"

"You'll probably say that for a while when we're dying. I'll go first. I have longer reach than you." Brian lowered himself over the edge and then decided he needed to be facing the rock. He climbed back up and turned around.

"Sure about this, are you?" Suzi asked.

"Yup." He lowered himself again, this time facing the rock. Feeling for the next foothold, he decided the double suicide might be a nice way to go out. "There's plenty of places to hang on. Come on down."

She shook her head, turned, and started down, giving him an uninterrupted view of her rear. The daily running regimen worked. Every morning for the past month he'd gotten up at eight so he could stand at his bedroom window and watch her walk to the top of the steps, stretch, and jog away. She used four different routes without any pattern. After about forty-five minutes, she returned. At first he'd told himself he was just curious. After a while, he started to feel like a peeping Tom watching her through the curtains, but by then the habit was ingrained, and he got up every morning without fail to watch her jog away and then jog back before breakfast.

"This is an easy climb. It looked worse from above," she said. Then the piece of slate she was standing on snapped.

Brian tightened his grip on the stone just in time for her to slide into his arms. He held perfectly still, not even breathing for a few seconds. She hadn't made a peep the whole time she was falling. The only sound around them was the chatter of the stream and bird song.

"Or not." Suzi glanced over her shoulder at him with wide, black eyes. "Thanks."

"Anytime."

Her warm body rested against his a moment longer. He soaked in the sensation. This is what she would feel like in bed. The way her curves fit against his body and the sensation of her heartbeat and breathing. This was going to keep him up nights. "My, what strong hands you have." She giggled.

"Side effect of the job. Are you ready to go on?"

"Wait a minute." She found handholds and lifted her body off his. "Whenever you're ready."

Never. He was never going to be ready. He wanted to spend the rest of his life hanging from the edge of this waterfall, cradling her in his arms. Reaching down with his foot, he found the next hold and shifted away. She followed after he'd gained a little distance. When he stepped back onto the little sandy beach at the bottom, he noticed blood seeping from her ankle. "You're bleeding."

"Shit."

When she twisted sideways trying to see, he stepped forward, ready to catch her.

"Where at?"

"On your ankle."

"At least it's not the bottom of my foot." She jumped the last bit, landing on her feet beside him. Limping to a fallen tree, she sat down and inspected her ankle. "That's ugly."

"It's not so bad." It was horrible. Blood streaming down her foot and dripping off her toe. Brian checked his pockets, though anything there would have been soaked from falling in the water earlier.

"Grab me some of that moss over there." She pointed toward a moss-covered tree. Then she scooped water out of the pool to rinse off her foot.

Brian brought her the moss. "What's this for?"

"Nature's absorbent. I'll keep pressure on it for a few minutes, and the bleeding will stop." She pressed the moss over the wound and smiled at him. "Well, if we were undecided about whether to go forward or turn back, I think this waterfall has made the decision for us. The point of no return."

The section of rock where she'd slipped was almost smooth now because she'd broken off so much slate in her fall. Every handhold was gone.

"Eventually this stream has to come out at the bottom of the mountain someplace. We'll find a way home from there." Brian crouched on the ground, sifting through the rocks, pretending to search for more fossils. If he sat down beside her, he'd want to put his arm around her, and that would be weird. She was dating another guy, and he was still married.

Of course, he didn't have to be married. The public expected rock stars to divorce. All he needed to do was call Tessa to get him a divorce lawyer, file some papers, and send Sandy a nice fruit basket for insisting on the prenup. While that was happening, he could be working on getting Suzi away from Logan. Six months from now, he could be sitting on the couch with her, admiring the Christmas tree while his kids, squealing with delight, tore open their gifts. She'd be wrapped up in a plush bathrobe with bed-tousled hair, wearing whatever sparkly he'd given her and smiling at him as he sipped a cup of her fantastic coffee. There'd be a fire in the fireplace of the big beautiful house he'd bought to live in with her. Like some kind of Norman Rockwell scene.

Brian rocked back on his heels.

Was he really sitting here plotting to leave his wife and steal another man's girl just because he thought he could?

He stood up and walked a little farther downstream, still pretending to fossil hunt.

When had his ego spiraled out of control to the point he felt he had the right to take someone else's girl? Logan wasn't hurting Suzi. He loved her, and she loved him. Everything she did was to make Logan happy. Bonnie used to be like that. Brian leaned on a tree, remembering when Bonnie wanted to make him happy in places other than bed and to spend time with him on purpose. She used to smile.

What had changed to make Bonnie stop smiling? What did a woman want?

"Can I ask you something?" Suzi said in a small voice.

"Of course."

"Logan's been edgy." Suzi started chewing her lower lip. "I don't think he gets along with Jason, and I don't know what to do about it."

"Oh?" Brian used the excuse of talking to her to go sit down next to her, though he kept a good foot and a half between then. He hadn't spent as much time in the studio for the past month, but when he had stopped in, Logan seemed the same as always. Unless Suzi was in the room, too. Then he turned into a giant asshole.

Suzi shook her head. "You guys are his heroes. He was so excited when he got the call. We were still in that initial courtship dance, and he called me effervescing over the phone. 'You're not going to believe who just called me. He never produces anybody, and he wants to produce us.' I don't think George Martin would have gotten him that excited. But now that he's here, in the middle of it, he just seems frustrated and angry. Like it's not quite what he thought it would be."

"Jason is tough to work with." Tough? Jason played an excellent asshole, too, and Brian had known him for nearly thirty years.

"Yeah, I guess. I guess I didn't understand what a producer did. I thought it was analogous to an editor, but editors don't contribute much at all to the creative process. At least, mine don't. With mine, it's more of a stretch this here, shorten that there, does the comma on your keyboard work?" She leaned back and bumped her head on another tree that had fallen behind the one she was sitting on. It had a weird pattern of peeling bark. "I'm sorry. You don't want to hear all this."

"No, it's fine." Brian licked his lips, wondering how deep he wanted to get. He wasn't the world's greatest expert on relationships, but she didn't seem to have anyone to turn to. Unless he counted Greg. She seemed tight with Greg, especially now that Charity had gone home. The idea of her talking to Greg about this burned him, though. He wanted to be her hero. "You know what I think the problem is?"

Suzi turned sideways. "What?"

"Logan's jealous."

"Jealous? Logan? I've never seen it."

"When you're not there, he's fine."

"So you think I'm the problem?"

"Not unless you are planning to leave Logan for Jason." Brian winced and tried to cover it by batting an imaginary fly off his face. Suzi with Jason. What fresh hell would that be?

"That's ridiculous. Jason's married. Even if I was leaving Logan, I wouldn't be leaving him to steal some other woman's husband." Suzi shook her head. "There's a hole in your story."

"What's that?"

"If he's worried that I'm going to run away with Jason, why isn't he worried about you? I just spent most of the last month with you."

"And the kids."

She shrugged and bumped her head again. "I'm clever. I could have gotten rid of the kids. Or I could have been using the kids as a reason to get close to you."

Brian wished they weren't in the middle of the forest having this conversation. Being lost gave his imagination too much privacy to run away. She could have been using the kids as an excuse to hang out with him. Maybe she wanted him as much as he wanted her? Or maybe he was more delusional than he thought. "I don't know, but I'm pissed off about it. I mean, I'm threatening, too."

Suzi laughed and peeked under the wad of moss she had pressed over her wound. He could see her putting the pieces together, but couldn't be sure what puzzle she was working on. "Logan can't be jealous. He didn't act at all like that around Karl."

"Who's Karl?"

"My ex-boyfriend." Suzi shrugged. "Logan was never jealous of him."

"Because you dumped him. Karl was the past."

"Karl dumped me."

Brian's mouth fell open. "He dumped you? Is he crazy?"

Suzi put her hand over her face. "See, now you're making me blush." When she lowered her hands, she was indeed blushing, and it was very fetching. "My friend Laurie says she thinks the competition was too much for Karl."

"Was Karl a writer, too?"

"No, an English major, but he was poised to be the big dog among the English majors. Then I showed up with my publication credits, such as they are, and started turning the heads of the profs."

Brian nodded as if he understood. Things must be different at college. He couldn't imagine a teacher dating a student, but he could understand any man alive wanting to get closer to Suzi even if it wasn't quite kosher. After all, that's why he was sitting here. "But you weren't with him anymore so he wasn't your type. Logan thinks he's your type, and if he's your type, then Jason is, too. Only more so."

"How more so?"

"He's got lots of money. He's established. He's really fucking famous."

"Then you should be just as big a threat. You have all those characteristics in common with Jason, and you're separated from your wife."

"But I'm not leaning over your shoulder when you're doing something." *Dammit.*

"I suppose not." Suzi frowned. "So if I were your girlfriend, and you thought I was drifting toward some other man, or some other man was trying to steal me, what would you want me to do?" She stared at him with her wide brown eyes as if he had the answers to the universe.

If you were mine, there would be no question. I'd trust you even if I didn't trust the other guy. I wouldn't even have to think about it. "How should I know?"

"Because you're a guy, and you're more similar to Logan than any other man I've ever known. You're what Logan aspires to."

Brian cocked an eyebrow. "Why?"

"Because you're a famous, respected musician." A blush spread across Suzi's cheeks giving him hope she saw more to this similarity that stringed instruments. "And you've got good insights."

"Do I?"

"Yes. I love Logan, and I want to make him happy, but I don't know how."

Brian glanced at the peeling bark of the tree. Did she know she'd just handed him the keys to make her his? He could give her bad advice, set his divorce in motion, and wait until Logan was out of the picture. No one would ever figure out he'd orchestrated it all. The perfect crime.

Chapter 9

Except for the victim sitting next to him. He couldn't do that to her.

"I wouldn't want to you to pretend to be someone you weren't," he said. "If you started to act different, and I found out later you were just pretending to be someone you thought I wanted, I'd be mad. I'd just want you to keep reminding me you loved me and I had no reason to doubt you."

"I didn't realize I'd given him a reason to doubt me." She stared into the stream.

Brian wanted to hug her, but resisted. It wouldn't stop there. She was far too vulnerable right now. "I bet he's not doubting you. I bet he's doubting himself. I don't know what his other producers were like, but every producer's different, and Jason's making him question everything he does. And he's just new with you, so he probably feels like a jerk."

"Because he—he's not confident." Suzi peeked under her wad of moss again and tossed it into the stream. Blood had smeared across her ankle, but the scrape through the middle was no longer bleeding. "And if he's not confident, he's afraid he won't be able to hang onto me, so he's projecting that fear and making a monster out of the nearest target."

"Sounds likely." Brian shrugged. It wouldn't be the first time someone had made a monster out of Jason. He usually had a hand in creating the image himself.

"So you think I should just keep doing what I'm doing?"

"I guess so." Brian decided he was an idiot. There were a thousand things he could have said that would have sabotaged her relationship with Logan and still kept him sitting pretty when things fell apart. Instead, he'd gone and been Mr. Nice Guy and screwed himself.

"You probably think this is kind of stupid."

"No. I wish someone would worry about me as much as you worry about Logan." Brian bit the inside of his cheek. He shouldn't venture into that territory at all. Not with this woman. Not in this place.

"I just—" Suzi swallowed. "I just want so much to make him happy. I can't remember who I was before because I want to be what he wants me to be so much. And I want him to be happy. I want everything to be perfect for him. And I'm afraid—I'm afraid—I'm—afraid—" Her eyes filled with tears.

"Hey, calm down. Logan's not going to leave you." *And I'm not going to try to steal you away. I couldn't do that to you.* "He loves you."

"But for how long? What am I going to do without him? When I'm not with him, I feel like I can't breathe." Her voice had risen to a painful squeak.

Brian caught her chin and made her meet his gaze. She didn't seem to be breathing. "Suzi, he's not going to leave you. And if he ever does, I'll be your oxygen."

She gasped, and he decided it was supposed to be a laugh. Turning her head, she took a deep breath. "Bonnie doesn't worry about pleasing you?"

For an instant, Brian was dizzy. Images of Bonnie's idea of pleasing him flashed through his mind, only it was Suzi in her place. Soft and sweet in his bed with her satin hair spilled across his pillow, smiling at him. "In her way. We've been together a long time. I guess things have gotten stale."

"That happens." Suzi examined her fingernails. "So there's no hope?"

"Not that I can figure." Suzi wasn't going to leave Logan. Ever. But as she'd said, she was clever. Maybe she could think a way out of this crate he'd sealed himself into. "What would you want if you were in Bonnie's shoes?"

"Me? I'm not an expert."

"But you are a woman, and you know what it's like to be in Bonnie's shoes." He grinned. "I told you what I thought about Logan."

"True." Suzi stared at her hands for a minute. Her fingers had a little blood and dirt on them. "If you're not happy, why don't you just leave her?"

Brian shrugged. "Seems like quitting, and who's to say I won't just wind up in the same situation with some other woman?"

"True." She nodded. "The kids are both in school now. Is she suffering a little empty nest syndrome?"

"Bonnie couldn't wait until the kids started school. She had a party the first day of Bub's preschool."

"Bubbie does have a real name, doesn't he?"

"Brian junior. It's easier to call him Bubbie."

"I suppose."

Brian frowned, wondering what that meant. One of the things he liked about her was that she had eight or nine things going on in her head all the time, but right now, he wasn't liking it so much. He couldn't even remember how Bubbie had gotten it now.

"You know, she might want the kids out and still miss them when they go. Weren't you on tour when your son started school?"

"Yeah, but we had a break the week he started."

"But you were on the road until the middle of October last year."

"Sure, but I'm on the road a lot, and Bonnie and me were drifting apart a long time before that. Things didn't get bad until Jason and Cassie got together."

"What about when Bear met Maureen?" She leaned her head against the log. "Did anything start to change when Bear met Maureen?"

"I guess so, but that was when Tess started school, too."

"And how did you feel about Tess starting school?"

Brian shifted back. "When did this become about me?"

"You asked me for my opinion, and I'm trying to give you an educated one. How did you feel about Tess starting school?"

"I was glad. It meant she was growing up. She was going into a good system, and she's doing well."

"And what about when your son started school?"

"Same thing. Good school system. He got the same teacher Tess had. He's doing good."

"And how did you feel when Bear met Maureen?"

"I feel like I'm being psychoanalyzed."

"I can't give you an educated opinion unless I know all the factors."

Brian sighed. "I was happy for him and jealous as hell."

"Jealous as hell?"

"They're perfect together."

"And when Jason met Cass?"

"About the same. Happy and jealous as hell." A bug crawled along the log above her head. Like a ladybug, but it was gray.

Suzi nodded, and her eyes darted toward the bug. She jerked away from the log, twisting. The wood behind her was covered with clumps of little gray bugs. Shrieking, she jumped off the log and hopped a few steps into the middle of the stream. "Why didn't you tell me those were there?" Yanking her ponytail out, she threw the elastic in the water and began scraping her fingers through her hair. "Are they in my hair? Get them out. Get them out!"

"Hold still." Brian grabbed her shoulder and ran his fingers through her hair. "Calm down. There's no bugs in your hair." He shouldn't be enjoying this as much as he was, but the satin soft strands felt exactly the way he'd imagined.

"Why didn't you tell me I was leaning into a mass of little bugs?" She pulled back and then leaned forward, studying them like they all might take flight at that very second, aimed right for her head.

"Because I didn't see them. They were on the other side of you." He ran his fingers through her hair once more, just to be certain, and inspected at the log himself. What he'd taken for peeling bark were colonies of tiny gray beetles. They ranged in age from little wiggling things to full-grown adults, writhing and crawling over one another.

Suzi shuddered. "They're disgusting."

"If there was only one of them, it would be cool." Out with the kids, it hadn't been beyond her to pick up a bug and let it crawl over her hand so they could look at it, but confront her with a whole bunch of them, and it was freak-out time.

"But there isn't one of them. There's eight billion of them."

"There's not eight billion. There might be a few hundred."

"Exactly. A few hundred." She bumped him with her shoulder. "You think this is funny."

"Of course, I think it's funny. What am I supposed to think?" Other than it was adorable. Her panic had kicked up his protective instincts. He reached down and fished her hair elastic out of the water.

"Men. You're all the same. Let's get going before those bugs decide to swarm and devour us." Suzi started downstream.

"Yes, because the ten minutes we were sitting next to them wasn't a good enough chance." Brian followed her.

"This whole adventure is starting to resemble Alexander Tomm's *Follow the River* a little too closely. Did you ever read that? It's wonderful. It's about a woman who's kidnapped by Indians right around this area and taken all the way to Southern Ohio, and then she escapes and follows the river back home. At the end, when she walks out of the woods, the men who find her just think she got lost in the forest the whole time." Suzi stopped in front of a fallen tree and inspected it before ducking under. "It was an excellent book."

"Just not a good thing to live."

"No. At least not for me. I think she's nervous that you don't love her anymore."

Brian navigated a deep section that passed almost directly under the exposed roots of a tree. He knew she was talking about Bonnie without asking. She could hang onto a conversation despite gaps better than anyone he'd ever met. A year from now they'd meet, and she'd pick up right where they left off as if no time had passed.

"Think about it. Maureen had an established career when she met Bear. Cass had an established business when she met Jason. Both of them married women who were successful as individuals first. And you, by your own admission were—"

"What?"

"You said you were jealous of them. You saw two of your friends fall for women who were independent and had their own lives. Cassie still owns the campground, doesn't she?"

"Yeah."

"And what is Bonnie without you? She doesn't have a career. She doesn't have a business. She's the mother of your children, and those children are growing up."

"So what should I do? Help her start a business?"

"Beats me. Ask her." Suzi stopped. The water rushed around her calves. She swept her hair up and twisted it into a bun on top of her head. "The road up to the house is not this long."

"It isn't?" Brian wiped his arm across his forehead. How long had they been walking? Half an hour? An hour? His jeans had started drying, but his shirt was soaked with sweat. He was filthy and hungry, and he couldn't remember the last time he'd been this happy.

"No. I've jogged down the mountain to the main road, and it's not this far." She turned to him. "We are lost."

"How can we be lost? We've been following the same stream, and it's been going downhill the whole time."

Suzi cocked an eyebrow at him. The expression was far too cute for being lost and alone with her in the forest. "You might have noticed that mountains are wider on the bottom than they are on the top."

"Ha ha. We haven't crossed a road, so we've got to be between the driveway and the road that leads over the mountain past the campground. We'll just keep going down and eventually we'll find civilization." He walked past her.

"You sound so confident." She splashed behind them. "I thought you didn't know anything about the great outdoors."

"I don't."

"So what makes you so sure?"

"You were sure when we started this little adventure." Brian lifted a branch and held it for her to duck under.

"And you're relying on me?"

"Yup."

She took the lead again, which he preferred. It gave him more time to consider what she'd said. Had he been assuming the marriage was over when all he needed to do was have a talk with his wife? Their last conversation hadn't gone well. He had said he was going to spend some time working with Jason and Savitar. She had told him he could fucking well spend the rest of his life out here. It went downhill from there. Before, when they fought, it had turned into passion. Now, it turned into ice. Passion he could understand, but ice drove him away. He could try waiting her out. See Bonnie through the lens Suzi gave him. Suzi had helped him see his kids for the wonders they were and shown him prehistoric West Virginia, so maybe she could help him see the Bonnie he had fallen in love with again. He could send the kids to spend a couple of weeks with his parents while he tried to rescue things. Maybe it was a little old fashioned, but he didn't want Tess and Bub to grow up in a broken home.

If he and Suzi ever found their way out of this endless forest.

"Are you going to write a book about this?" he asked.

"Stephen King already did."

"That doesn't mean you couldn't write one, too."

She glanced over her shoulder and shook her head. "You just want me to write a book with you in it."

"It wouldn't be a bad idea. I think I make a dashing hero."

"If you don't say so yourself."

"I rescued you from all the horrible bugs."

She shuddered. "I was trying to forget about those." She stopped. "I hear something."

Brian listened. It sounded like the hum of car tires on asphalt. The bushes hung lower to the stream, and he had to lift them up so they could duck under. Ahead, a deep shadow covered the path. He pulled away the last branch over a three-foot high concrete drainage pipe under the road.

"Hallelujah!" Suzi scrambled up the embankment with Brian right behind her. Across the road was the pasture of the riding stable, and beyond, the first houses at the edge of town. "Now all we have to do is follow the road back to the driveway and walk back up."

"Or." Brian grinned at her. "We could walk into town, go to Ida's, and get some food while we wait for somebody to come pick us up."

"I don't have any money on me."

Brian put his arm over her shoulders. "I can get us a line of credit."

* * * *

Suzi stared at the rocks in the bottom of the stream. The rose quartz assembled on a section of black slate spelled out a word. Yes. She didn't remember seeing rose quartz in the stream. Yes to what?

"He must be nuts," Brian said.

"Who?" Suzi asked.

"Logan. He left you alone with me." Brian started kissing her neck.

"But he's worried about Jason, not you."

"He should be worried about me."

"You?"

"I love you. I want you. You belong to me." Brian pulled her down into the stream. The water was warm and his lips were hot.

"What about your wife?"

"She doesn't mind. We do this all the time. Didn't you know? The invitation said orgy, not dinner." He stripped off her clothes in one motion. "Jason's coming later. And he's bringing Cassie."

Something started beeping. "We're lost in the woods," she said. His hands felt glorious caressing her overheated skin.

"Are you excitable?" Brian asked, thrusting into her.

* * * *

Logan could hear Suzi laughing upstairs and a fire alarm beeping. He was standing at the bottom of a sweeping staircase that wasn't in Jason's house, but in the logic of dreams was, and Suzi was somewhere at the top of it with Jason. "Come on, we've got work to do," Logan shouted.

"Fuck off, buddy. I've got my work right here," Jason shouted back.

Suzi laughed. It was the high joyful laugh Logan loved to hear, but not with another man.

"We're going to go over budget." Logan cringed at the whine in his voice.

"I don't give a fuck."

"Yes, you do," Suzi said laughing.

"Oh, yes I do," Jason answered. His tone was heavy with desire. Logan heard Suzi moaning in response. The bedsprings started squeaking.

He wanted to scream her name, but it bottled up in his throat as if there were a cork stuck in there. He reached for the banister.

His hand found her naked shoulder. He pulled her onto her back and climbed on top of her, thrusting inside her before he opened his eyes. "Suzi. My Suzi. I love you," he gasped, riding her.

"Logan, yes. Oh, God, yes." Her fingernails tore his back. "Harder, harder."

The headboard banged against the wall. "Tell me, Suzi. Tell me you want me."

"I want you, Logan. Only you."

She closed around him, dragging him under. Her hot mouth on his neck. Her legs tight around his hips. Her fingernails digging into his back. The world went black.

The beeping was still going, and now there was a knock at the door.

"Shit," Suzi hissed. "Shit, Logan baby, I'm sorry. We overslept." She started to pull away from him, but he held her tight. "Logan, we have to get up. Everyone else is up." Twisting, she slipped out of his grasp.

"What?" Logan lifted his head enough to see the clock. Nine thirty-five and still beeping.

Suzi had pulled on a T-shirt. "I have to get breakfast. You guys are all going to be late, and you've got a five minute commute across the lawn so you can't blame traffic."

Logan crawled out of bed. He located some clothes, and by the time he left the bedroom, he could smell smoke and hear Suzi in the kitchen scolding Toby for starting a minor kitchen fire. He had to stop having these fucked-up dreams. She wasn't even with Jason yesterday. Most of the day she'd been roaming the woods with Brian. Nobody had noticed they were missing until they climbed out of the backseat of Cassie's parents' car not long before dinner.

"Randy Mirandy strikes again, huh?" John said.

"*Logan, yes. Oh, God, yes. Harder, harder*." Greg snickered.

Logan punched Greg's shoulder and went into the kitchen. Suzi was frying eggs, and the toaster was dripping in the sink.

"I'm sorry. I don't know why I overslept." She kept her eyes on the eggs, and her face was red. They must have been needling her, too.

"It's not a big deal." The shirt she'd grabbed wasn't quite long enough. Her smooth, white ass peeked out. He stepped behind her and slid his hands over that pale flesh. He wanted her again, now. "Let's go back to bed."

"You have work to do."

"They'll be fine without me for a couple of hours. Let's go back to bed." He kissed her neck.

"I have to finish breakfast first."

Something about her voice was strange. Tight and too high. "What's the matter?"

Her breath hitched. "I love you."

"I know, sugar. I love you, too."

She nodded, still focused on the eggs. "I'm sorry."

"About what? Waking up late? It's nothing. Even people who wear suits are late to work sometimes."

"About yesterday."

"Oh, that. That's no big deal, either." He slipped his hands around her thighs. She was still hot and slick. "It's a lot easier if you leave a note rather than a pair of shoes and a coffee cup."

"Logan, don't." Suzi twisted.

"Don't what?" Logan slid his fingers between her legs.

"They're in the other room."

"So?"

"Please stop."

Logan moved his hands back to her waist. "Okay. What's wrong?"

"Everyone is in the next room."

"Yeah, and they were this morning when you were screaming my name, too." He bit her shoulder.

"I know." She scooped the eggs out of the pan and put them on a plate. "Please, just go eat your breakfast."

He picked up the plate. "Sure, whatever." Fifteen minutes ago, she was all over him. Zero to passion in ten seconds. Now she wanted him to just go eat his breakfast? What the hell? At the table, he got plenty of ribbing. She didn't come out of the kitchen.

"You comin'?" Greg asked. "I mean coming with us, not coming with Suzi."

Logan glanced at his plate and then at them. He had two untouched eggs. "I'll be there in a minute."

"Round two!" John stuffed the last bite of egg into his mouth as he jumped up from the table. "We'll see you in about five minutes."

Greg and Toby followed John out, arguing over how long they would take.

Suzi was scrubbing the sink.

"Hey Suz?"

"I thought you guys all left." She didn't turn around.

"You're being funny this morning." Logan wasn't sure if his stomach hurt because he hadn't eaten or because of the way she was acting. "Everything okay?"

"Don't worry about it. It's probably PMS."

Logan wasn't the brightest guy in the world, but he could count. She'd just had a period two weeks ago. Unless her cycle was speeding up, she wasn't having PMS. So she was lying. Why? "Is there anything I can do? Chocolate? Jewelry? Massage?"

"I just need to get some sleep. I'm kinda tired, and I've been having weird dreams."

"Yeah, me too. I warned you recording was stressful."

"I know." She rinsed off her hands and turned around smiling. "I wish I could help." She wrapped her arms around his neck, rubbing her lovely body against him.

"This is helping." He kissed her. She'd woken from a nightmare to having sex with him. And she was always kind of embarrassed when somebody heard them having sex. That's all it was.

"You should go," she whispered, teasing her lips across his. "You're already late. I promise tonight will be wonderful."

"Tall promise."

"You know I can deliver. Now get going so I can clean up." She swatted him on the ass.

Logan was out of the house and halfway across the lawn before he remembered what she'd said that morning.

I want you, Logan. Only you.

Why only? Did he need to ask who else she might be wanting? Or who might be wanting her?

* * * *

Suzi smacked a mosquito on her arm and leaned against the deck. So far Logan believed the nightmare-PMS story she'd come up with this morning. Acclimating herself to having kinky dreams about Brian was going to take time. Brian? She liked him. With the exception of those first couple of awkward meetings, she was destined to like him. As a friend. They could never be more than friends. She couldn't allow it to be more. She had a boyfriend. Logan was hot, famous, and seemed to like her right now. It wouldn't last. She knew that. She could count on one finger the number of rock stars who had a serious relationship, but the ride would be worth it.

Except now she was losing her mind and imagining she was in love with Brian Ellis of Touchstone. Because Logan Fitzpatrick of Savitar wasn't good enough anymore. Oh, God!

Suzi hugged herself. Brian had left this morning. Flown home to salvage his marriage based on her brilliant encouragement.

Good. That was good. She'd done a good thing. And once he was out of sight, she wouldn't be convinced she was falling in love with him anymore. Everything would be fine.

Jason strolled over with a beer in one hand and a Coke in the other. "What are you doing over here in the dark? The party's over there. You know, where the fire is." He handed her the Coke.

"I know. I was just standing back and enjoying the view."

"Observing so you can put it in a book later? Remember, I'm very charming."

"I know." Suzi opened the bottle. He'd been so nice remembering her drink preferences, she felt obligated.

Jason draped his arm over her shoulders. "I wanted to thank you. You've been a huge help with Andi, and you gave Brian a good pep talk yesterday."

"It's nothing."

"Says you." He kissed her forehead.

"What the fuck are you doing?" Logan demanded, suddenly right beside them.

Suzi jumped and dropped her pop. She wasted a moment grabbing for it. Logan had Jason by the shirt and was pressing him back against the deck railing. Shock had vanished from Jason's eyes, replaced by something a bit more dangerous.

"Keep your fucking hands off my girlfriend," Logan snarled.

"Fuck off. I'm not doing anything to your girlfriend." Jason tried to shove Logan back, but only managed to gain a few inches. Suzi heard Jason's shirt rip.

"Logan, stop it. Just stop it," she said, trying to maintain a calm tone but failing, judging by the squeak. If Brian were here, he'd be able to defuse this situation.

Logan tried to get back in Jason's face. "You need to stay away from my fucking girlfriend."

"Why?" Jason demanded.

"Jason, stop it. Both of you, stop it." Suzi wedged herself between them, facing Logan. It was like a nature show with two rams facing off with her getting crushed between. "Logan, let him go."

"I know what you're doing," Logan snapped, focusing over her head on Jason.

"And what's that?"

"Jason, stop provoking him," Suzi pleaded. She worked her arms up in front of her and planted her hands on Logan's chest. "Can you stop being crazy for a minute, please?"

"You're not going to take her away from me."

Suzi forced her arms straight, shoving Logan backward. He tripped and staggered back a step. Losing Logan's support, she stumbled and Jason caught her arm before she fell. Lunging forward, Logan drew back his arm, preparing to swing. Suzi threw herself forward in time to get clipped on the temple and thrown back into Jason's arms.

The silence was shattering.

Suzi shook her head, and the whole world swayed around her. Jason had his arms around her, supporting her weight. The fire crackled, but no one spoke for a long time. Suzi touched her temple, expecting to feel dampness or a lump or a dent, something, but there was nothing. Her motion seemed to spur Jason into action. He stepped in front of her, shielding her from Logan.

"What's wrong with you, hitting a girl?" Jason demanded.

"Jesus, Suzi—" Logan reached for her. "I'm sorry. Did I hurt you?"

Rubbing her face, Suzi jerked away from him and walked toward the steps to the guesthouse. Her head rattled with broken thoughts. She blinked away tears that had sprung to her eyes.

Logan followed her. "Suzi, I'm sorry. I didn't mean to hit you."

"Are you all right?" Jason was half a step behind him, and everyone else was on an intercept course.

She shifted her jaw. "I'm fine." She just wanted to go inside and hide for a minute.

"Are you sure?" Jason asked. "You want some ice?"

"What happened?" Cassie asked.

"Nothing," Suzi said before they could speak. "I just want to go to the bathroom."

Jason stopped at the top of the stairs, but Logan, Greg, and Cassie followed her down.

"Suzi, I'm sorry." Logan opened the cabin door.

"Let me take a look at it." Cass reached for her.

Suzi pulled away. "It's nothing. I'm fine." She walked through the door and tried to pull it closed behind her, but Logan squeezed in and followed her to the bathroom.

"Suzi, it was an accident."

"Was it, Logan?" She turned to him. Jason, Cassie, and Greg were now all hovering by the front window where they could see some of the bathroom. "You were planning to hit somebody. Why not me?"

"I wasn't thinking straight."

"Ya think?"

"I saw you guys and I thought—"

"Jesus, Logan, it's not like you caught us *en flagrante delicto*." She peered into the mirror. There was a red mark on her temple. Grabbing a washcloth, she wiped her face. Good thing he hadn't seen her in the woods with Brian. She shivered at the memory of sliding into Brian's arms on the waterfall. But she hadn't done anything. She hadn't taken it any further than that moment. That should get her some points. "Don't you trust me?"

"I trust you."

"Un-fucking-believable. Like I'm going to run off with a married man." Like Brian. Suzi blinked at her reflection. She did want to run off with a married man. Logan just had the wrong one.

"I turned around and saw him with his arm around you, kissing you—"

"On the forehead?"

"I couldn't see that. I just—it looked like—" Logan ran his hands through his hair. "I've been having these really awful nightmares."

"About what?" She glanced at him in the mirror. He was blushing.

Logan closed his eyes. "I love you, Suzi. I keep having these dreams of you and Jason together, and it's making me crazy. The idea that you might... That I could lose you."

Suzi turned. Brian was right. Jason was making Logan question himself, and in questioning, he'd started to wonder why she was with him. "You tried to deck Jason Callisto."

"I know."

She set down the washcloth and put her arms around him. Logan was so afraid of losing her, he was willing to ruin his career. No one had ever loved her that much. Her heart twisted. She had never loved anyone this much, either. Why had she ever thought she was falling for Brian? "Logan, you have to trust me. I'm not going to leave you for another man. I love you and want to be with you."

"Unless someone better comes along."

"No." She stroked his cheek. "There's no one better." Rising up on her toes, she kissed him. Instantly, he relaxed, opening her mouth and bending her back.

"Suzi," he murmured, kissing her throat. "God, I love you. I don't even remember what it was like to be without you. I can't live without you. I'm so sorry."

"You were aiming for Jason. You should apologize to him."

"Yeah. I guess so."

Suzi brushed her fingers through his hair. "He's trying to help you get better. You understand that, don't you?"

Logan stared at her, uncertainty clear in his eyes.

Suzi put her finger over his lips. "*Bayonet Ball* sold eight million copies and had five hit singles. *Lucky Charmer* sold six and a half million copies and had four hit singles. He knows how to do that. And even if he can't pull it off for you, there's legions of Touchstone fans who are going to say, 'Jason Callisto produced this. I need to hear it.' It's going to give you so much exposure."

"It doesn't really work like that," Logan muttered.

"I was a consumer for a long time before I became a creator. Trust me, it does. You're getting Jason's seal of approval. You need to learn everything you can from him while you have the chance, and you can't muck it up by being defensive."

"You're so smart. How did I get anywhere without you?" He nuzzled her cheek.

"Sheer determination. Now, Jason's standing at the door." She nodded toward the door. Jason, Suzi, and Greg still peered through the window.

Logan allowed her to pull him to the door and open it. When she turned to prompt him, he clenched his teeth. She smiled, and his expression softened.

"Everything okay?" Cassie asked.

"Yeah, um, Jason, sorry about that before. I thought I saw something— y'know..." Logan held out his hand.

"S'all right. I understand. I wouldn't want anyone messing with my wife." Jason shook his hand.

The moment the one pump handshake finished, Logan wrapped his arm around Suzi's shoulders. His grip was tight and reassuring. Suzi laced her fingers through his and leaned her cheek on his shoulder. He did love her. Enough to fight for her. That was precious.

Chapter 10

Wally parked the rental truck in the drive. "Are you sure about this? I can move your stuff out for you."

Suzi stared at the house. No, she wasn't sure, but she needed it. She had to get it together and start living something that resembled an adult life. Even if it was an adult life that included roadies willing to move stuff for her.

Every window was sealed against the August heat, and there was no central air. The house was going to be an oven. The grass was long and straggly, and the city had nailed a threatening note to the porch.

"Give me a minute in case Logan is in there."

"I'm not giving you more than a minute. He's in there," Wally told her. Wally had been trying to dispel her hope that she could do this without confrontation since he'd picked her up at the airport. She wasn't exactly sure when he'd gone from being a Savitar man to being hers, but she appreciated it.

She forced herself out of the car and up the steps to the back door. The screen door and the inside door were closed. Very bad signs. She braced herself before opening them. Hot, fetid air rolled over her. Shaking her head, she backed down a step to let the first blast pass before stepping inside. She left the back door standing open as she walked into the kitchen. The counter was littered with empty liquor bottles, moldy plates, and crusty baking dishes. A couple of the pieces belonged to neighbors or his mom. They had tried to feed him, but most of it was uneaten and alive with mold. No bugs at least, but then maybe the house was shut up too tight for anything to get in.

She walked around the first floor gathering bottles and opening windows. Most of the food had stayed in the kitchen. All she found were liquor bottles. Lots of them. When Wally came in, she asked him in a whisper to put all the bottles into the recycling bin while she scraped the food into the trash. As he did that, she took the bag outside before putting the dishes into hot water to soak.

Wally had set to work putting fans in the windows by the time she finished. Already, the smell was clearing. "I'll be down here with an ear open."

Suzi nodded and started up the stairs. Sweat ran down her face, stinging her eyes. Another large collection of bottles crowded her office door, but the office appeared untouched. A coating of dust lay on everything. Her carefully tended African violet had shriveled on the sill. Outside the bedroom door, she chickened out. Instead, she went up to the attic, opened those windows, and put in a fan to draw out the worst of the heat. Moving back to the second floor, she started opening windows, not sure if the heat was already dissipating or if she was just getting used to it. Her stomach clenched as she opened the last window in the guest room. The only room left was their bedroom. Anything could be in there. Piles of dirty clothes. Logan. Logan's dead body. Another woman.

No. No one else would have allowed the house to get this hot and this smelly. Any other human would have at least opened windows and gotten the rotting food out of the kitchen. Not even the most hardcore and desperate groupie would have allowed it to go this far. And if there was another woman, the neighbors and his mom wouldn't be feeding him.

The smell wasn't bad enough for Logan's dead body to be up there, either. According to her research, dead bodies had a repellant, frightening stink to them, and nothing like that emanated from the bedroom. Poor hygiene, yes, death, no.

She eased open the door and peered around it. The forest green carpet was buried under cast-off clothing as if he'd intentionally hidden the floor. The matching drapes were drawn against the sun, plunging the room into darkness. After he bought the house, they'd spent months decorating. Logan had loved picking out colors and finding just the right furniture. While they worked at the house, he'd kept saying he wanted this to be the place they grew old in together. For some reason, she'd bought the story. The filmy curtains around the bed were drawn, making it easier to spend time opening windows and putting off the inevitable.

Then she walked to the bed. Taking a deep breath, she pushed back the curtain. Logan lay in the middle, twisted up in the sheets with only an empty Jack Daniels bottle to accompany him. His hair was greasy and tangled. He had about two inches of beard that was also matted. Suzi didn't like to think what with. His ribs poked out like a xylophone. He reeked like he hadn't seen the inside of a shower since she left. She leaned over the bed, grazing his jaw with her fingers.

His eyes snapped open, and he grabbed her wrist, pulling her forward. She squealed and jerked backward.

"Suzi?" he whimpered.

"Y-yes." She shuddered. His eyes had always been dark, but now they were black and dangerous. His grip on her wrist was so tight she could feel the bones grinding together. "Logan, you're hurting me."

Staring down at his hand around her wrist, he blinked, frowning. "You're really here." He loosened his grip, but didn't let her go. "Are you coming home?"

"What's happened to you?" She knelt on the bed and touched his cheek.

"I can't live without you Suzi. I need you to come home."

"Logan, please let me go."

"I don't want to live without you." He released her. "Go away so I can die faster."

"No. No, it's not fair." Suzi pulled her wrist against her chest, rubbing it. "If you give up, I can't ever come home." She scuttled backward and fell off the side of the bed, banging her head on the wall.

"I can't live without you." Logan mumbled into the mattress.

"And I can't live like this." She crawled away from the bed. Her gut hurt as if she'd been punched. On her hands and knees in the middle of the room, she pressed her cheek against the carpet, remembering the day they chose it. The rich, beautiful shade to contrast with the pale yellow walls. The dark wood of the bed frame with the bright white, filmy curtains around it like a dream. Right now, she wanted nothing better than to disappear into that fantasy.

"Suzi?" Logan touched her shoulder. "Suzi, do you want to come home?"

"Of course I want to come home. Don't be an idiot." She sobbed. "This is my *home*."

"Then come home. Now. Please. I need you." He stroked his hand down her arm. The touch was agonizing. "I can't."

"But why? This is where you want to be, isn't it?"

"You gave up. You disappeared into a bottle, and you left me alone out here."

"You left me," Logan said.

"I'm here now. I thought— I hoped—" She pulled herself into a tighter ball. "I'm so tired, Logan."

"You look tired, sugar. Why don't you come to bed and rest? Let me take care of you." He pushed up her T-shirt, nuzzling her back. "You taste so good, Suzi. Sweeter than wine." He shoved her shirt over her head and reached for her bra. Moaning, she dug her fingernails into the carpet wanting to roll over and take him into her arms, into her body. Just like always. As if none of this ever happened. She'd closed her eyes to his behavior for years. Why couldn't she keep doing that? "You are the most beautiful woman I have ever known."

Overhead, something fell with a bang. The fan in the attic window. Suzi jerked. He was drunk, filthy, and disgusting. "No. Stop. Don't." She pushed away from him and scrambled to her feet. "Stop it, Logan. You can't just take me to bed and all is forgiven this time."

"Why?" He staggered toward her on his knees.

"Everything okay up there?" Wally called.

Logan sat back on his heels. "You brought a bodyguard?"

"I brought Wally to help me move." Suzi chewed her lip.

"Wally, you fucker. You are never going to work again," Logan roared.

"Sure thing, boss," Wally answered.

Suzi turned to the bed. Yanking the sheets off, she threw them on the floor. "You need to shower."

"I thought you were packing."

Suzi unhooked the curtains. They carried an aroma, too. "I can't leave you like this."

"Why should I shower?"

"I can't come home if you stink."

"You might come home?"

Suzi turned to him, clutching the curtains in front of her. This was her home. She had nowhere else to go. Closing her eyes, she sat down on the bed.

He sat down beside her. "I'm sorry," he whispered.

"For what?"

"Everything. I'm a jerk. The house is a mess. I'm a drunk."

"Sh. Not now. Let's go shower."

"Us?"

She tensed. How many times had they made love in that shower? How many times had he touched her and told her he loved her as he washed her hair? He loved to shave her legs. Never once had he even nicked her. "I meant, you need to shower."

He walked out. She followed him into the bathroom. It was vile. Logan had been sick and had very bad aim. She picked up a barrette from the counter to put her hair up. The butterfly he'd bought her in Japan. She started wiping down the counters. Logan picked up two moldy towels and dropped them into the trash. Suzi sprayed out the shower area and left the room. It needed more, but she wasn't up to the temptation of climbing in there right now. "Don't forget to drink some water."

Bundling everything into the fitted sheet, she carried it downstairs. Wally was attacking something crusted on a clear Pyrex dish. The basement door stuck before it popped open. At the sound, Wally turned around.

"You're gonna stay, aren't you?" His soft, sweet face had gone hard, his eyes glittered like ice chips.

Tears welled in her eyes. This was her home. How could she not stay? But how could she stay?

"He's gonna stomp on you again."

She nodded.

"You've got other places to go." Wally stalked across the kitchen, dishwater dripping off his big, scarred hands. "Why won't you call your friends? Somebody from fucking Touchstone has been on the phone with me almost every day. Sometimes twice a day. The band, the management office, their fucking publicist. I lied to Marc yesterday and told him I hadn't heard from you because you told me to. I got an email from Jackie at the SendDown office wanting to know if I'd heard from you. They just got back from fucking Europe and want to know where you are. All those guys are worried about you, and you go back to him? You have eight thousand places to go, and you want to go back to him?"

"I love him."

"No, you don't. You think you're responsible for him." Wally leaned in. His effectiveness as a security guy didn't come from his six-foot-eight height and weightlifter's build. His real success came from his scowl. "I am not leaving you here tonight, and I am not leaving you alone with him."

"He would never hurt me."

"He already is. And you are letting him." Wally walked back to the sink to attack the dish again.

Suzi scuttled down the basement stairs and stuffed the sheets into the washer. On the way back up, she grabbed a clothesbasket to clean the bedroom floor. Wally had finished the dish without breaking it and moved on to the next. He didn't speak as she reached around his legs to grab her bottle of bleach water from under the sink. As awful as the house smelled, the scent of bleach would be an improvement.

She collected all the clothes on the bedroom floor into the basket and left it at the top of the stairs. Then she went back and sprayed the mattress and pillows.

"Hey sugar, do we have pair of scissors in here?" Logan yelled from the bathroom.

"Little ones in the drawer by the sink. Drink water."

"Drink water," he repeated. Then the faucet turned on and a cup filled.

She wiped the mattress with a rag to spread the bleach around and started on the other surfaces. What he needed in here was a carpet cleaner. Why had the cleaning people stopped? They came once a month to handle heavy stuff, but the entire house was coated in dust, and she couldn't imagine them letting those dishes grow in the sink. She'd have to give the cleaners a call.

"Hey sugar, what do you think I'd look like with a mustache?"

"Like some other woman's boyfriend." Oh, no. Suzi sucked in a breath, trying to pull the comment back, but it hung in the air like feedback. She peered out the bedroom door.

Logan stood in the hall, his face slack as if he'd just been smacked in the face with a mic stand.

She cleared her throat. "I'm sorry."

He shrugged. "S'okay."

Suzi hurried down the hall and grabbed the basket. Before she could make her escape, Logan grabbed her arm. "Where are you going?" There were traces of shaving foam on his cheeks. Without the beard, he appeared even more gaunt.

"Downstairs to sort the laundry. Then I'm going to run to the grocery store. I'm willing to bet everything in the refrigerator is spoiled."

"But you're coming back, right?" His eyes pleaded with her.

"I'm not going to drive all the way to California with groceries." She tried to smirk, but it hung on her face lopsided. "I'll be back in a little while. Wally will be here."

Chapter 11

Wally. Like that was a treat. Logan watched her run down the stairs with the overflowing clothesbasket in her arms. Why the fuck had she brought Wally with her? Wally had become "her" security guy on tour to protect her from the fans, not from him. In the basement, he heard her banging around. Maybe if he made more of an effort, she'd stay. Logan went back into the bathroom and finished shaving. Then he cleaned it up to her standards using the bleach she'd left behind. He never should have let everything get this out of control. No wonder she thought she needed a bodyguard. He'd scared off the cleaners and the yard guys. Next on the to-do list should be calling them with hefty tips and apologies.

From the kitchen, he heard her talking to Wally and then her car started in the garage. The refrigerator made a sick sucking sound, and Wally gagged. Wally, who had dragged ODing guys out of bathtubs and done CPR on them, was grossed out by his fridge. He had let things get way too out of hand.

In the bedroom, she had stripped the bed that now smelled of bleach. He touched it to make sure it was dry, and then found some fresh sheets to make it up. When he finished that, he had to sit down for a minute because the world was spinning. When was the last time he'd eaten anything? Of course, there was nothing edible in the house. That was why Suzi was out shopping and Wally was gagging in the kitchen. In the closet, he found some clothes he'd managed to not destroy and put them on. Wally was on his knees in front of the fridge, pulling everything out and throwing it away. All the windows were open, but the stench lingered. Logan located the baking soda in the cupboard, took it upstairs, and sprinkled it on the carpet.

He let it sit while he checked the laundry. Passing through the kitchen, he noticed Wally had moved on to wiping out the fridge and acted as though Logan wasn't in the room. Suzi probably told him to. Wally had an unnatural attachment to his girlfriend. As soon as he got her back, he had to talk to management about getting her a different bodyguard, or at least mixing things up a little. The washer was just starting the first spin cycle, so he ran upstairs to vacuum the bedroom. When he finished, the place already smelled better.

Suzi had the grocery store down to a science so she wouldn't be long.

If it hadn't been so awful when she got here in the first place, she might have stayed.

But she hadn't left yet.

What could he do to keep that from happening?

She liked drying stuff outside. Claimed it smelled better. He tossed the wet sheets in an empty basket and loaded the washer with the next load. Then he carried the wet stuff out and hung everything on her precious clotheslines.

The lawn was bad. Really bad. Once, a month or so ago, there had been a kitchen garden right outside the back door. Now, it was a jungle that spilled into the rest of the yard. He could fix that, too. If she gave him the chance, he would fix it all.

Heading back inside, he heard Wally upstairs thumping around. He opened the refrigerator. It was empty and blinding white again. The various dishes people had been dropping off in an attempt to get him to eat were all clean and drying on the counter. It sounded like Wally was in Suzi's office.

What the fuck was he doing in Suzi's office?

Logan ran up the stairs two at a time. Wally was dusting off her books before he packed them in boxes. "What the fuck are you doing?"

Wally pulled another book off the shelf, wiped it off, and put it in the box.

"I'm talking to you," Logan shouted.

Wally repeated the process with Suzi's big Riverside *Shakespeare.*

Logan grabbed the book and tried to yank it out of Wally's hands. He might as well have been trying to pull a branch off a tree. "Let go."

"You."

"Why are you packing her stuff? She's not leaving."

"Yes, she is."

Logan grabbed a handful of books out of the box and shoved them back on the shelf. "No, she's not."

Wally stood up and took a step toward Logan. "She made me promise I wouldn't hurt you. Don't make me break that promise."

Logan backed toward the door. He stood for a minute, watching Wally get back to his task as if he hadn't been interrupted. Panic clawed at his throat. If she took her books, she was really gone. Could he get the house clean enough, turn himself around fast enough, to keep her from taking those boxes out of the house? He went to the bedroom to get the baking soda and took it downstairs to put on the rugs in the living room and the parlor. While he left it to work, he went down to the basement for the next load.

She'd been gone an awfully long time.

Maybe the grocery store was a cover.

Maybe she wasn't coming back after all.

But she left Wally here. She made Wally promise not to hurt him.

He hung the second load outside. While he was out there, Wally carried out two boxes and loaded them into a truck. When Logan had finished hanging the laundry, he went back in and vacuumed the rugs. The sound of the vacuum drowned out Wally's thumping. Would she take the desk? The shelves? They were hers from before. She'd never let him buy her better ones.

The bathroom downstairs was in as bad a shape as the one upstairs. No one would want to come home to this. He started working on it, peering out the window every few seconds for her car.

How long could it possibly take her to run to the store for a few things? She usually set a land speed record there.

But Wally had thrown out every single thing in the fridge including the mustard, and she probably needed to scout around for stuff he needed.

They needed. *Please God, let it be for stuff they needed.*

He went down to the basement to check the laundry. It was spinning. So was his head. He sat on the washer until it stopped. Then he loaded everything into a basket and hauled it upstairs.

She was unpacking a plastic grocery bag.

"You came back." He dropped the basket and hugged her.

"Of course I did. I said I would." She leaned her head against his chest. "I stopped at the farmer's market to get some corn and some salad stuff. Did I take too long or something?"

"No. I just wondered. You're usually quicker."

She frowned at the basket he'd dropped on the floor. "You're hanging all the laundry out? You don't like the laundry hung out. Did you think I wasn't coming back?"

"I don't—I guess…" He worked his fingers into her hair. "It just took you a long time."

"Logan, I promised I would come back from the grocery store."

"Will you come home?"

She turned her face away and closed her eyes. "Please, Logan…"

"Not now," he finished for her. He leaned down and kissed her. "I'll go hang up the clothes."

Outside, he hung the current load and took down the first one. Except for Wally loading boxes into the back of his truck, it could have been any normal day. When he walked back in, Suzi was on the phone. She had a pot of water boiling on the stove. "Well, thank you, Jason. I'll keep that in mind. Tell Cassie I said hello. Bye." She hung up the phone.

"What did Jason want?"

"To see if you were sober." She started chopping something. "He's called a couple of times, and apparently every time you answered, you were hammered."

He didn't even remember talking to Jason. Who else had called or tried to talk to him? He didn't even recognize most of the dishes, now dry and stacked on the kitchen table. A couple belonged to his mom. Shit, when had his mom been by, and how bad had he been for her to leave him like this? "What are you making?"

"Jell-O. You need fluids. Don't worry. I bought Cool Whip. I'm making potato salad, too. And I picked you up some hot dogs and veggie burgers because those are easy to cook."

Easy for him to cook. She could cook anything she set her mind to. Which meant she wasn't staying no matter how fast he cleaned or how he dried the laundry. Logan sat down at the table. "Is it time now?"

"Time for what?"

"Time to talk."

"No Logan, it is not time to talk. The time to talk is over."

"It can't be. You wouldn't have come back if it was."

Wally walked through the room carrying two more boxes. A large, sweaty reminder that it was time for her to pack her things. The bastard had amazing timing.

"Logan, I can't continue the way we have been." She plucked a piece of potato out of the boiling water and tested it.

"So I'll change."

"I've heard this tune before." Suzi poured the potatoes into a strainer. Steam curled around her head.

"I know, I know." He moved to stand behind her. Brushing aside her ponytail, he kissed her neck, and she shivered. Her neck was the best public place to touch her, and she loved when he kissed her there. He loved kissing her there, too. The velvet texture of her skin and the neat curve reminded him of more private nooks. "Sugar, listen. I'm serious this time," he whispered. "I'll do therapy or whatever you want. We can do couples counseling." He slid his hands around her waist. She had such a tiny waist he could almost wrap his hands all the way around.

"How am I supposed to believe you?" Her voice had the squeaky thread of tears in it. "You've made promises like that before."

"But this time I know what it's like when you leave me, and I can't take it." He dipped his tongue behind her ear, testing that sweet sensitive spot. "Please, sugar. You can see I can't live without you."

The kitchen door banged behind them.

Suzi jumped.

Fucking Wally.

Suzi eased away from Logan. "Please don't make this harder than it is."

"It doesn't have to be hard." But it was, in more ways than he wanted to think about. Just touching her turned him on. If Wally hadn't walked in, he'd have forgotten all about talking her into staying in favor of seducing her. Seducing her always had worked before. Two birds, one stone. He glared at Wally. "Did you need something?"

Wally gave him a hard stare, and then turned to Suzi. She must have given him the order to stand down because he stomped up the back stairs.

Suzi dumped the potatoes into a glass bowl and threw the celery and onions she'd been chopping on top. "I stocked you up with enough food to keep you for at least a week. I'm assuming you'll go out some. The house already looks better, but you should call the cleaners and the lawn guys."

"Do you want to come home, Suzi?"

"Have Emily come in and look around first. This isn't an average job. The carpets need cleaned. The drapes need washed." She squeezed mayonnaise into the bowl. "It's going to take her a few days to do it all."

"You didn't answer my question."

She mixed the potato salad. "I was pregnant, Logan."

Logan took a step back and grasped the edge of the table. "Was?"

"I lost it. Right after the party."

The party. "I didn't know."

"Would it have made a difference?"

"Of course, it would have. Do you really think I'm that big a monster?"

"Logan, it shouldn't have made a difference whether I was pregnant or not," Suzi shouted.

"Don't ask me trick questions and get pissed off when I answer them wrong."

Suzi snatched up the bowl and smashed it on the floor. "She was sucking your fingers."

"It was an accident."

Wally thundered down the stairs.

"An accident?" she shrieked.

"I spilled some of my drink on my hand."

"That is what napkins are for, Logan. Napkins!"

"What is going on?" Wally growled.

"We're having a fight. Is that all right with you?" Logan yelled at him. He buried his hands in his hair. More than life, he wanted to walk through the potato salad and glass, bend Suzi back against the counter, and remind her why she loved him. He could take a few cuts. He deserved the pain.

"It's time to go." Wally stepped over the mess and grabbed Suzi by the arm. "Come on. You need to be out of here."

Suzi resisted for a second, staring across the room at Logan. Tears streaked her beautiful face. Then she let Wally lead her out. Logan followed and watched Wally help her into the truck. As Wally drove away, he put his arm around Suzi's shoulder. Logan should be glad she had somebody to take care of her, but he couldn't get past wanting to beat the shit out of Wally.

He went back into the house and sat at the kitchen table, watching the potato salad spoil on the floor. All she took this time were books. Her clothes were still upstairs in their closet. She had bought him healthy food that was easy to fix and had given him instructions on how to clean up the place, but she never said she wasn't going to come back. In the bedroom, she had told him she couldn't come home if he stank. Didn't that mean she wanted to come home? Hadn't she given him the answer?

The mayonnaise on the floor was turning clear, and the shadows were getting long. He had to do something. Too bad about the potato salad. Suzi made the best potato salad.

After he'd cleaned up the kitchen and taken down the laundry, he sat down with the phone. The cleaning service was hesitant to return, but agreed when he promised a nice bonus. The lawn service told him to fuck off. Apparently, he'd thrown bottles at them, and the high weeds in the front yard were now laced with broken glass. He'd have to find another service and hope they hadn't talked to the first guy, otherwise he'd be out there mowing his own lawn. He also picked a therapist at random from the phone book and made an appointment.

Last, he dialed Jason. "Hey, you called before."

"And Suzi answered. How goes things?"

"Wally hauled her out of here a couple of hours ago."

"Wally?"

"He's kinda her personal security guy."

"She brought a bodyguard?"

"Yeah. She brought a bodyguard."

"Did she need one?"

He should have remembered that Jason fell into Suzi's protector camp. Greg always said the first time a guy met Suzi, he didn't know whether to fuck her or protect her from all the other guys who wanted to fuck her. As a married man with sisters, Jason had gone for protector. "No. I would never hurt her. You know that. I just didn't want her to leave until we had a chance to talk."

"And you didn't."

"No, we started yelling, and she broke a bowl on the floor. It was just— it was bad. It's probably good Wally got her out of here. But I can fix this. I know I can." Through the phone, he heard Cassie say something.

"Cassie wants to know what you're doing to fix it."

"I'm getting the house cleaned and the lawn taken care of. The place was kind of a mess when she got here."

"So were you."

"So was I." Logan hung his head.

"And what about the problem with groupies?"

"You know what they're like."

"I do, and I'm still married to a woman with a thing about faithfulness. What are you going to do about groupies?"

Picking a therapist had been a lot easier than admitting to starting therapy. Logan guessed sticking to it was going to be harder yet. Might as well get the little stuff out of the way. "I made an appointment with a therapist. I want to figure out what I have to do to not make the same mistakes."

"Mistakes?"

"You know. Getting caught up in that."

"Bear once told me to remember that groupies are hamburgers, and I've got filet mignon at home. And my filet has a shotgun. Ow!"

The *ow* had been preceded by a smacking sound and followed by the murmur of Cassie giving Jason further instructions. Logan crossed his fingers because that was all he could do at this point. Cassie and Suzi were close. Her opinion would carry a lot of weight. Cassie on his side might very well get Suzi back by his side.

"You are going to stick with the therapy."

"I am. I swear. I can't lose her, Jason."

"Okay, we'll try to help."

* * * *

"Jason talked to Suzi today," Marc said when Brian answered the phone.

"He did?" Brian held his breath, trying not to give anything away. Every lead he'd followed had come up empty. No one admitted to having any clue where she was. And she fucking called Jason? Why Jason? "Where is she?"

"She answered the phone at Logan's."

Brian's stomach hit the floor. He hadn't intended to hope and had convinced himself he wasn't, but there it was. "So they're back together?" Because he needed to twist the knife.

"No."

Brian sat up. A "no" was hopeful, at least from his perspective. "Then what was she doing at his house?"

"Moving out."

Now *that* was promising.

"She took along Wally, and when they got into a fight, he dragged her out."

"Wally?"

"Her bodyguard."

Brian picked up the folder full of dedication pages from her books. He'd printed them out so he could make notes on them. There it was. She'd dedicated *The Power Behind* to *Mrs. Helen Wheals for the great name and Wally Henderson, the best security a girl could have.*' He'd found an email for Wally, but never gotten a response. "Wally Henderson?"

"Yeah. I just talked to that bastard, and he said he hadn't heard from her."

"You know him?"

"Sure, I've met him a couple of times. I called him a few days ago because I knew he was tight with Suzi, and I wanted to know if he'd heard from her."

"How did you meet him?"

"I don't remember. Shows, hotels, studios. Who the hell knows? I've bumped into him a couple dozen times. He's a huge guy. You can't miss him."

"Often enough to have his number."

"At least I'm not badgering Suzi's publisher."

Brian licked his teeth. Lying was going to make things worse. "So I called her publisher. I was concerned."

"All of them."

"I'm a customer, and I thought they might have information. Anyway, how do you know?"

"Because they told me when I called them."

Brian wondered if he should stop worrying about Logan and start worrying more about his bandmates. No, not Marc. He'd worked too hard to catch Alex to leave her, even for Suzi. Ty wasn't even in the running. But if he and Marc were tracking her, how many other guys were too? "So did you call Wally again?"

"The bastard didn't answer his phone. He's avoiding me."

Just like Jason must be avoiding me. What did he know? Had he figured it out? Is that why he was keeping the news about Suzi going to Logan's from him? When Marc branched off into another conversation, Brian made the appropriate noises to convince Marc he was listening.

Why would Jason keep the news from him? He might be plotting something. He would want to keep Suzi and Logan together because he hated to see a relationship fail. Couldn't he see that Suzi was far too good for Logan? Cassie could be behind this, too. She liked Suzi and had a pathological need to make sure everyone was happy. If she was trying to get Suzi and Logan back together she'd...

Send them to West Virginia. That was Cassie's answer to everything, as if her hometown could heal the hurts of the world if they would simply spend a week walking through the woods and eating at least once a day at Ida's. Ida's did have the best pie in Eastern Standard Time, but it probably wouldn't solve the problems in the Middle East or get that guy from North Korea to chill.

"Are they going to WVA?" Brian asked.

"Who? The Rams? I don't think West Virginia has a pro football team."

"Jason and Cassie."

"Probably, he didn't say. Why?"

Why? If he'd bothered to pay attention to what Marc was talking about he wouldn't be in this fix. "I don't know. I was just thinking I could use a little peace and quiet."

"Give him a call and find out. You're a little distracted today. Coming up on the anniversary of the divorce, isn't it?"

"Yeah." Any excuse in a storm. Brian checked his calendar. It was coming up on the anniversary, but only because it had taken three fucking years to reach a settlement.

"That sucks. What is this, your second? WVA might be just the thing."

"Yeah, I think I'll give Jason a call. Talk to you later." He disconnected and dialed Jason. "Hey, I hear you heard from Suzi today." Brian rolled his eyes to the ceiling. Idiot, idiot, idiot.

"Yeah, did you just talk to Marc?"

"I just got off the phone with him. He said she was at Logan's." Now that he'd stepped in this, he might as well stomp around a little.

"Moving out."

"How did she sound?"

"You know. Fragile. I talked to Logan, too. He's a changed man."

"Yeah." The last thing Brian wanted to hear about was Logan's brand spanking new attitude. If Logan had a brain to his name, he'd have figured out how to take care of Suzi a couple of years ago instead of fucking her over every time he thought she had her back turned.

"I'm serious. He sounded sincere when I talked to him."

"I'll believe it when I see it. Anyway, that isn't what I called to talk to you about. Are you guys going to be in WVA anytime soon?"

"Maybe in a couple of weeks. Why?"

"I just thought I could use a little peace and quiet. It's coming up on my second anniversary." Brian almost felt like a heel for using that excuse. Almost.

"Is that why you've been such a bastard lately? Sure. Cassie's parents have the keys. You might have some company in a few weeks."

Then they did plan to lure Suzi to WVA. A few days to make his play was all he needed. And if Logan was there, that moron would make it easier for Brian to be Suzi's knight in shining armor. "That's okay. It's a big mountain."

Chapter 12

Three years ago

Logan parked his car in front of the office. He didn't like being summoned in like this. It always reminded him of being in trouble in school. The worst thing he'd done in the last twenty-four hours was screw around with Suzi in the back of the limo, and nobody knew about that.

"Logan." Elizabeth wore a crisp white blouse and a shell-shocked expression. Were they being sued?

"What's up?" He leaned on her desk.

"You better talk to Jim about it." She fixed her gaze on the desktop.

"He in his office?"

She nodded without meeting his eyes.

Logan headed to the office, but he could hear the shouting from behind the closed door at the end of the hall. Jim's big roar. Diana's high-pitched shriek. Frank's throaty growl. He knocked, and the yelling stopped.

Frank jerked open the door, and the fury melted off his face. "Logan. You're here."

"Yeah, because you told me to get my ass down here." Logan stepped into the office. They were all crowded around Jerry's big desk, looking guilty as hell.

"You didn't bring Suzi, did you?" Frank asked.

"No. Why? What's this about?"

"You better sit down," Diana said. "Something has come to light. Something potentially embarrassing for you and Suzi." She turned the monitor on Jerry's desk so Logan could see it. The three of them arranged themselves to the sides where they couldn't possibly see the screen.

"Me and Suzi?" Logan's gut froze solid. The image on the computer looked way too much like the back of the limo they'd been in last night. He'd done it as a treat for her. Last week, he'd called Elizabeth to arrange it. Ride to the premiere of her friend's movie in a limo. He'd gotten a couple for her friend and his costars, too. They said it was like a real Hollywood premiere.

"Logan, as part of my job, I search the Internet daily for any mention of your names," Jim said. He'd put on his cop face, the one used to tell you your wife was hit by a drunk and killed about an hour ago when you thought she was out getting groceries. "I follow up on anything that doesn't look kosher. This morning I was doing my usual check, and this popped up." He reached back and tapped the mouse, but also kept his face away from the screen.

The title card was sub-amateur and read *Logan Fitzpatrick and Suzette Miranda Bazian go to Town in a Limo.* The title disappeared. He and Suzi climbed in the limo. First, they were kissing. She said something about rewarding him for his good deed. And then she got down on her knees.

"Turn it off," Logan said hoarsely. The picture vanished. "This is for sale somewhere?"

"Yeah." Jim said. "We've already started proceedings against the limo company, and they are very interested in finding out who planted that camera in the ceiling of your car. And the website has already been shut down, but it was one of those pay-to-download sites, so who knows how many of these things got out before I stopped them. We're trying to get a court order to access all their records, but the courts move a lot slower than the Internet. It's already available on the piracy sites, too. We're working on getting it taken down, but the minute we do, another one pops up."

Logan put his face in his hands. Suzi was going to die of humiliation. Ten seconds after she found out, she was going to start hating him for putting her in an X-rated video, and she'd have every right to hate him. Two minutes after she found out, she was going to pack her bags and be out the door so fast his head was going to spin. If there wasn't a way to keep this from her, he'd already lost her. She just didn't know she was gone.

"You can't let Suzi know about this," he said.

Frank moved to the front of his desk. "I know this is embarrassing, but you're going to have to face it head on."

"Why?" Logan peered up, pleading with his eyes for Frank to come up with a way to cover up the whole thing so he would never have to tell her they were on video having sex.

"You can't hide from this." Frank patted his shoulder. "It's going to come out, and I think she'd rather hear it from you."

"You're wrong about that. Can't *you* tell her?"

Frank blanched. "No. I shouldn't be the one to break the news, but I can talk to her after."

"I can talk to her, too," Jim said. He looked as if he'd rather wrestle a live crocodile than talk to Suzi about the sex tape, but he would do it if he had to. "I can fill her in on all the work we're doing to get it off the market and the precautions we're taking to make sure it doesn't happen again."

"What am I supposed to tell her?" Logan clutched the arms of the chair. All he'd done was have a little fun with his girl in a limo. Millions of high school kids had done the same thing. Why did he have to get clobbered for it?

"Just tell her the truth." Diana's voice had a rasp from screaming.

Logan pushed himself out of his chair. "Can I take the video?"

Frank ejected a DVD from the computer and dropped it in a jewel case as if it was radioactive. "I'm sorry about this. I should have seen it coming."

"I should have had those cars checked thoroughly." Jim snarled. "Those cameras are getting smaller and smaller and smarter and smarter. And the two of you are such a good-looking couple. It's no wonder somebody would want to watch you. I should have thought of it myself."

Logan clutched the jewel case in his hand until he heard it crack. If he lost Suzi over this, it was going to become his life purpose to hunt down the people who did this kind of crap and destroy them.

He swept out to his car, not even noticing Greg and John chatting in the parking lot.

"Hey, Logan, wait up!" Greg shouted, stopping him at his car door. "What's up? Why the summons?"

"Some asshole put a video camera in my car last night."

"In your car?" John asked. "At that movie thing?"

Logan watched as the truth soaked through them. In seconds, they wore matching expressions of horror.

"So they caught…something," Greg said.

"Yes, they caught me and Suzi fucking." Logan's face burned, and tears welled in his eyes. When she found out about the damn video, it was all he was going to have left of her. He sniffed, trying to control the sobs that wanted to break out of his chest.

John drew a deep breath. "Jesus."

"So what are they doing?" Greg asked.

"Frank is suing the limo company, and they already shut down the Internet site. Jim said he was getting a court order so they could run down all the people who bought—" Logan sobbed. "Who bought the download." Filthy strangers sitting in front of their computers watching his darling Suzi like she was any cheap slut working a sex show for them.

John put his arm around Logan's shoulders. "So it got stopped fast. You just did that last night. How many people could have gotten it?"

"It's being pirated." Logan buried his face against John's shoulder. Sobs shook him. He had to go home to her. Tell her. Show her the DVD. Then watch her walk out. And for the rest of his life, guys were going to be winking and nodding because they'd seen the nice piece of ass he'd once had. How far did the tape go? Did it show them cuddling on the seat? Him helping her get dressed again?

"Suzi will know this isn't your fault," Greg said. "It's not like you set up a camera in your bedroom and taped her every time or something." He patted Logan's shoulder.

"Yeah man, she'll understand," John said.

Wiping his eyes, Logan pulled himself away from John. He had to get it together. If she saw him like this, she was going to lose any respect she had for him. He sagged against the car door. By sunset, she was going to be at least a state away. Back to college to find herself a nice quiet professor. She could be anybody's baby now that she wasn't going to be his anymore. More sobs crowded his throat.

Logan stood. "I have to go tell her." He rubbed his face, trying to clean away the tear tracks. "I'll talk to you guys later."

Logan climbed into his car and pulled out. In the rearview mirror, he saw them lingering beside his now empty parking place as Toby drove in. Above them, the curtain in Frank's office twitched. They were his buddies, and soon they were going to be all he had again.

Following the familiar route home, he wished he had some reason to stop and put off the inevitable, but all the lights turned green as he approached. He was at his own driveway all too soon.

He walked in through the kitchen door. She wasn't in her second favorite haunt, the kitchen. Part of him was relieved she wouldn't have access to knives when he told her. He'd prefer she kill him before she left, but he didn't want her to spend the rest of her life in jail. Not in the living room either, but as he tried to summon the courage to peek into her office, she walked down the stairs.

"I thought I heard you come in." She smiled. Her hair was dripping down her back from the shower she must have just stepped from. She'd pulled on one of his concert T-shirts, but he could see by the way it molded to her body that she hadn't bothered to put on anything else.

"What's the matter?" Her warm smile melted as he stood like a stone, unable to open his mouth. "Logan?" Panic suffused the word. She reached for him, but he stepped back. "What is it?"

"Something…h-happened."

"What? What is it? Logan, tell me what happened." Her voice rose shrill with fear.

* * * *

"Movie time!" Ty popped the DVD into the player the hotel had loaned them and threw himself on the bed beside Brian, kicking Bear in the process.

"Hey, watch it," Bear shouted.

"You're the one laying on my bed." Ty juggled remotes, trying to find the one that operated the DVD player.

"I can't believe we have an evening off, and the best we can come up with is a movie," Marc muttered. "What happened to the girls? The parties? The debauchery?"

"We all got married and turned boring." Rudy leaned the chair back and propped his feet on the desk. "Start the fucking movie, Tyler."

"Wait a minute. I can't figure out which remote is which." He pointed one and pressed a button.

"You should have turned everything on from the TV like I told you to." Rudy picked his teeth with the hotel comment card.

"Yeah Ty, you should do everything the road manager tells you to do," Jason said.

"Wait, go back." Brian sat up. He hadn't seen what he thought he'd just seen. He *couldn't* have seen what he thought he'd just seen.

"What?" Ty hit another button and screen read *operation not permitted*.

Brian snatched the remote out of his hand and shut off the DVD player. Regular TV came back on to the entertainment news program that had flashed across the television before.

"Can't say I'm shocked," the blond coiffed anchor said. "But it is a serious invasion of privacy."

"It is, and I think they are going to have a very hard time snuffing this one out." Her male counterpart turned to the camera. "In other news…"

Brian bolted out of the room and down the hall to his own. Behind him, he heard the other guys trying to figure out what was going on as they stampeded after him. Her website wouldn't say anything yet, but Savitar's might. Or the entertainment program's. He searched Logan, Suzette, and sex.

"What is the crisis?" Rudy demanded.

His search pulled up fifteen pages of links. Clicking on the first one opened a page with a screen cap of Suzi straddling Logan in the back of a limo. Brian was paralyzed between wanting to slam the laptop closed and wanting to scroll through more pictures.

"Holy shit," Jason whispered. "Well, it can't be them. It's got to be fake." He clicked through.

Brian closed his eyes. He pushed away from the desk. That bitch on TV said she wasn't surprised. Boy, was she going to be surprised when she got slapped with a lawsuit for that stupid remark. The image of Suzi and Logan imprinted itself on the backs of his eyelids.

"Jesus, would you look at the number of downloads," Ty said.

A phone started to ring. Marc answered, so Brian assumed it was his.

"We just heard," Marc said. "It looks like somebody filmed them having sex in the back of a limo, but it could be fake. Oh."

Marc's "oh" lingered in the air. Ty kept running his fingers through his hair as if the motion would help order his thoughts. Brian tried to cope with the fact that, even with his eyes closed, he could see that picture. He also remembered Suzi the last time he saw her. She'd been at one of Sandy's backyard parties. Smiling and laughing. The joy in her eyes like bottled sunshine.

"I don't believe it," Bear snarled. Brian focused on his friend. Bear's face was dark red and a vein throbbed at his temple. "It's fake."

Brian slouched against the window frame, mind blank. There was nothing to think. Nothing to cover what had happened to the sweet, innocent girl who'd come to dinner the first night with a bottle of wine, wearing a knee-length skirt and a turtleneck. Who had gone barefoot most of the time Savitar was in West Virginia. Suzi didn't want to be the center of attention. She preferred to sit at home and write her stories.

"Candy says it was them. They were at a movie thing for one of her friends last night, and they were wearing the same clothes as in the video." Marc shook his head.

"How could they fucking let this happen?" Bear paced across the room. "Didn't anyone check out the limo company? You don't think Logan did it on purpose, do you? You can't see him as well as you can see her. Naw, he wouldn't do that." Bear started chewing his fingernails. "Do you suppose someone at their office was in on it?"

"Why would they do that?" Ty asked.

"To break them up. What better way? She'll be so upset she won't ever want to see him again. Sons of bitches." Bear stalked into the hall, ranting.

"You don't think Logan did it, do you?" Jason's face was white and rigid. "He's terrified of losing her. She won't want to be without his protection and his lawyers now."

"Unless she left him already," Ty said.

"I gotta call her." Brian snatched his phone off the dresser and found her number.

"Good idea. We need to talk to them."

Them, yes, talk to them. Both of them. It rang and rang until it went to voicemail. He shook his head as he redialed. Jason stomped out of the room. Ty, Rudy, and Marc leaned over the computer. Brian caught snatches of their conversation through the ringing, but none of it made sense. Bear stomped up and down the hall cursing.

Jason walked back into the room with his cell to his ear. "Logan? It's Jason. We just heard." Jason stopped as if he didn't know what to say beyond that.

Brian tossed his phone back on the dresser. Ty danced around Jason as if he wanted to climb through the phone.

"What's your plan?" Jason asked.

Brian folded his arms. Logan was a guy. He was probably thrilled the world got to see him boning his hot girlfriend. Who cared what his fucking plan was?

"And Suzi…? No, I don't need to… Here, she can talk to Ty." Jason thrust the phone into Ty's hands like a hot potato.

"Hello?" Ty paused. "Hello? Suzi? How are you?"

Brian sidled closer, not sure what would be worse, talking to her or not talking to her.

Jason sat down on the bed. "Logan said they've shut down the website, and they're suing everyone and their brother."

Ty frowned as if he was trying to do trigonometry in his head. From the sound of his questions, he was getting very short, direct answers. Not at all the chatty Suzi they knew.

"What about Suzi?" Marc asked.

"Logan said she went into shock. They had a doctor come look at her."

"A doctor?" Brian asked. Now, it did feel like someone had reached into his chest and ripped out his heart. Poor Suzi.

"Logan said she was catatonic when he told her. She threw up, and then she wouldn't move. Doctor said she was acting like she'd been raped."

Rudy crossed himself.

"Brian's here. Did you want to talk to him?" Ty shoved the phone at Brian.

Brian grabbed it before Ty dropped it. "Hello Suzi?"

"Hello."

What did you say to someone who felt like they'd been raped? "You need anything?"

"No." Her voice was thin and distant. She almost sounded stoned. Had they drugged her?

"You know if you need anything, you can just ask."

Ty walked out of the room.

"I don't think that will be necessary."

"Well…" He glanced at Jason, trying to figure out what to say, but Jason backed away as if he thought Brian was going to hand him the phone. "At least it's off the Internet now. Not many copies could have gotten out, right?"

"It's a download. All the pirating sites Jim checked have it."

Whoever Jim was. Savitar's head of security? "Yes, but you can get that pulled down."

"It doesn't work that way."

"What d'ya mean?" He heard the soft, wet sound of her licking her lips and then a sigh. She liked being smart. Fortunately, he'd never minded having things explained to him. He knew how Internet pirating worked, but if it made her feel better, he'd listen. As long as she was talking and sounding like herself, she could talk about anything she wanted.

"As long as one person has the file on their computer, they can just post it as another torrent. It's the head of the hydra. We cut off one, and two more sprout." Her voice was sounding warmer, more like her.

He sat down on his bed beside Jason. "So as long as somebody has it, anybody could get it."

Jason snarled at him.

"Yeah," Suzi muttered, sounding at least fifty percent normal. "Though I can't understand why."

She wouldn't. Unfortunately, Brian was stuck between wanting to see how beautiful she was when she made love and sick over the fact that weirdoes were spying on her for their jollies. "People are nosy. Your publishers are probably loving this."

"They're in shock."

"But it's good advertising."

"Good is relative."

"Didn't you say all advertising was good advertising? Scandal, death, all that stuff is good for sales."

Jason buried his face in his hands, obviously certain that Brian had lost it.

"I don't think it was as bad as that."

"It's relative," he said.

She almost laughed.

"Candy said you were at a movie. Was it any good?"

"It was wonderful, but I'm required to say that because a friend of mine is in it. Logan fell asleep."

"He fell asleep?"

"At least he doesn't snore. It was a period piece. Not his thing."

"We were just about to watch a movie."

"I'm sure Logan would rather have seen the movie you guys are watching than the one we saw. I liked it, though."

"You like Keats."

"I love Keats." He thought she might be up to ninety percent normal. Now, she mostly sounded tired. "Did you get my email?"

"I haven't looked today."

"I sent you a story yesterday."

"It's not romance, is it? You keep trying to trick me into reading romance."

"You'd like my romance."

"I don't read romance."

"Fine. It's not romance."

Now she sounded like the girl he adored. "Good. I need new reading material. I'm in the middle of a divorce, and I'm depressed. I need something creepy to cheer me up."

"You're depressed? My life just went through a blender," she grumbled playfully.

"You know if you need something, you just have to ask. We're in— where are we?" he asked Jason. Jason shrugged. "We're on tour, but if you need anything…. Have you talked to Tessa?"

"Jason's sister? She called not long before you did."

"See, the Touchstone machine is already working for you."

She laughed. The genuine, lovely Suzi laugh. "Did you want to talk to Logan?"

"Sure." Brian didn't want to talk to Logan, but couldn't think of a delicate way to escape it. "Just remember. If you need us, just call. I mean it."

"I know. Something about you and oxygen, right? Here's Logan."

Brian grinned. She remembered that comment about him being her oxygen. Good. If things ever did go south between her and that idiot who couldn't manage to protect her, he'd be right at the front of the line.

"Hi Brian," Logan said. A door closed on his end of the phone.

"You talked to Tessa?"

"She was doing her fire-breathing lawyer thing. I'm glad I'm not on the wrong side of her. I heard you ask about sales. We've both had an uptick. Suzi's been out of it, so I've been talking to people. Shitty way to make sales." Logan's misery leaked through the phone, making Brian feel bad for him, too. No way had Logan rigged this. "Hey, thanks for talking her down."

Making a phone call in the middle of a crisis? A buck or so. Getting to be the guy who talked her out of shock? Priceless. "S'nothin'. She's all right then?"

"She comes and goes. Sometimes, she's just like normal, and then five minutes later she's wigged out again. I thought she was going to have a nervous breakdown when I told her."

"But you stopped the guy who did it."

"We shut down the site, but the jackass is still out there. He didn't get away with a big payday because it immediately got pirated, so we figure he'll pop up again. When he does, our security guy wants to crucify him live on network television at prime time, but I think we're going to have to settle for a civil suit."

"Maybe we can catch him in a dark alley."

"Yeah, you can hold him for me." Logan paused, and Brian could hear the other man cracking his knuckles through the phone. Logan was a lot more freaked out about the whole thing than he was playing at. "I can't believe she didn't leave me. I can't believe some dickwad taped us. And seriously, it was just a spur of the moment thing. We never do stuff like that. What the fuck is next?"

"If I were you, I'd just be careful." Brian clenched his teeth. *Logan better fucking be careful. Suzi couldn't take too much of this shit.*

"Yeah. That's at the top of the list."

"You'll have to start paying a lot more attention to one another. You're all you've got out there." Brian was starting to feel like Logan's dad.

"Yeah. I'm thinking about moving back to Rochester. LA is such a fucking fish bowl."

Brian swallowed against tightness in his throat. If they moved to New York, he'd never have a chance to see Suzi. They couldn't meet up for coffee or go catch a movie like they had been. "You could do that. You know, we're going to England to record in a few months. You guys will be on the road by then. She could come along with us."

"Yeah, maybe. I'll ask her. Thanks for calling. We'll keep you posted."

"Talk to you then." He hung up.

"She's all right?" Rudy asked.

"Logan says she has good times and bad ones. I think she'll be fine with time. Logan is thinking about moving to Rochester."

"Might not be a bad idea," Jason said. "I know I feel a lot more relaxed in WVA. Everybody in Potterville is looking, but they aren't staring the same way. You know what? I bet a nice little getaway would be good for them. Suzi would love to go back to my place out there." Jason grabbed his phone and walked out dialing. Marc followed him.

Brian sat on his bed. Meeting up with her all the time in LA was excruciating, anyway. If she was on the other side of the country, he could limit his pain to a couple times a year.

Chapter 13

Logan stopped outside the office door and took a deep breath. Picking a therapist out of the phone book was starting to sound stupid. Suzi would have researched it. Asked around for recommendations. Studied credentials. She was going to ask him how he picked his therapist, and he was going to have to tell her he found the name in the phone book. No wonder she thought he was an idiot. Maybe he should scratch this and start over. Do it right.

But it had taken two weeks to get this appointment, and he was going to WVA in a month. If he didn't show up with some serious therapy under his belt, Jason and Cassie were never going to let him near Suzi. They would kick his ass all the way back to New York and fix her up with some nice guy who wasn't going to break her heart on a routine basis.

That might not be such a bad thing. Suzi didn't deserve all the shit he put her though.

Logan opened the door before he chickened out. The reception room was small with soft beige furniture and a coffee table fanned with magazines. The receptionist smiled. "Mr. Fitzpatrick? Good afternoon. Dr. Kennedy will be with you in a minute. Would you like something to drink while you wait?"

"No thanks." Logan sank into a chair. Her desk didn't have a panel across the front so he had a perfect sightline under it. Her skirt rode up to mid-thigh, and great thighs they were. She either jogged or spent a lot of time in a gym to get those gams. No stockings. Stockings had their appeal, but the idea of her long, bare legs was pretty fucking appealing, too. She wore standard high-heeled pumps, black, but she only had on one. Her legs were crossed and she was dangling the other shoe from her toes. Nice toes, too. Purple polish. Good feet, nice arches, soft heels. Suzi had hard heels because she was barefoot most of the time. She buffed them to keep them from being scratchy, but they were still tough.

Suzi. Jesus, he was sitting in a therapist's office to save his relationship with Suzi and was checking out the receptionist.

Logan slouched to the other side of the chair so the arm of the couch blocked his view under the desk. He should have brought something to read. Some save-the-world shit about feeding starving kids or housing the homeless. Something that would impress the therapist so she'd help him get Suzi back.

A door opened at the side of the office. A woman came out, sniffling, and walked by without acknowledging him or the receptionist. Logan leaned his elbows on his knees. He'd written a lot of new material since he'd sobered up. The record company had been real flexible about them delaying their album. Toby thought they were looking for a reason to break the contract.

"Mr. Fitzpatrick? Dr. Kennedy will see you now."

Logan stared at her for a second before he stood up. Was that a smirk she was hiding? Was she going to be on the phone the second he walked through the door to tell all her girlfriends about the screwed-up celebrity who was in with the doc right now? Maybe they'd make a date to meet for drinks after work so they could talk over Cosmos, or whatever the hot chic drink was at the moment, about what he'd worn and what a jerk he must be to have lost Suzi. They'd probably pull the video up on their phones so they could watch her run out on him again. He swaggered through the door. Never let 'em see you sweat.

Dr. Kennedy stood up. And up. She had to be over six-foot. Her brown hair was short and threaded with gray, and she had biceps like a quarterback. At least he didn't have to worry about hitting on her. "Hello, Mr. Fitzpatrick. Or would you rather I called you Logan?"

"Logan's fine." He shook her hand and sat down in the big brown leather wing chair across from the one she stood in front of.

"Would you like something to drink?"

Was this a test? Did his choice mean something? Did it mean something if he said no? "No, thanks."

"Why don't you tell me about yourself?"

Logan frowned. "I sent in all the paperwork."

"I know. I just want to hear it from you."

Logan shifted. The paperwork had been a pain in the ass. He didn't want to go over all that crap again. "I'm Logan Fitzpatrick. I play guitar in Savitar. I'm thirty. Thirty-one." Dr. Kennedy had a calendar over her desk.

He squinted at it. "I missed my own birthday because I was hammered. I missed hers, too."

"Whose?"

"Suzi's. The reason I'm here. The reason I keep breathing. It was her birthday, and I was too drunk to notice. Jesus, I'm an idiot."

"Why do you say that?"

"Because isn't that like a woman's biggest pet peeve? Their guy forgets their birthday. I always remembered hers. It's ten days before mine. I always did something big. This year was supposed to be a haunted castle tour thing in Spain and Portugal. We wouldn't have even been home yet." Logan lolled his head against the back of the chair. "I didn't even remember to say happy birthday when I saw her."

"Because you were hammered."

"Yeah. When I came home after the party, the house was just too empty, so I started drinking. I didn't stop until she came back to get her stuff."

Dr Kennedy leaned forward. "Why do you say 'The Party' like that?"

"Because it was The Party where she caught that groupie sucking on my fingers and took off with that fucker Cherney."

She nodded.

"It wasn't my fault. She didn't let me explain. I went to the bar to get Suzi a Coke. She doesn't drink. Well, not often. The results are usually pretty bad when she does. Gillian went with me because she's a groupie and there's no getting rid of her. When we were walking back, somebody bumped me and some of Suzi's Coke spilled on my hand. Gillian said she'd take care of it, took the Coke, grabbed my hand, and stuck my fingers in her mouth. It was an accident." He jumped up and started pacing the room. "I knew I shouldn't have been anywhere near Gillian. I knew Suzi wasn't feeling good that day. That's why I got her the drink. I thought it would make her happy. She didn't tell me she was pregnant. I was trying to do the right thing, and it just got all screwed up."

"You sound very defensive."

"Of course, I'm defensive. Every fucking person in the world has decided I'm the biggest jerk in the universe. Have you read the comments on the YouTube video? There's pages and pages of people talking about what a dick I am. They're even trying to pin that sex video on me again. I had nothing to do with that. Why would I risk it? Especially when we could have just set up a camera in the bedroom."

"Did you ever ask her to?"

"What?"

"Put a camera in the bedroom."

"No. That shit's for amateurs. It's too dangerous, too. Computers get hacked, and the videos end up online. I wouldn't risk that with Suzi."

Dr. Kennedy folded her hands on her notepad. "How did you meet Suzi?"

"I emailed her. She wrote this story about a three-hundred-year-old vigilante witch who goes after this guy. He's a high school basketball coach, and he's screwing all the little girls. These girls hire Desdemona to take him out, and she tears him up. It was the hottest, scariest thing I ever read. She wrote a whole bunch of Desdemona stories, but that was the first one, and after I read it, I emailed her. We emailed back and forth for a while, and when my tour went near her town, I put her on the list, and the minute I met her I never wanted to be away from her." Logan dropped back into the chair.

"But you were on tour."

"We emailed for a couple more weeks, and the next time I had a break, I went to her place, and we packed her shit into a U-Haul and moved her in with me. She tried to finish her college, but between my schedule and her publishing schedule, it was impossible, so she dropped out before she graduated."

"How did her family feel about this?"

"They went ballistic. She's an only child, and her dad never wanted her to leave home. She hasn't spoken to them since."

"Did that put a strain on your relationship?"

"Shit, yeah. I mean, it could have been worse. I was living in LA at the time so I wasn't near my family, and none of my friends were near their families, so it wasn't like she was the only one. And then the next summer we went to record with Jason Callisto. His wife is from this little town so they sort of adopted Suzi. Everybody who meets Suzi loves her." Logan smirked. "She was always way too good for me. I knew I was going to lose her someday."

"Why do you say that?"

"Because she's really nice and smart and so fucking talented and really…good. Suzi is just a good person. And I'm not."

"Do you think she loved you?"

"Yeah. I know she did. I just couldn't figure out how to hang onto her."

"It sounds like you were trying."

"I was. I really was." Logan clenched his hands. At least the therapist was on his side. "But she never wanted much. Suzi isn't a material girl. Expensive jewelry made her nervous that she'd lose it. She was always afraid she'd spill something on designer clothes. The only thing she let me get her was a Tesla car, and she left that behind. It's sitting in the garage. All I could do was…drug her with sex."

Dr Kennedy's eyebrows went up. "Drug her with sex?"

Logan swallowed. "It was stupid. I knew it was stupid."

"No, please explain."

"I just thought…if we had sex enough, she wouldn't ever leave me." A boulder started to grow in his throat. "She was a virgin when we met, and up until The Party, I would have sworn to you that I was the only man she'd ever been with. She loved sex. Loved it. Anytime, anywhere. She was always willing to experiment, and she's so creative. And flexible." Logan licked his lips. Thinking about it was making him hard.

"And she wasn't doing it to please you."

"Hell no. She wore me out sometimes. But I knew great sex was something I could always give her, and I thought if I gave her enough, she'd stay."

"You know a relationship can't survive on just physical attraction."

"I know, but it was the only thing I had to offer."

* * * *

"What is your plan?" Trisha asked. "You have to have a plan."

Suzi gritted her teeth and changed the channel.

"Suzi?" Trisha lifted the remote out of her hand. "Susan."

"Don't call me Susan."

Trisha smoothed her neat blue skirt and sat on the coffee table. "Suz, you can't sit around my apartment watching TV forever. Have you even written anything in the last month? In college, you never stopped."

"I'm grieving." Suzi estimated her chances of getting the remote back to be slim to none. Trisha had a good grip on it, and her mood wasn't advantageous.

"You're sitting on the couch doing nothing. You won't even go to the gym."

According to Trisha, that was her biggest sin. The not writing. The hiding from all her other friends. The sitting on the couch watching TV all day. The not eating. None of that trumped not going to the gym. "Trisha—"

"I'm not listening." Trisha stood up. "I understand you were madly in love with Logan, and you just broke up with him—"

"Publicly."

"Yes." Trisha groaned. She tossed the remote onto the table. "Suzi, you've been sitting on that couch for a month. You need to do something."

Suzi sat up. "I will. I swear." She checked her watch. It was a gift from Logan. For two months now, she'd been taking it off every night and putting it on every morning without thinking. Unbuckling it, she tossed it on the table. "You're going to be late for work. Why don't you go, and I'll figure something out. I promise, by the time you come home, I'll have a plan."

Trisha narrowed her gaze at Suzi before grabbing her purse and walking out.

"Not all of us started kindergarten with a detailed life plan to become a marketing genius," Suzi muttered as she opened up her email.

A plan.

Her email was full again. She hadn't checked it since she got here. Wally wanted to know what to do with her stuff. He'd stashed it in his garage where it was safe, and it was no problem, but... Okay, what he wanted to know was where was she, and was she all right? Fair enough. So did everyone else who had emailed. If she sorted the email alphabetically by subject, the list wouldn't change—almost every one of them started with the word *where*. Except for Brian's. His first one read **tap, tap* Is this thing on?* The one after that read *Nature Girl! Come out, come out wherever you are!* She opened that one.

Hey Suzi, here's another bottle in the ocean. I'm at Jason's in WVA. If you want to fall down that waterfall again, give me a call, and I'll pick you up. You can talk. You cannot talk. You can lie in the hammock and watch the trees grow. I don't give a shit. I'll even run interference for you for free. That's got to be the best deal going because quality interference-running is hard to find, and I'm the best in the field. I'm your oxygen.

She clicked open a couple of his other emails. They ranged from silly to frustrated. He'd heard she'd seen Logan, and it hadn't gone well. Brian said he remembered what it was like to be where she was, and back then she'd been there for him so he thought he owed her one. Remember? England? When Brian smashed that bottle on the wall fighting with her, and she ended up playing Trivial Pursuit as a drinking game with Marc and Ty and getting so wasted that he had to carry her to bed where absolutely nothing whatsoever happened? Remember?

Most of it, she didn't remember, and what she did, she'd been trying to forget. Ever since she woke up fully dressed and alone that morning, she had known he was trustworthy, too.

And since he was offering to let her lie in a hammock and watch the trees grow to her heart's content, she decided that sounded like a great plan.

Chapter 14

Three years ago

Suzi swallowed and braced herself. Brian was wallowing, and she couldn't take it. His eyes hadn't been this dim since the first time she met him when he was still married to Bonnie. Did he still love her somehow? "I just don't think it's a good idea for you to spend every day sitting on the veranda drinking."

Brian sneered and bobbed his head, continuing to stare across the lawn.

"You wanted to come to England to write the new album." Suzi hooked a lock of hair behind her ear. Feet together and back straight, she felt like she was trying to give a speech to her whole university. "We could take a break and go sightseeing. Just to get out."

"I don't want to go look at a bunch of fucking castles. I'm perfectly happy where I am."

Suzi clasped her hands together. She should never have mentioned castles last time. Those she could do alone. All she was doing here was hanging out, waiting for the Savitar tour to swing past and pick her up for a couple of weeks. Supposedly, she was also helping Brian with his depression, but he wouldn't let her. "I wasn't thinking of castles. There's a nice Beatles tour in Liverpool. That wouldn't be a bad day trip."

"I don't want to go to Liverpool." He took another swig from the bottle. He'd given up glasses, too, but she figured that was to annoy her.

If the Beatles didn't work, she wasn't sure what to try. He'd already nixed Sheffield, and nothing on Earth was getting him over to Dublin. Jason had asked her to come stay with them for a while because Brian had become unbearable as his divorce progressed. They thought she could cheer him up or at least distract him. So far, no good. All she seemed able to do was irritate him more. "I was planning on making cookies. You in?"

He rolled his eyes toward her, took another ostentatious drink, and went back to glaring into the distance.

"Brian, this is ridiculous. You're just being childish."

"Leave me alone."

"I can't leave you sitting here sulking and drinking. It's unhealthy."

"When did you become my mother?" Brian snapped.

Suzi drew a quick breath to bolster her confidence. His mother? Is that what she sounded like? "I just don't like to see you like this."

"Then go away!" Brian threw the bottle onto the flagstones on the other side of his chair.

Suzi recoiled. None of the glass came anywhere near her, but the violence in his voice stung. Brian had never yelled at her before. She blinked to keep her tears back. She ached to wrap her arms around him and soothe his hurt, but that was a bad idea. "Fine." Snatching up the second bottle of whiskey from behind his chair, she tucked it under her arm. "But you've had enough."

She made it to the kitchen before the trembling made her stop. Her whole body shook. She set the bottle on the counter before she dropped it. The huge manor house kitchen had delighted her when she arrived. Now, she couldn't do much more than lean on the table and shiver. This was Brian. Sweet Brian. Yelling at her to go away.

Before she ended up blubbering, she started mixing the sugar cookies. Suzi had the recipe memorized, and the cook had made sure all the ingredients were handy before she left after supper. Brian hadn't joined them for the meal. He'd already been out on the veranda.

Marc wandered in as she put the second batch in the oven. "How's it coming?" he asked.

"Fine." She focused on moving cookies from the pan to the cooling racks.

"Cookies, huh?" Marc picked up the whiskey bottle.

"Cookies."

He put down the whiskey bottle. "They look good."

"They're still too hot."

Brian yelled at her to go away. And he broke a bottle. Brian.

"What's going on?" Ty asked, strolling in. He leaned over the bowl of dough. "Can I just eat the raw cookies?"

"If that's what you want. I'm not your mother."

Marc winced.

Ty laid his head on her shoulder. "I'll let you be my mom if you want to be."

Marc growled.

"Maybe later, Ty." Suzi slipped away from them. "I'm gonna go get some work done. I'm probably falling behind on a deadline somewhere. Take those out when the timer goes off or the house will burn down."

"Don't go hide." Ty grabbed her hand. "You know he's just being an asshole. Tomorrow, he'll be guilty and beggin' your forgiveness. You know what you need? You need to get drunk."

"I don't drink," Suzi protested.

"Exactly, it'll be easy," Marc said. On the way out of the kitchen, he grabbed the whiskey bottle. "Come on, we'll play a game. You love to play games."

"The last time I got drunk, I propositioned somebody," Suzi pointed out.

Marc chuckled. "I solemnly swear if you proposition me while you are drunk, I will not take you up on it."

They were not going to take no for an answer. They wanted to see her drunk. It might not be so bad.

"Me, too. I will not turn you down— er, take you up to my room— ah—on it. On it. I will not take you up on it." Ty draped his arm around her shoulders. "Seriously, I promise. I will be a perfect gentleman."

"Don't strain yourself on my account," Suzi muttered, allowing him to pull her toward the parlor.

Marc veered toward the liquor cabinet while Ty dragged her to the closet where the owner of the house kept a stock of board games. Half a dozen of them she didn't recognize. On the bottom of the stack was Trivial Pursuit.

"You know all the answers to that one," Ty said. "The point is to get drunk, not avoid getting drunk by being smart like a freak."

"I don't know all the answers, and it won't take much for me to get drunk."

Marc had collected three shot glasses and another bottle of whiskey and was headed their way.

"All right." Ty winked at Marc. "Every time you get a wrong answer, you have to take a shot. Now, how do you play this game?"

Suzi rolled her eyes and explained the rules.

* * * *

Brian stared at the stars. He was hungry. Starved. But he didn't have the courage to go into the kitchen to find food. Suzi might be there. Five-foot-three and a hundred pounds soaking wet, Suzette Miranda Bazian was someone to be feared.

It wasn't her. It was her eyes. Fury masking shattered hurt. The fury he could handle. He'd earned that. The hurt, though. That had been like a knife to the chest. He'd forgotten she wasn't like his other friends. She couldn't take his foul mood. Hell, most of his friends couldn't handle his foul mood right now. That's why she was here. The guys in the band were ignoring him. The cook avoided him. Suzi had come here just to be nice to him.

Her being nice wasn't what he wanted. He wanted her in his arms, in his bed, in his life on a fixed, permanent basis. But she was still with that idiot Logan, and that didn't seem likely to change. The whole plan three years ago when he pulled the trigger on his divorce was to wait until Logan screwed up enough that Suzi would leave him so Brian could catch her when she fell. She didn't leave him after the sex video. Or after the multitude of times she called asking about this groupie and that groupie, and were they something to worry about? Nights, he lay awake and alone imaging how it would play out when she finally called and told him she'd left Logan. His grand plan to wait sucked. Tom Petty was right. Waiting was the hardest part.

He needed to apologize for being an ass because he'd run out of patience.

Dragging himself out of his chair, he went into the house and up the back stairs. It was late, but she never slept well when she was upset. She might be up writing a whole book or big sections of one, at least. Her door stood open, and the room was empty. He ventured in far enough to make absolutely sure she wasn't hiding in a corner or something. Maybe she'd gone for a run. When she was upset, she ran, too. She could be out pounding the pavement. He wasn't going to sleep until he'd spoken to her.

On the way down the front stairs, he heard Ty in the lounge. He sounded smashed. "That didn't take mush."

"Aw, she's a lightweight. She was winnin', too," Marc answered.

Since there was only one woman in the house now the cook had gone for the day, he went that way instead of the kitchen. Suzi lay passed out on the parlor floor beside a Trivial Pursuit board. Marc and Ty slumped against the couch and a chair respectively. An empty bottle of whiskey sat between them, and Ty held a half full one.

"What are you two doing?" Brian demanded. Suzi had an overturned shot glass in her hand with whiskey soaking into the carpet.

"Protectin' Suzi from you, ya asshole," Marc snarled and then laughed.

"How much did she have?"

"Oh, please. She had like five shots. She knows too many of these answers," Ty snickered and took a swig from the bottle. "We should have made her take a shot for every one she got right."

"Naw, she'd have been down hours ago, and she wouldn't have had time to lord over us how smart she is."

"Both of you should be beaten." Brian knelt beside Suzi. He took the shot glass from her hand and pulled her upright. Her head lolled onto his shoulder.

"Boshten," she slurred, waking up.

"Nope," Marc said. "That's another shot, kiddo."

Brian lifted her off the floor. "No, it isn't. It's time for you to be in bed."

"Now wait a minute." Ty straightened, weaving. "We promised we would be good."

"We promised. He didn't," Marc reminded him.

"Oh well, in that case, have fun."

Brian shot him the evil eye as he started up the stairs. Suzi shifted in his arms, cuddling against him. "That's right. You didn't promise," she said.

"Promise what?"

"They promised not to take advantage of me." She traced her fingers along the neck of his T-shirt. "You didn't promise."

"I'm not going to take advantage of you." *No matter how much I want to.*

"Why not?"

He made the mistake of glancing at her as he walked down the hall. Her drowsy, drunken brown eyes stared up at him with so much come-hither he wanted to press her against the wall and take her right here. Dodging into her room, he prayed he'd be able to escape this situation with some dignity. "Into bed with you."

"Come on, Brian. Kiss me. Please."

He tried to lay her down gently and back away, but she had his shirt in her clutches. "Let me go, Suzi."

"Come on. You know you want me." She pulled herself upright and draped one arm over his shoulder. "You're the only one who doesn't joke about it. Everybody else makes lewd comments, but not you. This is our chance. You could have me because I'm too drunk to stop you, and everybody knows I get horny when I'm drunk."

He sat down before she pulled him on top of her, and then pried her fingers off his shirt, but her other hand had found its way to the base of his skull. "I don't have a good excuse, though," he told her. He struggled to take a deep breath. Being this close to her with her fingers tangled through his hair, he didn't know how he managed to think straight. What had he done to deserve this? Oh yeah, he'd been an ass for three days that led to yelling at her today. Karma was a bad bitch with a nasty sense of humor.

Tomorrow, he was going on one of those castle tours with her. The next day they were going to do the Magical Mystery Tour in Liverpool. And the day after that, Sheffield. Or wherever else she wanted to go.

"Sure, you do." She started nuzzling his neck. "You've been drinkin' all day. We were just victims of circumstance."

"Hey." Brian grabbed her hand he'd just gotten out of his shirt and pulled it away from his fly. She'd gotten the button open before he realized what she was doing. Not only was she randy, she was an octopus. "Suzi, no. What would Logan say?"

Suzi laughed, the hot pulse of her breath swept across his skin. "I don't care. What's good for the gander should be good for the goose, too." She licked his throat. "I can make you feel all better."

He caught her shoulders and pushed her down on her back. Then he stopped. He could lean down and kiss her. A moment after, he could have her shirt off and be tasting her bare flesh. Even if he took time to close the door, he could be sampling her delights in a few seconds. And he could be doing it all night. On five shots, she wouldn't sober up for hours, and by then the damage would be done.

Damage. For almost three years now, he'd been giving her advice on how to keep Logan. Overruling his own desire to destroy their relationship so he could be the one to help her pick up the pieces, he'd been helping her salvage it. "Suzi, you love Logan. If you wake up next to me in the morning, you're gonna hate yourself." *And me.*

Suzi groaned. "Do you have any idea how long it's been since I got fucked? And the amount of testosterone floating around this house is ridiculous. I'm gonna have to spend a solid week in bed with Logan to work it off. It might kill him." She reached for him again, but he caught her hand before she connected. Thwarted, she licked her lips. "You could be saving Logan's life."

"I'm afraid it's a chance I'll have to take." He kissed her hand. "I'm sorry, sweetheart."

"Aw shit," Suzi muttered.

Brian stood and threw a blanket from the foot of the bed over her. "G'night." He risked leaning over to kiss her forehead. When she didn't

Christa Maurice

make another grab for him, it felt enough like kissing his daughter good night that the room stopped spinning.

Pulling the door closed behind him, he sighed having escaped his own lion's den. She was hot, she was randy, and she wanted him. How stupid did he have to be to walk away?

No, not stupid. Tomorrow morning there would have been screaming and tears. She'd have left within the day. The other guys in the band would forgive him for being a greedy bastard, but he'd still have to live with himself.

Then he noticed the door down the hall standing open. Ty's room. Ty, who had promised not to take advantage of Suzi. Ty obviously took that promise seriously. Brian walked down the hall, calling a cheery good night on his way past the door.

Chapter 15

When Suzi opened her eyes the next morning, they were sticky. Her brain throbbed with the effort of focusing. *Play a game*, they'd said. *It'll be fun*, they'd said. *You need a drink to relax*, they'd said.

Delinquents, both of them.

But this was her bedroom. How did she get up here?

Brian. Oh Jesus, Brian. And she distinctly remembered asking him to kiss her. Suzi groped under the blanket. T-shirt. Shorts. Everything still intact. Plus, she was alone. She was alone, wasn't she?

She sat up, and the room lurched around her. The door was closed, and there wasn't another soul in sight. Okay, apparently Brian brought her up here, refused to kiss her, and left her here to sleep. Hopefully, all she'd done was ask him to kiss her.

Stumbling across the room to the bathroom, she drank two glasses of water before stripping down and stepping under the shower. What was the likelihood that all she'd done was ask him to kiss her?

Well, she'd only been drunk four times in her life. The first time she'd been with friends in her dorm room at school, and she'd tried to seduce her very straight roommate. The second time she'd been with Logan, and he said the sex had been fun. She didn't remember too well. The third time she'd been with Logan and Greg in Portland. What she did remember of that, she wished she didn't. She never had planned to be that kind of girl. And last night, she'd gotten drunk with Marc and Ty and, at the very least, had asked Brian to kiss her.

"Crap," Suzi muttered. She shut off the water, dried off, and stepped out. Checking herself over in the mirror, she decided it could have been worse. Much worse. She could have needed to explain to Logan how she ended up in a compromising position with Marc and Ty in the scattered remains of a Trivial Pursuit game. They'd promised to behave, but Logan had told her that when she was drunk, her persistence bordered relentless. Now that would have been something for the resume.

Pulling on some clothes, she brushed her hair and then braided it. No run today.

In the kitchen, Betsy was cleaning up from last night's dinner. "Good morning, Miss Suzi. How are you this morning?"

"Little headache. Too much to drink last night."

"I have a remedy. Would you like it?"

Suzi rubbed her forehead. "Is it worse than the headache?"

Betsy laughed. "Could anything be worse?"

"Okay, I'll try it." Suzi made some toast and sat down at the table, trying not to watch what Betsy was putting in the blender.

Marc walked in and stole one of her pieces of toast.

"Good morning, Mr. Marc. Do you have a headache as well this morning?" Betsy glanced at Suzi.

"No." Marc grinned. "Does kitten have a hangover?"

Suzi growled at him, and he put his arm around her shoulders, still munching on her toast.

"Breakfast?" Betsy asked.

"Yes, thanks Betsy." Marc said to her, "Admit it, you had fun."

"I would have had more fun if you two hadn't started cheating."

"Cheating? We weren't cheating."

Suzi glared at him. "You weren't even reading questions off the cards. You were asking me random shit about sports."

"The point was to get drunk, not answer a bunch of silly questions." He gave her a squeeze and let her go so he could finish her toast.

Betsy set a glass full of purple slush in front of Suzi.

Bracing herself, Suzi picked it up and drank it as quickly as possible. It was vile, horrible, and grotesque, but better than the headache. Ty waltzed in and had a quick conversation with Betsy about breakfast before sitting across the table from her and Marc.

"You bastard," Suzi muttered.

"Suzi has a bit of a hangover," Marc said.

"You know how to fix that. Hair of the dog." Ty grinned.

"No, it's not." She held out the glass. "Rinse this out and fill it with water, cheater boy."

Ty took it. "What do you mean, 'cheater boy'?"

"Did you think I wouldn't notice the last three questions you asked me were baseball questions? You didn't even pull a card for the last two, and I'm almost certain you just made up that other one," Suzi grumbled.

"You were getting too many of them right," Ty protested. "When you play a drinking game, you're supposed to drink." He set the water in front of her just as Betsy brought over Marc's breakfast.

"You're reprobates and bad influences." Suzi picked up her glass as Brian walked into the room. His eyes were drawn and red from more than a hangover. He hadn't been awake all night screwing her. He also hadn't slipped away after the deed and spent the night guilty. "I'm going to tell Jason and Bear they're never allowed to leave me alone with Mad"—she pointed at Marc—"Bad"—she pointed at Ty—"And Dangerous to Know." She tossed her head in Brian's direction because she didn't want to look at him. It was a serious mistake. The kitchen sloshed like a ship in a heavy sea. "Ever again."

"Aw, how come he gets to be Dangerous to Know?" Ty protested. "I'm dangerous. Brian's not dangerous at all. He should be Mad."

"Naw, Ellis is a prince, isn't he? Sweeping in to rescue poor little drunken damsels from bad boys like us." Marc smirked at Brian.

"Fuck off," Brian muttered. "Suzi, can I talk to you for a minute?"

Suzi considered telling him to go right ahead and talk, but since there were big sections of last night she didn't remember, she was afraid of what might come out. He wouldn't blurt out anything too horrible, but Marc and Ty might spin gold from straw. She stood up and walked out to the lounge. "What happened last night?" she asked before he could say anything.

"I know. I was a jackass. I just wanted to tell you I was sorry."

Suzi stiffened. Had she, for some unknown reason, had sex with him and then put her clothes back on? "What?"

"For yelling at you last night." Brian rubbed the back of his neck. "I know I've been mean, and I shouldn't have been. You're only here to be nice to me. Everybody is here because they're trying to be nice to me, and all I can do is be a big asshole. So I just wanted to tell you I was sorry. I'll get to everybody else later."

"Sorry," Suzi repeated. "And nothing happened last night?"

"Before or after I smashed a bottle on the ground?"

Had he been up all night fretting about the fact that he'd blown up at her? "After. When I was drunk. You carried me to bed, didn't you?"

"Oh, that." He blushed.

Suzi stomach tightened. What had she done that would make him blush?

"Nothing happened."

He was an awful, awful liar. His hands were behind his back, and his eyes were fixed on the wall over her shoulder.

"What happened?"

"I carried you upstairs and put you to bed." He shrugged, still staring at the floor with his hands stuffed in his back pockets.

"And I did what?" Suzi chewed her lips.

He rolled his eyes. "You asked me to kiss you. I told you no, and then you passed out."

"I passed out."

"Yeah."

As shifty as he was acting, it wasn't the whole truth.

"Don't worry, I won't tell anyone."

And he would absolutely keep his promise. She threw her arms around him. "You know what, Ellis? You're a prince."

"That's me. A prince." He rolled his eyes again, and she was afraid to ask why. "So tell me about this Beatles tour in Liverpool."

"You'll go?" She brightened. Maybe yesterday hadn't been so bad. If she could cheer him up a little, achieve her objective here, make him happy, wasn't that worth a little heartbreak and a massive hangover? "It's supposed to be fun. Come on, I'll show you the website."

Chapter 16

Suzi fell into his embrace. She wrapped her arms around his waist and pressed her cheek to his chest. "I missed you so much," she whispered.

When he saw her headed for luggage claim, he almost hadn't recognized her. The bright light of her personality was gone. Her hair frizzed out of its ponytail, and her eyes were downcast on the way to baggage claim. Never had he seen her get off an airplane, or even get out of a car, so wrinkled and limp. How had she gotten that old, that brutalized, in just a few weeks? Then she glanced up and caught sight of him. A weak smile lifted her lips, and his heart clenched. He met her halfway.

He'd hunted and manipulated and misdirected and plain-old lied to be right here, right now.

Stroking her hair. "I missed you, too. You have luggage?"

"I have a blue Halliburton case. You'll recognize it. It's covered in alcohol labels and bumper stickers."

Brian whistled. "You have a Halliburton case?"

"Brett loaned it to me." She'd made quote marks with her fingers at the word loaned.

"Was he trying to get you to leave?"

"No. He wanted me to stay forever no matter how badly I was cramping his womanizing, but if I was going to leave, he wanted to make sure I was as safe as possible."

"Why did you leave?" Brian bit the inside of his cheek. The last thing he wanted to do was encourage her back to Cherney.

"It's hard to swan around in a post-break-up fugue when your host is bringing home a party every chance. He was great when I needed him, but I felt like I was imposing." She stepped back.

Brian wished she'd stayed in his arms. He could protect her there. "New computer bag?" He reached for the leather bag draped over her shoulders. For a second, she tensed, but then she relinquished it.

"New everything. Mr. Discover loves me."

The luggage carousel clanked to life behind them. Brian put his arm around her shoulders to walk her back to collect her things. The aluminum case appeared first. Brian almost couldn't see the metal for the stickers. He yanked it off the belt. "What the hell do you have in here?" Brian laughed.

"My whole life."

He glanced back at her. A little girl lost in a big world again. "Hey, come on Suz. Let's go home." He set the case on its casters and pulled out the handle. Settling the computer bag on top, he glanced at her again. Her eyes were on the computer bag. No matter what she said, her life wasn't in the Halliburton case. It was in the computer bag. And she'd trusted him with it.

She didn't say anything on the way to the truck. As soon as he got on the road, she turned to the window and fell asleep. He'd planned to ask her if she wanted to stop for a bite on the way, but decided, based on how thin she was, she wouldn't. This time, Cassie might be right. A little bit of Paul's cooking might be vital.

* * * *

Suzi wiped her hands on her napkin. Fried chicken. The minute they walked into the restaurant, Ida had insisted what Suzi needed was fried chicken. Suzi assumed there had been a plan in place before they left the house. The entire town was in collusion with Brian to cheer her up.

Brian had insisted they go to town for dinner and hadn't even let her stop for shoes on the way out. At the time, it hadn't seemed all that unusual a request, even if he was in an all-fired hurry to go. She'd been congratulating herself on the drive down on how agreeable and nice she was being by letting him take over. For five days, she'd lounged in a hammock, refusing most food and all conversation, and he'd let her. Now, she could go with the flow for a little while. Let him do what he thought would cheer her up. Then go back up the mountain and sequester herself in the guest cabin to stare at the scenery for several more days.

When they'd arrived in town, she knew something was up. People on the street were smiling at them. They got a booth in the restaurant when every other seat in the place, inside and out, was taken, and their meals were already prepared.

Paul swept out of the kitchen bearing tartlets already packed in a clear plastic container. Paul insinuated himself in the booth beside her and gave her a fierce hug. "You poor dear. You're just skin. And over that barbarian. He was never good enough for you." Paul kissed her cheek. "I have been just wild to go up there and tell you, but that man"—Paul aimed a glare across the table at Brian—"wouldn't let me. Now, tell me you ate enough."

"I ate plenty."

"Good. I packed these up to go because I knew you would be full. They're Mountain Berry Tartlets. It's just whatever berries are in season that we find, but I remembered how much you liked blackberries, and these are blackberry heavy. You are so different from Cassie. When Cassie was depressed, all she wanted to do was eat, and you—you look like you've just been freed from a concentration camp." Paul pinched her cheek. "Poor thing." Something banged in the kitchen. Paul bounced up and sprinted for the sound.

"Gotta love the local color." Brian grinned. He had such a great smile. Warm and welcoming. "I need to wash the grease off my fingers. I'll be back."

The minute he left, Ida swooped in. "I'm so happy to see the two of you together. You were always so cute."

"We're not together together." Suzi shook her head. "We're not even sleeping in the same building. He's in the house, and I'm in the guest cabin."

"Why not? He's obviously in love with you. Paul said it the first time he saw you together. You remember that day you walked in here, both of you barefoot and covered in dirt and twigs? You just looked like a match made in heaven. Or West Virginia. Close enough. We half thought the reason he went home that summer was to get his divorce going so he could settle down with you, you being so good with his kids and all." Ida tapped her wicked long, hot pink fingernails on the table.

"No, he went home to salvage his marriage. It just didn't work." Suzi bit her lip. She remembered walking in here that day. It had been her bright idea to follow the stream. That was the day she'd started imagining she was in love with him. A delusion she'd been battling ever since.

"I think there's a very good reason it didn't work."

He had gone home right after that foray down the mountain, and he had filed for divorce within six months. Thinking back, the timing was… interesting. "We're just friends."

"Friends is a very good way to start." Ida levered herself out of the booth. "Don't you forget those tartlets now. Paul made them special for you."

Special. Something was up. Those tartlets had been baked hours ago. Long enough to have cooled before they were packed up.

Brian came out of the hall from the bathrooms and stopped to talk to someone. He glanced at her, and her breath caught in her throat. She'd forgotten how tall he was. Not in an imposing way, but solid. Safe. After clapping the man on the shoulder, he returned to the table. "So, do you want to head back up the holler, or do you want to see if there's something interesting going on in town?"

"You know there's at least six things going on in town tonight."

"Yeah, but I didn't know if you'd be up to the craft show in the middle school gym." He laced his long fingers together on the table. He'd made no effort to reach for her hand, but he was in reach. Brian had always been in reach, starting six months after they met. Because they were friends.

Just friends. Nothing more. "Maybe another night."

"All right. I'll go settle the bill, and we'll head home."

Home. As if it belonged to either of them. But it already felt more like home than anyplace she'd been in the last two months. She gathered up the tartlets and followed Brian to the counter where he was joking with Ida. After he'd collected his change, he draped his arm over her shoulders, and Ida batted her eyes as if blinking back tears. Shaking the Suzi-and-Brian rumor was going to be nearly impossible. No way was Brian in love with her. He was just a good friend. A very good friend.

A very good friend whose kids she loved. Who made her heart pitter patter when he smiled. Who she hunted for excuses to talk to and dreamed about. In the past four years, she'd written a ton of short stories just because it gave her an excuse to email him.

"I'm not going to be able to eat in town often. Between Ida and Paul, they're going to fatten me up like a Christmas ham," Suzi said after they'd pushed through the door into the humidity outside.

"They just want to take care of you. Everybody feels bad about what happened."

"Including you."

"Of course. We were in Japan finishing up the tour. Everybody was climbing the walls, trying to figure out what happened, and then you disappeared. Don't ever do that to me again."

We. Everybody. Neither was specific. Ida had lost her marbles. But then, there was that *me* at the end. "Just to you?"

"Yes, I thought you knew you could always rely on me, and I hated thinking of you out there alone."

"I was with Brett first, and then I went to stay with a friend."

"But I wasn't there, so as far as I'm concerned, you were alone." He gave her a playful squeeze.

The sidewalk was still hot from the sun, but the air was cooling. His body heat did more than keep her from getting a chill. It comforted. He was right. She had been alone. Until she threw her arms around him at the airport, she'd been isolated. Even when he didn't press her to talk, or even expect her to sleep in the same building with him, she'd felt cared for. To be honest, his almost daily emails from the time she'd left the party until she came here had made her feel connected even when she was flying around like a balloon with all its air escaping. Suzi sniffed.

He stopped. "What's wrong?"

She shook her head. "You're right. I was alone. I just didn't know how to stop."

"You pick up the telephone"—he leaned in close, staring meaningfully into her eyes—"and you make a call. And the person on the other end says, 'When are you arriving? I'll pick you up.'"

"I know. It just felt so awkward. You're all Logan's friends."

"Oh, my God! You're Brian Ellis, aren't you?"

Brian turned to the two middle-aged women, and his public persona kicked on. Suzi stepped back. He'd been about to say they were her friends, too. She should have known that. Jason and Marc were probably half out of their minds worrying. Or had been. The emails had stopped. Brian would have let them know when she called. No, Brian wasn't in love with her. He was a very concerned friend. She just wished it was more.

One of the women gasped. "You're Suzette Miranda Bazian."

Suzi pasted on a smile. Naturally, they would recognize her, too. Hanging out with these guys had been a fantastic sales boost, and she'd been photographed with them often. "It's very nice to meet you."

"Oh, my God. I had to read one of your stories just because Brian liked it. It was so good." The other woman pressed her hands over her heart. "I bought an e-reader so I could read them all."

"I was so sorry when you broke up with Logan Fitzpatrick. That must have been so awful. Breaking up is so hard anyway, and having to do it in public like that?" The first woman sighed, clenching her hands together like she wanted to throw her arms around Suzi. "I'm so sorry."

"Thank you."

The other woman glanced from Suzi to Brian. "Are you dating? I always thought you looked so good together. Every time I saw you together, you just looked so natural. Can I have a picture of the two of you?"

Suzi positioned herself next to Brian. He did his fan photo-pose, one arm around her shoulders, slouching toward her with his head tipped in her direction. Of course, she had to admit she was doing what she always did in photos with fans, too. Standing straight, hips twisted just a bit to make her appear thinner, head tilted toward him. She remembered a photographer friend taking pictures one day in college and snapping at her, "For chrissakes, Suzi, be in the moment. This is supposed to be fun."

She was in homey little Potterville with someone who cared deeply about her. Someone she had always been able to trust. And these people, these total strangers, cared about her, too.

The flash popped in her eyes. Suzi blinked so she could see to autograph the slips of paper the women produced. As she wrote her name under Brian's, she imagined the women would frame their picture together with the autographs and tell people they once went on vacation in Potterville, West Virginia and bumped into Brian Ellis and Suzette Miranda Bazian walking down the street.

"Can you send me a copy of that shot?" Suzi asked.

"You want me to send my picture of the two of you?" The woman's eyes were so round Suzi was afraid she'd go into shock.

"If you wouldn't mind. Just go to my website and click *contact me*. I think my fans might like to see a recent picture." Suzi smiled.

The women giggled and said their goodbyes.

"You ready to go?" Brian asked.

"You suggested coming out tonight."

"I thought it would please you."

"It did." Suzi leaned against him, wrapping her arm around his waist. Too bad he wasn't in love with her. Every moment with him was so easy. So natural. But he wasn't in love with her. He couldn't be. "Thank you."

"Of course." He opened the truck door for her and waited while she climbed in.

"So why did you ask for that picture?" Brian asked when he climbed in the driver's seat.

"The picture? Oh, I was trying an experiment when she took it."

"What was that?"

"A friend of mine once yelled at me to be in the moment when she took my picture. I was wondering if it would work now. I was thinking about how exciting this must be for them to come here on vacation and bump into the two of us."

"You know a bunch of people who come to Potterville are hoping to run into somebody from Touchstone."

Suzi shrugged. "That doesn't mean they weren't excited when it happened." She peered at him. The woman on the street had said they looked good together, echoing what Ida had said. In fact, most of the comments on the photos of the two of them together were about how nice a couple they made. Maybe in all those pictures, she'd been more in the moment than she'd realized. Maybe he had been, too. What if, when all those pictures were snapped, he'd been in the moment thinking how happy he was to be standing beside someone he loved? His message was mixed, not negative. Mixed enough to be positive.

Brian turned off the main road onto the long driveway up the mountain, and she turned sideways to study him, cradling the tartlets in her lap, and trying to decide how much of a gamble she wanted to take with this friendship.

"What?"

"You said everybody felt bad when I left Logan."

"Everybody did."

"But you knew I wasn't alone. I left the party with Brett."

Brian rolled his eyes. "Brett."

"Why do you say it like that?"

"Well, he's Brett. He's famous for going through women like toilet paper. And you were alone with him."

"I'm a consenting adult."

Brian either blushed or the light got strange all of a sudden. Nothing else in the truck had such an odd coloring so he must be blushing over the fact she'd been alone with a well-known sex fiend. Brian pulled around the house to the garage.

"Well, it was just weird to think of you with Cherney. He's…"

"A man?"

"There's that." Brian shut off the truck. "Why all the questions?"

"There's a shortage of answers." Suzi felt as if she was sitting on a crate full of live questions, hissing and growling, demanding to be fed. "Why did you leave Bonnie so soon after you met me? Why then?"

"We talked about it. You gave me some ideas on how to save my marriage. They didn't work so I threw in the towel."

She remembered sitting beside him in the warm sun, wanting nothing more than to lean forward and press her lips to his. "Marc told me things had been bad between you and Bonnie for five or six years before you divorced her. He said they all thought you'd never leave her."

"There were a lot of reasons."

Suzi clutched the container of tarts, making it crackle. "Was one of them me?"

Brian opened his mouth to speak. Then he closed it. The garage light cast weird shadows across his face. If she, Ida, and Paul, were wrong, it would be embarrassing, but the light made it hard to tell if his mouth had curled into a frown or not. Suzi held her breath. She didn't want to be wrong. She wanted, needed, to be right.

He reached over, slipping his hand behind her neck, and pulled her closer, pressing his lips to hers. With a heavy sigh, he drew her lower lip between his. Suzi unsnapped her seatbelt and put the tartlets on the dash so she could reach for him. Brian abandoned her lip to invade her mouth. He stroked his hand down her waist, sending a hot shower of sparks along her nerves. Clutching his shirt, she moaned.

Abruptly he pulled back. "Is that a good enough answer?" he asked.

Chapter 17

Suzi nodded, too breathless to speak for the moment. Her whole body trembled. Every time she was near him, she'd sensed some tension, but she'd always thought it was only hers. "When?"

"I wanted you the moment I saw your picture." He stroked her cheek with the backs of his long fingers. "Then I met you, and I fell in love with you."

"Why didn't you tell me?"

"I knew it would just upset you. I didn't want to hurt you."

"But I've been here for a week." Suzi cupped his jaw, a bristle of whiskers scratching her palm. All week long, she'd been moping around, wondering why he couldn't fall in love with her the way she'd fallen in love with him. Longer than that. Every time Logan hurt her, her first thought always had been *Brian would never do anything like that.* "Weren't you going to say anything?"

"I didn't want to pressure you. I wasn't sure you were ready." He put his hand over hers. "It drove me crazy you were out there alone, and I didn't know where or who with. I was afraid you'd find another man before I got a chance."

Suzi bit her lip, studying his blue eyes. He'd never once miscued her. Trusting him was automatic. "I think I love you."

"Thank God, because I've been in love with you for years." He kissed her again, light and sweet. "Can we finish this conversation inside? The car's not especially comfortable."

Suzi drew away and climbed out. Her legs still worked. That was a relief. Meeting him at the garage door, she ran her hands up his arms until they rested on his shoulders. Distantly, she heard thunder. A storm coming in over the mountain. "So what do we do now?"

"I'm letting you lead. You've been hurt, and I don't want to add to it." He rested his hands on her hips. "I also don't want to be your rebound guy. I've waited a long time for you. I don't want to lose you by rushing now."

Suzi twisted a lock of his hair around her finger. He was letting her lead. If she told him she wanted to sleep alone tonight, he would let her go without pressure. For her, the weight of his hands on her hips was pressure enough. Another volley of thunder shook the house. "Make love to me."

"Your place or mine?" He ran his fingers through her hair.

"Yours. Tonight, I'll let you have home court advantage."

He laughed. "I'll make sure the windows are closed and meet you upstairs."

Suzi hurried up to the guest room, her body sizzling with desire. Life with Logan had included sex at least once a day when he was home. Usually more often, but since she left him, she'd been solo. She missed regular, heated contact. The assurance she was loved and wanted. Based on how she'd always felt with Brian, sex would make her feel more loved and wanted than she ever had before.

Brian had thrown the covers over the bed this morning so she folded down the thin blankets. This was the first time she'd been in this room. There hadn't been any reason. She had always stayed in the guest cabin when she visited here with Logan. Tomorrow, they could exorcize the cabin.

Through the windows, she watched the storm coming over the mountain. Black clouds and flicking tongues of lightning blotted out the sunset.

"Big storm." He stood in the bedroom door with his head tilted, watching her. "Are you afraid of thunder?"

"No. Are you?"

"Not in the least." He crossed the room and ran his finger around her collar. "You're still dressed."

"I thought you might like to do the honors." Her skin tingled in anticipation.

"That was nice of you." Leaning down to kiss her, he pulled up her shirt.

So many concerts she had been backstage when he came off shirtless, or at least unbuttoned. So many times she had straightened his collar or adjusted his jacket before he went on or had his picture taken. Her palms slid over his skin.

"Hmmm, nice." He unhooked her bra and brushed it off her shoulders, kissing her bare shoulder. His tongue flicked against her skin.

"I thought you hated me at first. I thought you were disappointed because I wasn't what you thought I'd be." Suzi stripped his shirt off him.

Brian traced her nipple with his thumb, making her shiver. "You weren't. You were a lot more. So bright and cheerful. I didn't know how to talk to you."

Suzi dragged her lips across his chest. He tasted divine. Warm and tangy. She found his nipple with her tongue. The tight, hard bud rolled along her tongue as her fingers opened his jeans.

Brian tipped her face up to capture her mouth. When she succeeded in getting her hand around his member, a feral growl welled up from his chest, and he clutched her tighter. "Angel," he murmured against her mouth, pushing her back onto the bed.

But instead of climbing on top of her, he turned to the table and kicked off his jeans as he searched for something.

"What are you looking for?"

"Condoms." He threw a book over his shoulder and then a couple of picks and a crumbled piece of paper. "Shit. I don't have any."

Suzi wiggled out of her panties and tossed them to one side. "Don't worry about it. I'm safe. I was tested after I left Logan, and I haven't been with anyone since."

He pulled out the drawer and dumped it out. "Aren't you worried about me?" he asked, sifting through the mess on the floor.

"I trust you."

He turned to her, amazement blooming on his face. "You trust me?"

"You told me about the Paternity Suit Insurance Bowl in Sandy's office, and you have yourself tested once a year when you get a physical." Suzi rolled onto her side. "Besides, you're hunting for protection like it's a deal breaker. I know you, and I trust you."

He shuddered as if that was the most erotic thing she could have said. He pressed her hand to his lips. "Are you sure?"

Suzi slid closer to him so she could wrap her hand behind his neck. "I trust you. I've never trusted anyone the way I trust you."

Brian crawled onto the bed. "Angel," he whispered, kissing her fingers and then her cheeks.

Suzi ran her hands down his back, feeling the fine muscles under his skin. "I want you. I've always wanted you. The moment I met you, I knew I could trust you."

"My angel. You drive me wild." He sank into her.

Suzi moaned. The friction of their skin brought tears to her eyes. Being touched, held. His long, easy strokes filling her. He caught her earlobe between his lips. She gasped. He was so gentle. His hands touched her so carefully. The sweet sensation of his breath on her skin.

This man had always loved her. From that first moment when she'd shaken his hand. His touch had been gentle then, too. As if he knew he could crush her if he wasn't careful. Even when things got out of hand, when tempers ran high, he'd been aware of her tolerance level. The only time he'd pushed her had been England right when his divorce came through.

Every moment they had been together led them here.

Thunder exploded over the house, rattling the windows. The white flash of lightning filled the room. A sweet wash of joy overflowed inside her, and she cried out. "Brian, I love you."

He shuddered and groaned before sagging to one side of her. "Beautiful Suzi. I love you too," he murmured.

Rain lashed the window. Suzi curled against him, resting her head on his chest. Under her ear, his heart pounded. He seemed relaxed and well pleased. When she moved to lie beside him, his arm coiled around her shoulders.

But he wasn't saying anything. Logan always talked after sex. He always told her how good she made him feel. How much he loved being with her.

Brian snuggled her closer, kissing the top of her head. Still not saying anything.

The whole time she'd known him, they'd talked about everything. Almost everything. Not this. But everything else. And now—now he wasn't saying anything. What if she wasn't enough? Or was too much? Or was younger than he thought? Or he'd suddenly realized she made a better friend than lover? Or he was just horny, and now that he was done, he wanted her to go away?

Suzi blinked, fighting back a rush of tears. What if she'd just ruined one of the friendships she treasured most because she was rebounding and he was horny? How was she supposed to face him? He said he'd always loved her, but that could have been a line.

Or he might have made love to her just to make her feel better. It was just the kind of thing Brian would do. Going along with the pressure from Ida and Paul and the fans.

A sob hitched in her throat.

"Angel? Are you crying?" He turned her onto her back. "What's the matter? Did I hurt you?"

Suzi squeezed her eyes closed, forcing tears out the sides. She shook her head, hating herself for crying. The cloying manipulation of it sickened her. It felt too much as if she was taking advantage of Brian's sweet nature, twisting a one-night stand into something permanent.

"Then what's wrong? Come on, Angel. Talk to me." Brian stroked her cheek, and his gentle touch threatened to bring on another sob. Thunder rattled the windows again. "Are you afraid of the storm?" he asked lightly.

Suzi shook her head. She tried to force air into her lungs, but couldn't seem to get any.

He laid his head on the pillow beside her, nuzzling her cheek. "Tell me, Angel. Whatever it is, I can take it. I'm a big boy. Did making love to me make you realize how much you miss Logan?"

Suzi let out a sharp breath. "No."

"Then what's making you cry?"

Suzi turned to him. They were nose to nose. His eyes were close enough she could make out the uncertainty in them. The tone might have been light, but the question was real. "Was it…? It was okay for you?"

"It was fantastic, Angel. More than I'd ever hoped for." He rested his hand on her stomach. It fluttered at his touch. "Were you worried?"

"You don't think it was a mistake?"

"Do you think it was a mistake?"

"I…" Suzi bit her lip. "You didn't have to do this to make me feel better."

"I thought we were doing it to make both of us feel better." Brian stroked her cheek. "Suzi, I love you. What's going on in your pretty little head?"

"You didn't say anything."

"I'm sorry, sweetheart. I was laying here thinking about how happy I was. I guess I should have told you." He kissed her, teasing open her mouth.

She rolled onto her side and curled her leg around his hip. His skin slid against hers again. The sensation of his hands wandering down her body was gentle and possessive. Everywhere he touched, he claimed, until she was dizzy with need. This was how he'd always touched her, she realized. Taking her hand to help her out of a car, draping his arm over her shoulders at a function, hugging her in greeting or goodbye. Whenever, wherever he touched her, it had always had the same gentle possessiveness to it.

"You know it's going to be a while before I'm up for another round," he murmured. "The spirit is willing, but the flesh isn't twenty-two anymore."

Suzi chuckled, watching as the dark sound drew a flush to his skin. "I can wait."

He brushed his fingers through her hair, his expression turning serious. "I'm sorry. I didn't realize you were getting upset. I should have known you'd be a little nervous."

"No, I'm sorry. My brain just started spinning, and I thought maybe you only made love to me to make me feel better."

"I have waited years for you."

"And you're sure?"

"Absolutely." He kissed her again, nibbling her lips. "I love you, Angel. I've been waiting years to tell you that."

"You have?"

"I remember that first night at Jason's. Before you came out here." He propped himself up on his elbow. His leg slid between hers. "I shook your hand and couldn't think of anything to say. All I could think about was how much more beautiful you were than your picture."

"You couldn't think of anything to say?" Suzi cocked an eyebrow. She remembered that whole first meeting being miserable. All the guys had been so anxious. She'd had to cut Greg off after dinner because he was intent on getting hammered. All of them had tried to stop Charity from saying anything that popped into her head. "I thought you were angry."

"I was frustrated. I'd been so looking forward to meeting you, and I didn't know what to say." He sighed. "Marc wanted to put tape over your mouth and have you walk for us."

"Why?"

He smirked. "Because I said you had a great swing to your hips."

Suzi turned onto her side. "You said what?" This was more the kind of conversations she was used to having with him. "Is that all you were doing that night? Watching me walk around so you could stare at my hips?"

"No, I spent some of the time watching you talk so I could stare at your lips."

"My lips?"

"You have very nice lips." He brushed his finger across them, followed by his own lips.

She closed her eyes, enjoying his soft, sweet exploration. The weight of his hand on her waist anchored her.

"You have an impressive stride as well."

"There's a secret to that."

"What would that be?" He licked behind her earlobe.

"Thigh-high stockings. I was wearing them that night to please Logan."

"Then I'll have to make sure you have a good supply so you can please me."

"I'll be happy to please you." Suzi ran her fingers down his chest, making him moan.

"You already do." He kissed her neck.

"So tell me more about what you thought of me that first night."

"Are you going to get vain now?"

"I was vain before. You just never noticed. Why did you want to put tape over my mouth?"

Brian scowled at her with mock impatience. "I'd put some tape over it right now if I didn't have some better uses for it in mind."

Suzi pushed him onto his back, kissing him. This all felt so natural. Like this part of their relationship had always been there, but hadn't been used. "Tell me why you wanted to put tape over my mouth."

"Marc wanted to put tape over your mouth."

"Marc. When were you talking to Marc about this?"

"That night. He had to be in New York and couldn't come, so he called me."

"He called you." She trailed her tongue down his throat. Her hands strayed farther, stroking his belly and, ah yes, the flesh was willing. "Why did he want to put tape over my mouth?"

"Because you talked like the Queen of England." Brian gasped as she wrapped her hand around him.

"The Queen of England?" She stroked his hard length, trying to decide what she wanted more. Riding him would be fun, but so would sucking him. Sucking him would fulfill one of the better uses he probably had for her mouth. Riding him would allow her to continue the interrogation. She had him at her mercy now. If she timed it carefully, she could do both. Decisions, decisions.

"Angel," Brian moaned.

"What do you mean I talked like the Queen of England?"

"You're a bad girl, you know that?"

"But you like it. That's your real problem." She traced her thumb across his head making him shiver. "You know I'm not going to release you until I get an answer."

"I know you. You're never going to release me." He put his hand on the small of her back and tried to pull her closer, but she resisted. "You sounded…ah…stiff and formal."

"Stiff and formal?" Deciding, she inched down, kissing his chest as she moved. "Any other observations?"

"Suzi," he moaned.

She licked his nipple. His hand stroked up her back sending another shower of desire through her. "Well?" She swirled her tongue through his belly button, eliciting another low growl of pleasure.

"We thought you were an intellectual, but sexy, too."

That sounded good. "What else?"

"I don't remember. Suzi, please," he pleaded.

She kissed below his belly button, letting her cheek brush his swollen head. The room filled with the sound of rain and panting. "You don't remember anything else?" She released a slow, hot breath, knowing how it would travel across his skin.

"Jason didn't figure out the 'keeping you up' thing until after you left." Brian gasped. "He thought you were choking on something."

Suzi smiled. The bottom of the barrel. He did remember a lot of little details of their first encounter. That alone was proof he had been fascinated from the very first moment. She licked away a pearl of cum, making him shudder. She could taste herself on him as she drew him into her mouth. Closing her eyes, she relished their combined flavor. Everything had always been so easy with him. There had been tension, but nothing that ever overrode their friendship. That was one thing she'd never had with Logan. They had been lovers, but never friends.

Shifting, she straddled him. He opened his eyes, smiling. "That's better." As she sheathed herself on him, he groaned. "Much better."

She leaned down, letting her hair trail over his skin. "This is much better?"

He arched up to catch her in a rich, sweet kiss as he clasped his hands on her hips to guide her rhythm. Suzi let him have her, caught by the taste of his mouth, the strength of his hands, and the friction of him inside her. Her climax flooded her. Rushing down through her body to her toes. He caught her as she sagged forward, cradling her on his chest.

"You're a bad girl, Suzi," Brian murmured, stroking her hair. "Questioning me that way."

"You hated every moment, didn't you?"

"Pure torture."

She nestled her cheek against his chest. "You remember an awful lot about the first few hours you knew me."

"I was watching you." He ran his fingers down her back.

Suzi turned to rest her chin on him so she could see his eyes. He seemed sincere enough. "Why did you say this was much better?"

He blinked. "What?"

"When I climbed on top of you, you said it was much better. Why?"

For a long moment, he just stared at her face, running his fingers through her hair. "Because I want to see you when we make love. I want to know it's you and not some other woman I'm wishing was you."

"Have there been other women you wished were me?"

"Two or three."

She slid up his body, relishing the slick friction of his belly against hers. "Why didn't you say something?"

"I thought you were happy with Logan."

Suzi bit her lip. He'd been years thinking about her and too kind to want to hurt her by saying anything. Brian would have watched her marry Logan and kept his secret if he thought it would make her happy.

Kissing him, she let herself slip under his spell. He turned her onto her back, exploring her with his hands and mouth as if he might never touch her again. Suzi floated in a pool of heat while he tasted every inch of her. It seemed to be hours before he climbed out of bed and turned off the lights. She admired his long lean line as he walked back to the bed and settled beside her. Suzi raised his fingers to her mouth, kissing each one before nestling against him to watch the light show outside. His warm breath slid across her neck as he pulled her closer to his hard body.

Years she'd wanted this. Snuggling against Brian, she decided she couldn't have ended up in a better place. When she'd walked—run—out on Logan, she'd thought the world was coming to an end. The years of clinging to him because she adored him. Giving him space by ignoring his bad behavior. Knowing if they had a child, it would grow up believing Mommies took shit from Daddies because they had to.

But Brian would never do anything like that to her. She'd never seen him with a woman other than Bonnie. Not that she didn't believe there weren't any, but he was obviously beyond the need to chase every woman he saw.

Outside, the storm subsided to steady rain. The valley was lost to view. They were alone up here. Isolated from the world. His lips brushed her neck. Then her shoulder. Then he shifted up on his elbow to nip her arm, and she felt something hard to the south.

"I thought the flesh was weak," she murmured, arching her neck for him.

"You have a strengthening effect."

Chapter 18

Brian woke up because Suzi was moving. Swimming through grogginess, he reached for her, snagging her arm. "Where you goin'?

"To run." She kissed his cheek from an odd angle, so he opened one eye to see where she was. The room was bright. She'd managed to get out of bed and was leaning back over the side. "I'll be back soon."

"Just stay here." He fought the impulse to drag her back into bed with him. If she wanted to run, he should let her run, but he wanted her in bed with him until he was done with her, which might be never.

"I haven't run in ages. I'm going to be all blobby and unattractive if I don't." Pulling her hand free, she kissed his cheek again. "I'll be back soon and we can have breakfast. Or lunch as the case may be."

Scowling, he rubbed his suddenly empty hand over his face. The clock read eleven.

He remembered making love to her as the sun rose. Four times last night. Been a while since he'd done that. Been a while since he'd wanted to. Generally, one round was enough to burn off whatever lingering lust he had. With Suzi? No, with Suzi he'd wanted more. He'd wanted to touch her all night long. And had. If exhaustion hadn't knocked him out just after dawn, he'd have kept going.

He wished she was still here so he could touch her some more.

Most mornings, she ran for about forty minutes. Enough time to shower and meet her outside.

Throwing his legs over the side of the bed, the rest of him followed through a fast shower and a trip to the kitchen for coffee. Cup in hand, he went outside to wait for her.

She came around the curve of the drive, and her face lit, then she lowered her head, picking up speed. Shit. Brian dropped his mug in the grass and shifted his weight to one foot so when she plowed into him, she wouldn't throw him flat on his back.

Instead, she swung him around and pulled him down on top of her, laughing. "Hey baby, didja miss me?"

"Yes." He brushed sweaty tendrils of hair off her face. Four times last night, and her pressed under him again was giving his body ideas.

"Mmm, I can tell." She squirmed, running her palms up his chest. "I wonder what would happen if I went away longer."

"Don't do that." He tasted the sweat on her throat. "I don't think I could take it."

Suzi wiggled out of her shorts. "Well, I wouldn't want to cause you grief." Her fingers went to work on his jeans. She trusted him. She left Logan because she caught him with another woman, and she trusted him.

She wrapped her legs around him with a pleasured gasp. Ecstasy lit her face. Yesterday, he couldn't have imagined this. They were lying on the grass beside the pond in front of Jason's house with the sound of the waterfall and the birds and her moans. He'd fantasized about sex with her a lot, but most of his fantasies took place in bed. Less than a full day, and she was fucking him outside under the sun. She arched and shuddered, clutching him inside her. He gasped as the electric sizzle shot through him. Resting most of his weight on his elbows, he nuzzled her neck.

"Brian?" she asked. "What are we doing?"

"Other than having sex in the front yard?" He would have laughed, but he didn't have the energy. Raising his head, he smiled at her.

She met his smile with a hollow fear that made him catch his breath. He'd forgotten how much of a worrier she was. Two minutes after playful sex, and she was worried about something. Was she always this nervous, or had five years with Logan caused it?

"What is it, Angel?" He stroked her cheek.

"Are we in a relationship, or are we just burning off sexual tension? Is this friends with benefits or—or more? I just want to know. I'm okay either way." She tried to pull away from him, but he still had her half trapped with his body. "I just don't want to pressure you or— or not give enough or something. It's just, we've always been such good friends that I wouldn't want to ruin it. It's okay. I understand if you're not looking for—"

Brian put his finger over her lips to stop her. The logjam of words filled her eyes with anxiety. At least there was no confusion about what she wanted. She wanted forever, and that he'd be happy to supply. He sat up and put his hands on her shoulders. "Angel, I love you. I meant it when I said it last night, but I don't want to hurt you either. I understand you're nervous. I want a relationship. I want—" Brian caught himself before he said marriage. She was not going to react well to the thought of marriage after a twelve-hour sex marathon. "I want to build on the friendship we have."

"Ida said friendship was a good place to start."

"Ida?"

"She said last night that Paul knew we were in love five years ago."

He kissed her nose. "I wonder if Paul mixed something special into our dinner to help us along."

"He's a chef, not a witch doctor."

Brian stood and reached out to help her. "I wouldn't put anything past him."

Chapter 19

Logan threw another pair of jeans into the suitcase. "So Brian says she's okay?"

"Yeah. He said he'd heard from her, and she's still upset, but she's okay."

"But he didn't say where she was." Logan dug through the bag Suzi always packed for him. He didn't even know what to take. Dr. Kennedy said he was too dependent on her and intimidated by her, and that bred resentment, so he acted out by flirting and occasionally cheating. It all sounded pretty good. Suzi did make him feel stupid. Always throwing around her vocabulary. Dr. Kennedy said she might not even know she was doing it, and he needed to discuss it with her and put it in terms of how it made him feel. It sounded like a lot of daytime talk show stuff, but he'd give it a shot.

"No. He may have only talked to her on the phone or via email. He's already there, so you can ask him yourself. Don't forget to bring something warm. It can get very cold on the mountain," Cassie said.

Logan snapped his fingers and went to the closet to dig out his flannels. Instead, he opened her closet. She hadn't taken any of her clothes when she was here. What was she doing? Buying new? According to his office, she hadn't used her expense account, but she did have money of her own. He stroked the midnight blue velvet jacket she liked to wear when she dressed up. It had a tight waist and long tails. She could wear it with a skirt or jeans or whatever and she always looked hot and forbidding, like a vampire on the hunt. "So do you think you're going to be able to get her to WVA?"

"I don't know. Jason thinks we shouldn't tell her you're going to be there, but I don't think we should trick her like that."

"She hates to be messed with."

"Well, I'll warn Brian we're coming. I just hope he checks his email. He hasn't been answering the phone."

"Really?"

"It's the second anniversary of his divorce. Jason said he sounded a little depressed when he asked about going to Potterville."

"Oh, I forgot." Logan scratched his head. He'd never known, but he didn't want Cassie to think he was an insensitive jerk. Suzi kept track of all that stuff. He was lousy with dates. She sent all the cards and emails and junk like that.

"How is the therapy going?"

"Good. Dr. Kennedy says I just need to stay calm and tell her how I feel." And not to be embarrassed about being such a pussy.

"Well, that is a good start. Do you know what you're going to say to her when you see her?"

"I'm just going to tell her that I love her, and I'm willing to do whatever I have to to get her to come home." Logan surveyed the room. Her perfume bottles were still on the dresser. Her clothes still hung in the closet. When they went to LA for The Party, she'd left a pair of jeans draped over the back of a chair, and they were still there. The cleaners had wanted to move them, but he'd told them no. It made him feel like maybe she'd just stepped out and would be back. Having the house clean and the yard done helped the feeling along.

"We'll see if we can get Brian to convince her to come to Potterville. He's always been very close to her."

"I know. Better to see her with him than with Cherney."

"Is Brett that bad?"

"Yes. She probably picked up a disease from him."

"Logan, I doubt she ran right out and slept with the first man she found."

Logan frowned at his bag. Cassie had a permanent Pollyanna tattoo on her forehead. He could still remember chasing Cherney's fucking car out of the parking lot. If he forgot, the video was online with millions of hits and thousands of comments. "I don't care what she did while we were apart. I just want her to come home."

"Good. As long as you're willing to fix the things that are a problem."

"I know we can. Dr. Kennedy says she knows a couple's therapist she can send us to."

"Excellent. And you know, even if Suzi won't come to see you, a few days on the mountain will be good for you. Some fresh air and good food.

Brian will probably have some insights, too. She talked to him quite a bit about Bonnie."

"I know." Logan zipped up his bag. "You guys will make good character witnesses, too. You can tell her I'm different."

"Of course. We'll do everything we can to help you. When does your flight arrive?"

"The middle of the night. The first flight I could get lands at four-forty."

"You'll be there about an hour before we are. It's easier on the kidzos to fly at night. You can either rent a car and drive yourself or wait for us. My dad is coming to get us in the Wegman's B & B van since we haven't been able to get in touch with Brian. Just don't wait in the bar."

"I won't. I need to be sober to deal with all this crap."

* * * *

"What do you think?"

"I think we should let the poor little buggers go."

Suzi rolled onto her side, teasing her fingers through his hair. The fireflies floated around in the jar, seeking escape. Hundreds of their relatives beckoned from around the valley. None of them cast enough light to see by, but the full harvest moon hanging overhead did the job better anyway. They'd been outside all evening and never even turned on any lights in the house or the cabin. "So Jason bought this valley for Cassie."

"He did."

"That was sweet."

"Not at first."

"What do you mean?"

Brian propped his head on his hand. "He bought it out from under her as an excuse to stay close to her."

"So he kinda cheated her on a business deal."

"Kinda, but it worked out in the end. Even though she pulled a shotgun on him."

"Is that true?"

Brian pulled her closer. "I don't know the details, but there was a shotgun involved. She still has it. It's hanging up over the fireplace in the living room."

"That is the shotgun?" Suzi snuggled close to him. She hadn't been much farther than this all day. Or all last night. To think, yesterday afternoon she was lying in the hammock reading a book, and now she was all his. Keeping him outside after dark to catch fireflies in a jar. Sometimes she was such a little girl.

"That is the shotgun." He brushed his lips across hers. Such a little girl. On her last birthday she'd turned twenty-five. "Are we going to let these poor fireflies go before we get distracted and forget about them, only to come out in the morning to find we have their tiny souls on our heads?"

Suzi giggled. "I guess we can let them go now." She reached up and unscrewed the lid of the jar. "Happy?"

"Yes. I was worried we'd be haunted by fireflies for the rest of our lives." He traced her lower lip with his thumb. Was she going to be happy when she turned around and realized she was with an old man? "Does it bother you that I'm so much older than you?"

"You are?"

"Over fifteen years older." In the dark it was hard to see her expression. Did the news surprise her? Or did she not care?

"No." She stretched, draping her leg over his. "I'm very mature for my age, and you're immature, so I think we meet in the middle."

"Thanks." He pushed her over on her back. "Little brat."

"You love it."

He nuzzled her neck. "As long as you don't threaten me with a shotgun."

"I'll keep that in mind."

"You never wrote that story I told you to write." Her skin tasted so soft and sweet, and she had a precious little catch to her breath that told him how much she wanted him.

"What story?" She sounded disoriented. Good.

"The one about us getting lost in the woods." He worked his way down the collar of her shirt, licking under the fabric. "You need to wear more shirts with buttons. T-shirts are too hard to get into."

Suzi slid her hands under his shirt. His skin tightened under her light touch. "I wrote it. It was published, too. You didn't read it?"

"No."

"It was a romance."

He lifted his head. "That's why I didn't read it." He pulled her shirt up.

"Coward. The hero and heroine got lost in the woods, had sex, and came out a stronger couple."

"Mmmm, let's go act it out." He kissed her belly.

She giggled and pushed him away. "You're silly. Why don't we just go inside and have sex before the mosquitoes drain all our blood?"

He helped her up. "I'm serious about those shirts with buttons. And skirts. Those are easier to get into, too."

"Maybe I should just become a nudist."

He ran his fingers up her spine. She always arched like a cat when he did that. "Naw, people would stare when we went out to dinner. Look how much attention you get when you go out barefoot. Besides, you're mine. I don't want anybody but me getting peeksies."

"Peeksies? This is what I mean when I say you're immature." She slipped out of his arms. "Race you to the cabin." Then she sprinted away.

"I thought you were the mature one," he yelled after her.

Her laughter floated back to him, and in the moonlight he saw her strip off her shirt. By the time he got to the stairs, she was in the cabin, and her shirt hung from the railing. Brian scooped it up and pressed it to his face. She always smelled good, but he'd never been able to indulge in more than a whiff of shampoo when she was standing next to him. It was flowery, but a little musky, too. He'd never noticed another woman with the same scent.

She'd left the cabin door open and the lights off. As he crossed the common room to her bedroom door, his feet caught something. Her jeans lay in the middle of the floor. He picked them up. So this was how she was playing it. "If you think I'm going to pick up after you all the time, you're wrong."

By the time he got to the doorway, she was lying in the middle of the bed wearing only a smirk. "I bet if the reward was good enough, you'd pick up after me all the time."

Brian kicked the door closed and left her clothes on the chair. He crawled on the bed over to her. "You are so beautiful," he murmured and kissed her throat.

"Why, thank you."

"No, I mean just you. Everything about you." Brian lifted his head to study her. She lay back on the pillows with her hair haloed around her head. "You're beautiful. Your face, your body, your personality, your sense of humor. Being with you makes me feel so damn good."

Suzi blinked. "Why, Brian, that's poetic." Her mouth trembled. "I love being with you, too."

Brian kissed her, wishing he had more words to tell her what she meant to him. She slid his shirt off his shoulders and ran her fingers down his arms. He shivered. His member strained against his jeans. Ignoring it, he moved down her body, taking her left nipple into his mouth.

Suzi gasped. "Oh, Brian. That feels wonderful." She laced her fingers through his hair. "Make love to me. Please. I want to have my legs wrapped around you while you thrust into me. Please. I love you."

Brian stood up and shoved his jeans down. Then he crawled back onto the bed and mounted her, plunging deep into her with one long stroke. She shuddered, clasping herself to him. Brian pressed his face into the curve of her neck. She tasted warm and sweet. The heat of his skin matched hers. Her body wrapped around him like a vine, clinging to him. Her soft cries filled the room. This was what he'd always wanted. This rich affection. She gave a strangled cry and tightened around him. He thrust into her twice more before his own climax rolled through him.

She ran her fingers through his hair. "You are so sweet to me," she murmured.

"Sweet?"

She kissed his cheek. "That's the closest word I can come up with for how you make me feel. It's like my whole body is filled with wind and sunshine."

"You make the earth move for me, too." He shifted off her.

"Don't go," she pleaded.

"I'm staying right here."

Suzi curled against him. "I want to wake up where you are. I love you."

Brian leaned down, kissing her so he could taste the words on her lips. His whole body trembled, and so did hers. She tangled her leg through his, cinching herself to him. Her soft curves fitting to him. "I love you, too," he told her.

She drew in a jerky breath. "You're so good to me. The way you make me feel. The way you hold me." She nestled into him. "I want to wake up in your arms for the rest of my life."

Brian tightened his hold on her and closed his eyes, trying to get use to the feeling. Curling against her in the night. Waking up with her. He ran his fingers through her hair. "Go to sleep, my sweet. I'll be here in the morning."

* * * *

Cassie's father parked the van in the garage. The first blush of dawn was already creeping over the mountain. Logan climbed out with his bag and collected his guitar from the back. "I'm gonna go get some sleep." He gave Jason a salute. "See you around lunch."

"You'll have to make the bed," Cassie said, unbuckling Sonya. Andi already clung to her leg, rubbing her eyes.

"She's obsessed with bed-making," Jason muttered. He pressed a key ring into Logan's palm. "Take the keys in case it's locked up."

Logan hoisted his bag over his shoulder and crossed the front lawn. Beside the pond, he kicked something. Squinting in the half-light, he found a glass jar lying in the grass. What the hell was Brian doing with a glass jar outside? Maybe he'd been trying to catch fireflies. Suzi liked to do that when she was here. Jason said he'd been talking to her. Maybe it was making him nostalgic, too. Logan shuffled down the steps and into the cabin. The door was unlocked. Brian must have opened it up for him. Of the three bedroom doors opening off the common room, one was closed. Not the one he and Suzi used when they were here. Maybe Brian had decided not to stay in the big house. With two little kids in there, it wouldn't be a picnic. Logan dumped his bag on the floor. He'd intended to grab the blanket and curl up in the middle of the naked mattress, but staring at the bed where he'd slept, and not slept, so many nights with Suzi left him wired. He went to the bathroom.

On the counter lay a green, plastic wide-tooth comb with long brown hairs trailing from it. Logan picked it up and laid the hair across his palm. Definitely brown. Odd since Brian was blond. Had he picked up a girl? That would explain why he wasn't in the house. On the other side of the sink lay a familiar barrette.

The cheap metal had started out gold, but had turned coppery pretty quick. It was a butterfly with purple and blue cloisonné on the wings. He'd bought it for Suzi in…Japan maybe, while he was on tour from one of those street vendors when he'd been missing her. He picked it up. It had a long brown hair caught in it, too. Could there be another woman on Earth with brown hair and that exact barrette staying in Jason and Cassie's guest cabin? Maybe it wasn't Brian down here. What if he'd convinced Suzi to come? She could have been the one catching fireflies. She might not have been able to sleep in their regular room, either.

She could be in the cabin right now.

In the room beside the bathroom, the room with the door closed.

Logan pressed his ear to the door. Inside, he could hear the high, sweet sound of a woman's voice. Suzi sometimes read aloud to herself when she was trying to figure out if a conversation worked, and she didn't sleep well when she was stressed. If she knew he was coming in tonight, this morning, she might be up writing, trying to distract herself. She might be waiting for him. If he just opened the door and walked in, she might be happy to see him. The whole reconciliation could be over before the sun rose over the mountain. All except for the fun part. He planned on that taking a very long time.

He could also get a dictionary thrown at his head if he walked in on her unexpected. For some reason, she always seemed to have a big, hardcover dictionary with her.

He could knock. That would work. But what if she was just talking in her sleep? Then she'd be mad that he woke her up.

So he could wait until morning. Just sit on the couch and wait for her to get up so they could talk, and he could tell her all the stuff he'd been rehearsing with Dr. Kennedy. Then she'd cry and climb into his arms and tell him she was coming home. And it would all be fixed again. This time he was going to put a ring on her. Make it all permanent. His hands itched to touch her again. The heat in his groin was unbearable. He needed to be wrapped in her arms, making love to her again.

No way could he wait. If she was here, he needed to see her.

Of course, he could have been right the first time, and it was Brian with some girl who happened to have long brown hair and a barrette just like the one Suzi had. Brian had been in Japan a couple of months ago. He could have bought the same barrette for his little friend. The whole divorce anniversary thing could have been a smoke screen so he could meet his chicklet here.

Logan glanced around the room. He'd stayed in this cabin at least a dozen times. With the band and with Suzi. This room had a window that opened onto the porch. If the curtains weren't closed all the way, he could just peek in and see.

He left the bathroom and went out to the porch. It was starting to get warm with the sun shining in. The curtains hung most of the way open, allowing a shaft of sunrise across the room to bounce off the mirror on the dresser. The mirror then threw a spotlight onto the bed.

And Suzi.

Suzi knelt in the middle of the bed, straddled across a figure. The undulation of her hips was unmistakable. Strong male hands clasped her, guiding her. She clutched his wrists, throwing her head back. Her long hair bounced in time with her motion.

Logan stood, frozen, watching his Suzi make love to another man. She was gorgeous. Her perfect curves and animal grace.

Stumbling backward, he found a chair. He dropped into it, unable to breathe. That bitch. How could she flaunt her affair in his face? Bring another man here just to rub his nose in it? Did Jason and Cassie even know?

Wait.

Logan dragged himself into his own room. Jason and Cassie didn't know she was here. Brian said he'd talked to her, not that he'd convinced her to come. Had she arrived with the new guy in tow? With Cherney? Had Cherney been the man in that bed? Or was it another man? Logan frowned. He'd been consumed with the sight of Suzi making love, but he must have seen who she was making love to. The man's lean arms were wrapped around her body. His long fingers pressed into her flesh. Blond hair on the pillow.

Brian Ellis.

Suzi was fucking Brian.

Logan went back into the common room. He turned a chair toward the closed bedroom door. Then he grabbed his acoustic guitar and sat down to wait.

* * * *

Suzi lay down on Brian's chest, listening to his heart pound.

"I love the way you wake me up." Brian kissed the top of her head.

"Things like that happen when I'm too excited to sleep." She rubbed her cheek on his chest.

"Too excited to sleep. I like the way that sounds, too."

"I'm liking the way it feels."

"Me too. Want to try again?"

"I thought you weren't twenty-two anymore."

"I'm inspired."

"You're insane."

"I'm that, too."

"As much fun as this is, I have to use the loo." Suzi started to sit up, but Brian dragged her down for a deep kiss. She indulged him for a minute before pulling away. "I have to go to the bathroom."

"I'll let you go, but you have to promise to come back."

Suzi smiled. He was wrapping her up in him again. Cocooning her in passion and safety. "I'll come back. I promise." She drew herself out of his arms. "Chilly in here," she commented, grabbing his shirt off the floor and pulling it on. She glanced back at Brian with her hand on the doorknob. He was propped up on his elbow watching her. Winking, she opened the door.

Then she screamed.

Logan set aside his guitar and stood up. Raw fury etched his eyes with acid. "Trading up?" he asked.

Brian grabbed her from behind.

"What do you mean?" Suzi demanded.

"It looks like you went fishing for a bigger rock star."

"How dare you!" Suzi sobbed.

"Logan," Brian growled. His arms tightened around her.

"Did she have you fooled, too?" Logan stalked toward her.

Suzi shrank back. "What are you talking about?" What was Logan doing here? Was this a nightmare?

Logan glared over her shoulder at Brian. "Did she make you think she's not just the run-of-the-mill, gold-digging groupie?"

"You bastard." Brian lunged forward. The jolt of his wrath coursed through her. Suzi turned, wrapping her arms around his waist, holding him back. He was shaking.

"Please, please don't fight," she begged. "Please, Brian." She dug her fingers into his skin, reminding him she was there. It had to be a nightmare. Logan was in New York. They were alone on the mountain. In a second, Brian would wake her and tell her she'd been whimpering, and then he'd hold her until she fell back to sleep. It was not real.

Pounding erupted at the cabin door. "What's going on in there?" Jason roared.

"Logan get out," Suzi ordered.

The door burst open and Jason stumbled in. His gaze swept the room, and he cursed. "What is going on? Brian, you said she wasn't here."

"I said I'd talked to her," Brian shouted. "I never said where I talked to her."

"It looks like you've been doing a lot more than talking," Jason shouted back.

Logan stalked forward and leaned into her face. "Are you happy now? Or do you need to move further up the fame chain?"

Suzi slapped him, snapping his head around.

Cass and her father crowded through the door. Cassie put her hands over her mouth. "Oh, my God. This can't be happening with my kids here." She turned around and grabbed her father, pulling him out behind her.

"Is this what you want, Suzi?" Logan's breath hitched. "Are you really going to be any happier with him than you were with me?"

Suzi wrapped her arms around her stomach. It was trying to eat its way out of her body. Jason and Brian were shouting at one another. Logan stood in front of her as if he was either going to grab her and kiss her or humiliate her some more. The print of her hand stood out on his face. She closed her eyes, letting tears slide down her cheeks.

"Suzi? Sugar?" Logan reached for her. "Please don't cry."

Suzi sank into Logan's embrace. The simple familiarity took the gnawing edge off her panic. But it was Logan. Logan who she couldn't trust. And she was wearing Brian's shirt. She jerked backward, tearing away from Logan and blundering into Brian.

"Poor kitten." Jason grabbed her arm and pulled her out from between them. "You both get out. Look what you've done to Suzi."

"What I've done to Suzi?" Brian shouted. "I didn't ambush her with her ex-boyfriend."

"We called, we emailed, we texted. We practically sent smoke signals. Cassie's mom was going to drive up here yesterday but couldn't get away." Jason snapped. "It is my house."

Suzi twisted, escaping Jason's arms. "Please stop fighting. I—" She looked around at their expectant faces. "I have to go to the bathroom." She fled to the bathroom and locked herself inside.

She did have to go, a fact she had forgotten when she opened the door and saw Logan sitting in the other room. After she washed her hands, she splashed water on her face and stared at her reflection in the mirror. Shock radiated from her eyes. Through the door, she could hear them still fighting. They weren't shouting, but their voices were harsh and loud. She needed to escape this situation. Her heart slammed around in her chest like a wild bird beating at the bars of its cage. If she could slip out of the house for a run, it would help clear her head. Her running bra was still hanging where she'd rinsed it out this morning—yesterday morning—and she could run barefoot if need be, but she couldn't run in just Brian's shirt. The bathroom window was too small to climb though, too. She would have to face them to get out of here.

She stomped out of the bathroom and headed for her room with her head down. They fell silent as she passed between them. In the bedroom, she found underwear and a pair of shorts.

"What are you doing?" Brian asked.

"I'm going for a run." Suzi jammed her foot through the leg of her shorts.

"For a run?" Jason asked. "It's the crack of dawn."

"She's either going to run or she's going to cook something," Logan said. "Aren't you, Suzi?"

Brian stepped in front of her, shielding her from the door. He'd managed to pull on his jeans, but she was still wearing his shirt. "Are you sure you want to do this? It's dark and cold." He smoothed her hair off her face with gentle hands.

"I have to get out of here or I'm going to explode," Suzi whispered. "I can't be here now."

"I'll come with you."

"No. I need to be alone."

He nodded, not even offering a fake "I understand." He leaned down and kissed her forehead. Suzi wrapped her arms around his waist, pressing her check to his chest to listen to his heartbeat. It was steady and strong, like his arms around her. Brian had always cared for her. He knew she couldn't take much craziness. Pulling away, she sat down to pull on her shoes.

"You can't be letting her go," Jason snapped.

"Yes, I can. Just leave her alone. All of this would have been a lot easier if you could have just left her alone."

Suzi closed the cabin door behind her. If only she could run away into the mountains and disappear like the woman from *Follow the River*. But at the moment, she wouldn't want to follow it back home.

Chapter 20

"This was a bad idea," Cassie said, wringing her hands. She'd returned after putting the girls back in the van and sending them down the mountain with her father.

"It was a fucking brilliant idea until this moron got in the way." Jason gestured at Brian.

"You are not my mother or her mother. It was none of your business," Brian snarled. The room was chill, and she still had his shirt on. Had she wanted to wear his shirt, or had she just forgotten she was wearing it when she left?

"This wasn't fair to her," Logan said. "She hates being manipulated." He went into the room across from Suzi's and closed the door.

Brian arched an eyebrow at Jason. "Fucking brilliant idea." He walked to the house and into the guest room. Inside, he leaned on the door. Last night, she'd loved him. Begged him to stay with her. Curled into his arms as if she belonged here. She had belonged there. He'd promised her he'd be there in the morning, but would she want him now that Logan was here? She must still love the other man. She'd fallen into his arms like he was magnetized.

Logan hadn't treated her right. He made her feel like nothing but a sex toy. But that had been good enough for six years, and she didn't exactly hate sex. Or did she not know how to act when a man wanted her for more than sex?

If he fought for her, she would get hurt. That, he didn't want to see. The way she hurt now was too much. But if he didn't fight for her, she would end up with Logan, and Brian liked to think she'd be better off with him.

* * * *

Suzi stopped at the bottom of the path and bent over trying to catch her breath. Running up the mountain first had been wise. It burned off most of her anxiety. Unfortunately, running back down had made her feel out of control again. To get back to the guest cabin to shower, she had to pass the kitchen, and she could hear the raised voices from here.

"You remember what you were doing twenty years ago?" Jason shouted.

"Our first tour. What is this, a quiz?" Brian snapped.

"You know what she was doing? Starting school."

"She's not five years old anymore."

"She's still fifteen years younger than you."

"So?"

"Do you even think you can keep up with her?" Something banged on the counter. "You're a total bastard stealing her like that."

"She's not a ball." Oh good, Cassie was in there, too. "She made a choice. I don't see anything wrong with it."

"Oh, you don't? You were the one all hot and bothered to get them back together. You said they just needed to talk."

"Well, I was wrong."

"That's a first, isn't it?"

Suzi pressed her hands over her face. Jason, Cassie, and Brian fighting in the kitchen. She was going to break up a band and a marriage. Jason and Brian had been friends longer than she'd been alive, and she'd come between them. Helen of Troy had nothing on her. Turning back, she ran toward the cabin.

* * * *

Logan staked out the common room. He knew Suzi. She'd show up here soon enough. Breakfast was a requirement for her. Jason and Cassie might not have done the kindest thing in setting them up like this, but he couldn't pass up a golden opportunity.

"What are you doing here?" Suzi demanded when she walked back in from her run.

"I had nothing to do with your ambush," Logan said. He tried to keep his voice calm. Dr. Kennedy told him he needed to talk to her, not shout. "Jason and Cassie invited me here, hoping they could convince you to come so we could talk."

Suzi folded her arms. "I didn't mean here in West Virginia. I meant here in the cabin."

"I knew you would come here."

She blinked. Her jaw flexed. "Don't do this to me, Logan." She walked into the kitchen.

"Do what, sugar?" Logan followed her.

She tried to juggle a carton of eggs, a package of smoked ham, a hunk of cheese, and a carton of milk as she backed out of the refrigerator.

Logan lifted the eggs and milk out of her hands. "Sugar, listen to me, please."

"I listened to you for a long time. It didn't work." She went to the counter and spread out her ingredients before she went digging for utensils.

"I'm in therapy."

"Bully for you." She set out a bowl. "A little early for breakfast."

"I could eat."

Suzi's lush lips twitched with a smile. "You always could." She broke a couple of eggs into the bowl.

Logan leaned in the doorway, watching her. "Please listen to me. I'm trying to fix it. I really am."

"You should have tried earlier." She whipped the eggs, added some milk, and whipped them again.

"I know. I talked to my therapist about why I…did what I did."

"Seduced every female in fifty feet?"

Logan sighed. "She thinks I was trying to remind you that other women are attracted to me. To make you jealous."

"Right. I might have missed that." Suzi cut butter into the frying pan she'd set on the stove. "I hadn't noticed all the women throwing themselves at you all the time or the vast numbers of panties that arrived daily in the mail."

"It sounded stupid to me at first, too."

"At first?"

"Well." Logan focused on the counter, tracing the grain of the wood. "The more I thought about it, the more sense it made."

"You are grasping at straws. I don't know why, but you are."

"Because I love you." Logan slammed his fist on the counter. It hadn't taken him long to lose his temper. Dr. Kennedy would be disappointed.

Her beautiful face went completely blank. In one hand, she held a knife while she steadied the ham with the other, but neither moved.

"I fucking hate it when you do that," Logan snarled. He started pacing the kitchen.

"When I do what?"

"Look at me like that. Like I'm an idiot."

"I'm not looking at you like you're an idiot. If you want to read that into my expression, that's your prerogative."

"Would you quit using your vocabulary on me? Does he know you do this crap?"

Suzi focused on chopping the ham. "First, I'm not using anything against you, and second, he has a name, and you used to know it."

Logan leaned on the wall beside the door. "Yeah, I just can't believe you're fucking him."

"We have always been friends." Suzi smiled at the cutting board. "It was a natural progression."

Logan's stomach clenched at her smile. He had dozens of photographs at home of her with that same expression— aimed at him. She loved Brian. In the same way, she used to love him. There had to be a way to turn that smile back on him. Something between them that left Brian out. He leaned on the counter beside her. "I'm sorry about the baby."

"Why are you bringing that up now?"

He shrugged. "I just didn't get a chance to tell you before."

"It's water under the bridge. I always knew I couldn't have kids." Suzi shrugged. Anyone else would think she didn't care, but Logan had seen it often enough to know it was a cover.

"I know, but when you told me, my first thought was that we would have a beautiful baby, living and breathing. A child who would show the world how much we loved each other."

"And it's my fault that that child won't be born." Suzi scooped the ham into the frying pan.

"That's not what I meant. I just never realized how much I wanted us to be a family."

"Well, we're not going to be a family."

"We could be." Logan took her hand. "Just because you can't carry a child doesn't mean we couldn't have kids. We could adopt. Or we could hire some woman to do the pregnancy."

"A surrogate?"

"Is that what they're called?" Logan laced his fingers through hers. Her hands were sticky from the food, but small and warm and fit perfectly in his. "We could get a surrogate and have a child of our own. Children. As many as you want."

"So I can be left holding the babies when you went wandering off to check out other women?" Suzi pulled her hand out of his. "No, thank you."

"But I wouldn't. My therapist says that once I have you for sure, I won't do that anymore."

"Have me for sure?"

"You are the only one I ever wanted." Logan leaned toward her. "That's why I flirted with all those other women. To make you jealous so you would stay with me."

"Guess what?" She leaned toward him, too. She was close enough he could feel her breath on his cheek. Her lips curled with anger and misery. "It made me feel like shit." She grabbed the cutting board and stomped to the sink to wash it.

"I know that now." Logan followed her. This tack wasn't working the way he'd wanted it to. He'd hoped that getting her to think about them as a family would bend her back in his direction. The only other idea he had was sex. "And I'm sorry. I've changed."

Cass returned to the eggs, stirring them around. "The tune is familiar, but I think the words have changed, and I don't want to dance to it anymore." She dropped in cheese he hadn't even noticed her cutting up. "Did your therapist tell you this is a classic abusive cycle?"

"I never hit you."

"You engage in the behavior, and then you seek forgiveness. Then the cycle begins again." She made a circle in the air with the spoon before stirring up the eggs.

"I'll ask her about that." Abusive cycle? He needed to get Suzi in to talk to Dr. Kennedy. They spoke the same language. "I will. I promise. What happened between you and Cherney?"

"What do you mean what happened between me and Cherney?"

"Well, you left with him, but you didn't stay long." Logan picked up a kitchen towel and started pulling strings out of the fringe.

"You wondering if I had sex with him, too?" She took a loaf of bread out of the refrigerator and dropped two slices in the toaster.

"I wasn't going to ask."

She snatched the towel out of his hands. "I didn't."

Logan blew out a breath. That thought had been haunting his nightmares since he watched her drive away with Cherney. Boy, had he been off the mark. "That's a lot of food for the two of us," Logan pointed out.

"You said you could eat." She shut off the fire.

Logan rested his hand on her shoulder, waiting to see if she would shrug it off. When she didn't, he let his hand slide up to her neck. Her skin was so soft and supple. "Suzi," he whispered, "I still love you."

"Logan," Suzi murmured.

His breath caught. The raw tremble in her voice drew him forward a step to lift her hair off the back of her neck and kiss her. She tasted just the same. He traced his tongue down the back of her neck. "Suzi, you taste so good. You always taste so good."

"Logan, don't." Suzi moaned.

"Don't what? Don't stop?" Kissing the tender spot behind her ear, he slipped his hands around her waist. "It feels good, doesn't it?" He pressed his hands on her belly, pulling her tight. His member thickened.

Her body molded to his, soft and yielding. Her breath shortened.

"Let me show you how much I love you. Come with me now." Every touch, every glance, every breath they had shared came back to him. Logan drowned in her. "So sweet. So fine. I understand why you went to him. It doesn't matter. We'll put it behind us. Make love with me again."

She twisted in his arms. "It would be easier."

"What would be easier?" Her liquid eyes were dark with desperation. If she would give him the chance, he could fix that. Whatever it was. He could make her life perfect. Just having her in his arms, he felt better than he had since she left.

"If things just went back to the way they were."

"We can put things back and make it better." He brushed a lock of hair off her face. Her skin was softer than he remembered. "I promise you, Suzi. I want to work this out."

She touched his face. Her fingers were light, teasing. "I'm ruining his life."

"Whose?"

"Brian's. I heard him fighting with Jason. Cassie was there, too. They were all arguing."

Logan clenched his teeth. He should let the guilt eat at her. If she wasn't with Brian, he had a chance. He brushed his lips across hers. When she didn't slap him or hit him with anything, he pressed farther, teasing open her mouth to taste her. Her flavor was like no other woman. Rich and sweet. She responded with familiar eagerness. Her arms wrapped around his waist. "Suzi, please, come back to me."

"Back to you?" She made it sound as if she'd never really left.

"Being with you is…" Logan drew a breath. "Magic. Every time. All the time. You always made me feel like the hero of one of those books you write. Like the greatest guy in the world."

"Logan," she moaned. Her eyes were dark and soft.

"One more time, Suzi, please," he whispered, nipped her shoulder. "I'm begging you for one more time."

She bent to him. "One more time," she murmured.

Logan lifted her off the floor and carried her out of the kitchen. Drugging her with sex had worked for five years. It could work again.

Halfway through the common room, Suzi gave a strangled cry, twisting out of his arms. "No," she sobbed. "Stop." Dropping to the floor, she staggered to the back of the couch.

Logan froze. Another ten feet, and he could have had her. His thwarted body throbbed, but his heart ached more. The only things keeping her up were her pride and the couch.

"I'm not with him just because I couldn't be with you." Suzi rocked like someone had stuck a sword in her gut.

"I know that."

"I don't think you do." Suzi's face was streaked with tears. "How can you make me feel so good and so bad at the same time?"

"What?"

"I loved you. I gave you the most precious gift I had to give. I did everything I could to please you, and all you could do was treat me like crap."

"I never treated you like crap," Logan whispered. "I treated you like a queen."

"Who? Catherine of Aragon?"

Logan threw his hands in the air. "Who the fuck is Catherine of Aragon?"

"The first of Henry the Eighth's wives."

"I never cheated on you."

"It felt like you did. It felt like you had sex with every one of those women you flirted with right in front of me."

"And it's all my fault." Logan wasn't sure if he was serious or sarcastic.

"No, it's my fault, too. I thought I could be okay with it, but I never was." Suzi wiped her face. "I should have made my feelings clear sooner. Before I stormed out of that party."

"That might have helped. Not treating me like a moron might have helped, too."

"Logan, I never treated you like a moron, but I'm sorry if you felt that way." She straightened. "Eat your breakfast." She walked into the bathroom, and a second later the shower started.

Logan ground his teeth. Being this close to her made him crazy. He wanted to break down the bathroom door, throw her over his shoulder, and carry her to the bedroom so he could make her listen. He wanted to make love to her until they were both sweaty and sated.

Instead, he stomped into his bedroom and slammed the door.

* * * *

When she judged it safe to leave the bathroom, Suzi got dressed and left the cabin. At the top of the stairs, it occurred to her that she had nowhere to go. Standing here wasn't the most protected position. If this were a zombie movie, something would be snacking on her brains by now. It wouldn't make a very satisfying meal. Judging by her state of mind, her brains would be tough and stringy.

She wandered to the hammock. The day before yesterday when Brian decided they needed to go to Ida's for dinner, she'd left her book, and it was still lying there. She picked it up and wished she could escape back into its pages, but the rain the other night had soaked it through, and now it was a brittle block. Somehow that was symbolic, but if she ever put it in a novel, no one would believe it.

"Hi Suzi. Doing some reading?" Cassie asked. She stopped on the other side of the hammock.

"No. Just reminiscing about a simpler time."

"Ah." Cassie nodded. "I was going over to the campground to check on things. Want to take a walk?"

No. "Sure." Cassie was probably the best person to talk to. She would have a considered opinion. Suzi fell into step beside her.

"I swear to you, we didn't mean to trap you like this." Cassie led the way along a narrow trail into the woods. "We hoped to get the two of you together to talk. That was it. I just hoped to talk to Logan and find out how sincere he was about getting you back. Jason wanted to lure you here under false pretenses, but my husband has a bit of an underhanded side to him."

"I don't blame you. I had to face Logan sometime."

Cassie walked in silence for a minute. "So, you and Brian."

"Maybe."

"Maybe?"

"I don't know what to do, Cassie. I love Brian, but I still love Logan." Suzi bit her lip. "I think I still love Logan."

"You think?"

"We have so much history. It's hard to forget that."

"History is nice, but it can trick you. You end up staying with the known quantity even though it's killing you. Of course, jumping at the next thing along isn't a great idea, either."

"Wife, mother, campground owner, and amateur psychologist."

"You'd be surprised how often that stuff goes together. Let's focus for a minute on Brian. You and Brian were always close. When did you fall in love with him?"

"I think I've always been in love with him. I just could never do anything about it."

"So Paul was right."

Suzi frowned at Cass. "Paul told you?"

"Paul is the Google of gossip. That summer you two walked down the mountain and into town, he asked me if you were a couple, and when I told him no, he said you should be. And then he told everyone in town the two of you were good friends."

"Fabulous."

"Welcome to the wonderful world of small town living." Cass put her arm around Suzi's shoulders and gave her a brief hug. "When did the relationship...deepen?"

"The day before yesterday. I had a secret crush on him, but Paul and Ida both made comments about us, so I asked him and...well, that's when it deepened." Suzi shoved her hands in her pockets. How could she write all this stuff for strangers to read, but she couldn't say it out loud to a friend?

"So you only had one day."

"Yes."

"And what about Logan?"

"I've had years with Logan, but he's always flirting with other women, and you know what some of those women are like. They think *no* means *keep trying because my girlfriend isn't here*."

Cass rolled her eyes. "Tell me about it. If groupies applied their single-minded purpose to politics, we'd have world peace."

"I used to find him all the time with girls sitting in his lap or rubbing his shoulders. He swore it never went any further than that, but how do I know?"

"I know."

"And then you get the geniuses who figure out where the hotel is and show up at the door in nothing but a raincoat and high heels."

"That's not going to be much different with Brian. I've opened doors on some very interesting deliveries when the guys are on tour. You don't want to hear your four year old say, mommy, there's a lady in the hall with no clothes." Cassie shuddered.

"I'm sure, but Brian I trust. Logan, I could never take my eyes off."

"He is going to therapy about that."

"He told me." Suzi hunched her shoulders. "I almost had sex with him this morning."

"With Logan?" Cass stopped at a door in a privacy fence and stared at her wide-eyed.

"I didn't, but for a minute there it seemed like a great idea. I've just been with him for so long, and I heard you all fighting in the kitchen this morning. I just wanted everything to go back to the way it was."

"Oh, that. That was nothing. Jason doesn't like it when he doesn't get his way. He'll get over it. He already is. When I left the house, he and Brian were headed into the studio to play around and make up song lyric koans."

"They know 'Billy Don't Be A Hero' is a protest song, right?"

"It doesn't matter. What matters is, no woman is going to come between them. If Bonnie couldn't, you sure can't because Jason likes you." Cassie lifted the latch but didn't open the door. "Suzi, let me ask you the real simple question that led to my divorce."

"What's her name?"

Cassie smirked but didn't deck her, which Suzi figured she deserved after that snide comment. "My father asked me one day if my ex-husband made me happy. Does Logan make you happy?"

"He's trying to."

"What about Brian?"

Suzi smiled. She couldn't remember a time when Brian didn't make her happy. After the sex video broke, he was the first one who had reached her. In England, in the middle of his own misery, he had lashed out at her and then hunted her down to apologize, but didn't take advantage of her even though she was drunk and willing. When she arrived here, he had let her lay in a hammock for five days reading because he didn't want to hurt her more. He wouldn't have ever made the first move. This morning, he'd tried to protect her despite being naked.

"Well, there's your answer." Cass pushed open the door. "You should go talk to Brian. They're still in the studio."

Suzi nodded.

"Suzi." Cassie caught Suzi's arm. "You have to tell him about the near miss with Logan this morning."

"Do I have to?" Suzi cringed.

"You don't want him getting a ramped-up version from Logan. I'm sure he'll understand."

Suzi nodded. "Thanks Cassie." She watched her feet as she went back down the path, rehearsing what she needed to say to Brian. Her stomach knotted. At the time, getting back together with Logan had seemed like the best thing to do. Put everything back the way it was. She should have known. This wasn't a book she could delete half a scene and rewrite it to make everything work out. She couldn't just clip out the subplots that weren't working. If she could, she'd take out the whole scene of this morning. All of it, from midnight on. She'd reset it in Brian's room so they would be found by Jason or Cassie instead of Logan. Or go back two days so Brian called Jason and told him the good news before any of them arrived. Then they all could have laughed about it instead of fighting.

Chapter 21

At the studio window, Suzi had to stop rewriting her own past. She peeked through. Brian was sitting alone, scowling at the guitar in his lap. Cassie said he and Jason were the best of friends again. Was she wrong? Brian smiled when he saw her at the window. Setting aside the guitar, he headed for the door.

Suzi met him at the corner of the building.

"Where have you been?" he asked, guiding her into the shade of the trees.

"Hiding."

"From me?"

Suzi wrapped her arms around his waist. "Hold me."

"Of course, Angel. Of course." Brian held her close, leaning his head on top of hers. "What's the matter?"

"I heard you fighting with Jason and Cassie before."

"It's not the first time."

"But it was about me," she said. His eyes were so warm and understanding.

"You don't have to worry about it."

"I—" Suzi's breath locked in her chest. She couldn't tell him. It would hurt him so much.

"You what?"

"I had almost sex with Logan today."

"You—?" Brian took a step backward, releasing her. Suzi swayed, waiting for his response. "You almost had sex with Logan today? Jesus, you were just in bed with me three hours ago."

"I don't know what happened. We were talking, and it was nice. Like it used to be. And I started to remember…"

Brian stalked deeper into the trees. Twigs snapped and crackled under his feet. He raked a hand through his hair. "Remember what?"

Suzi clutched her hands. "It's just… We were together for a long time, and I was thinking it would be easier if I just got back together with him. Then nobody would have to fight anymore. We could all just go back to the way things were. But I didn't do it."

Brian crossed back to her in three strides, caught her by the shoulders, and pressed her against a thick oak. "The way things were? You want to go back to being his sex toy? You want to go back to him humiliating you all the time?"

"He swears he can change." Suzi shuddered. She hadn't expected violence, but somehow it seemed right. His hands dug into her shoulders, as if he'd never let her go.

"I can change, too. You want to be treated like a groupie slut? I can do that." He leaned into her face. "I can fuck your brains out ten times a day and treat you like shit in between times. I can ignore everything you say until you walk away, and then come crawling on my hands and knees, begging you to come back. Is that what you want?"

"It wasn't like that."

"Tell me, what was it like? I just spent five years listening to you make excuses for him. Watching him laugh at the way you blushed when they called you Randy Mirandy. I listened to him brag about how hot you were. How willing and flexible. Are you going to tell me it's not always like that?"

"He's trying to change."

"I bet. He'll change until the minute he has you back again, and then you think you're going to be able to run to me for advice on how to keep him happy." He pressed into her. "I'll do anything for you, but I can't be your friend anymore. I can't stand on the outside anymore."

Cass expected him to kiss her, or start taking off her clothes, but he didn't. Instead, he leaned his head into the curve of her neck and held her.

Abruptly, he dropped her and turned away. "You've gotta make up your mind, Suzi." He kept his back to her.

"Brian," she whispered. The sound couldn't have carried to him over the wind in the trees, but he flinched and then stomped back to the studio.

She wanted to chase after him, but her feet had intentions in the other direction. Instead of taking the stairs, she scrambled down the steep hillside to the ledge where the guest cabin sat. Skirting the far side of the pond, she concentrated on being invisible.

"Suzi!"

Shit, not invisible.

The porch door banged. "Suzi!"

"You son of a bitch!" she shouted. "What did you tell them?" A flock of birds shot into the sky overhead, screaming.

Logan stopped on the other side of the pond. His eyes went wide. "What?"

"What did you tell them about us? I'm willing and flexible? Did you tell them I was a whore or a nympho?"

Logan held out his hands. "I never said anything like that."

"You did. I know you did. Did you tell everyone about that night in Portland with Greg and the bottle of tequila, too? Did you make it sound like we did that all the time?" Too furious to go around the water, she splashed into the middle of the pond. "You bastard. I can't believe I ever trusted you."

"I never said anything to anyone."

"You never loved me. I was never anything to you but a good fun fuck." She scooped up a handful of mud and threw it at him.

"Suz!" Logan ducked but got splattered, anyway. "No. I loved you. I still love you. I know I made mistakes."

"Mistakes like talking about our sex life in public. You were the one who made that sex video and released it, weren't you?"

"No! I would never do that. How can you even think that?"

"It fits with the rest of the pattern." Suzi wiped tears off her cheek and succeeded in getting mud all over her face. "And now all you want to do is ruin my chances with Brian. That's why you wanted to get me into bed this morning. To wreck things with Brian, and I was stupid enough to consider it. He loved me, you know that?"

"I love you." Logan waded into the pond.

"Dammit Logan, it's over. Can't you see it's just time to let go?"

"What is going on?" Jason yelled from the stairs.

Suzi glanced at him and then back at Logan. The sound of the stream flowing down the mountain reminded her of a flushing toilet. She dove into the undergrowth at the edge of the ledge and plunged down the hill. A branch whipped across her cheek, bringing more tears to her eyes.

She'd ruined it all. Every chance she had at being happy. If she'd only gone to Brian's room last night instead of the cabin, Logan wouldn't have found them this morning. If she'd answered Brian's emails when she first left Logan, she could have gone to his house to lick her wounds and never left.

If she'd just kissed him that day they climbed down this stream five years ago....

* * * *

"What happened?" Brian asked from the top of the hill. Through the studio window, he'd seen Jason running across the lawn. When he walked out, there had been yelling, including Suzi's high pitched, panicked voice.

Logan waded across the little pond beside the guest cabin. He was spattered with mud. Jason had run down the stairs and around the corner of the cabin before Brian got outside. No Suzi. There was a hole in the bushes near the mouth of the stream.

"What the fuck is going on?" Jason roared.

"Suzi went completely cuckoo and ran." Logan started lifting away branches from the mouth of the stream. "Suzi!"

Something crashed down the hillside.

The knot in Brian's stomach tightened. He'd explored these woods with her. Snagging branches. Rocks covered in slime. Holes hidden under leaves. Ledges and small cliffs appeared out of nowhere. There were snakes and spiders and other critters. She was always careful because if she wasn't, she could break her neck.

She was following the stream.

Brian bounded down the hill.

"Where are you going?" Logan demanded, trying to block the way.

"After her." Brian ducked around him and slid down the first drop.

He should have kept his temper when she came to talk to him. He remembered the surprise in her eyes, but at the time, it hadn't penetrated. Surprise and something else. Brian frowned. When he had pinned her to the tree, her eyes had gone dark, excited. Like she'd expected him to make love to her.

She'd come to him to confess almost screwing Logan within hours of being in bed with him and not long enough after Jason insinuated he'd never be able to keep her satisfied. Why would she be turned on? Was it because he was mad? She and Logan had a stormy relationship. Maybe that was the way their relationship worked. They fought so they could make up. Bonnie had been like that. Most of the conversations he had with Suzi about her relationship had been about not getting into fights with Logan. How to keep things calm. Most of the time, when drama got whipped up around her, Suzi found a reason to leave. She ran, she wrote, she found a burning need to leave the scene. She was passionate enough about things without having to induce.

He didn't hear anything behind him or in front. Neither Logan or Jason was following. Suzi had been blundering through the undergrowth like an army. Why was she quiet now? Had she fallen and hit her head? He'd be glad she wasn't screaming in pain if he didn't have the image of her slumped at the bottom of a ledge unconscious.

His foot slipped, and he grabbed a tree branch before he went down. If he didn't slow down, he was going to crack open his head, and then he wouldn't do her any good.

If he'd kept calm when she came to him just now, they wouldn't be in this fix at all. Instead, he'd told her she needed to make up her mind and stormed away. What made him think he couldn't keep up with her? Over the years, she'd made comments about needing a break from Logan's demands. At the time, he hadn't put it together, but he doubted she was talking about cooking.

And she'd *almost* slept with Logan, not that she did. Logan had always had that hold over her, so of course he'd try to use it on her to get her back. If things were reversed, Brian knew he'd have done the same. He'd have given it a shot just to have one last time with her.

A fallen tree blocked the stream. He didn't remember it being here last time. In the mud, he saw footprints and a muddy smear on the trunk, but he couldn't see how she'd gotten through. He picked his way around and back to the stream.

"Suzi?" he called. "It's me. Brian. Where are you?"

Nothing.

Absolutely nothing.

No birds, no critters, no cracking twigs. Just the wind in the trees and the water over the rocks.

Brian searched around for prints and regretted quitting Boy Scouts when he was ten. He'd know a little more about tracking if he'd kept with it, but at the time, guitar had been more interesting. "Suz?"

He slogged through the water. The rocks were just as slippery as he remembered. Everything was slippery. Every action, every word.

She was standing in the middle of the stream, soaking wet, legs braced, staring over the edge of the falls.

"Suzi?"

She didn't turn around.

Brian walked up to her. She'd stopped at the edge of the waterfall. The handholds didn't look any better than they had before, and there was still no way around it. "If you're thinking of jumping, I'd have to recommend against. At worst, you'd sprain something, and it's a long way back up."

"I was trying to figure out a way to climb down," Suzi whispered. "Besides, I think I already sprained my wrist." She held one arm cradled in the other.

Brian put his hands on her shoulders and guided her back. Just because she wasn't thinking about jumping didn't mean she wouldn't slip and fall. "Why don't you come over here and sit down?" He led her to a boulder. The angle wasn't perfect for sitting, but it did well enough, and there weren't any bugs on it. "Are you hurt anywhere else?"

She shook her head.

Brian crouched in front of her and ran his hands down her legs. She had a collection of scratches and scrapes, but nothing too serious. Her arms had another collection, and there was a nasty slash across her cheek. Her eyes were swollen and red.

"I'm sorry," she whimpered.

"So am I." He gathered her hands into his and kissed her scraped knuckles. "I'm sorry about what I said before. I was just pissed you'd think about going back to him at all."

"I didn't know what to do. You and Jason were fighting." She blinked.

"I've been fighting with Jason since before you were born. Jason likes things to stay the same, and he doesn't like to be wrong. Don't you worry about a few cross words. Those fly around all the time." Brian smoothed his palms down her thighs.

"Does it bother you that I'm fifteen years younger than you?"

Brian frowned. "Why would it?"

"Jason said something about it this morning, and you said something the other day." Suzi licked her lips. "And isn't it a little bit of a cliche? The May-December romance."

"Suzi, that's every man's fantasy." He sat back on his heels, pulling her into his lap. "Every man in the world would envy me for having a hot, talented, wonderful girlfriend. Besides, like you said, you're very mature, and I'm immature, so we meet in the middle."

A little smile lifted the corners of her lips.

She did look awful. Dirty, scratched, frightened, and confused. She might be more mature than he was, but sometimes he had to be stronger. "Suzi, I love you. I want to take care of you. Marry me."

Suzi jerked back, and if he hadn't had a sure grip on her, she would have banged into the rocks behind her. "What?"

He ran his fingers through her wet hair. "I love you. You seem to love me. You know my kids, and you love them. They love you."

"You love your kids. Your kids love you," Suzi joked.

"Exactly. We can all be one big happy family."

"You're serious."

"Absolutely serious."

She leaned her head on his shoulder. "You want to take care of me," she whispered.

"Yes, I do."

She wasn't going to answer. The proposal took her too much by surprise. Next time he'd have to do it over a candlelit dinner with the ring in his pocket. "We'll have to get you out of here. I think up is going to be better than down this time. With a hurt wrist, you won't be able to get down the waterfall."

"Everything with Logan always felt like foreplay." She sat up. "Every glance, every touch, every breath was seduction."

Brian studied her eyes, trying to decide if she *had* hit her head. She was staring at him as if she'd never seen him before. The intensity of her gaze unnerved him.

"You were always more concerned with my wellbeing. You even got mad at me for thinking about going back to Logan because he would hurt me."

Brian shifted his grip on her so she didn't slide off his lap and into the boulder. Logan said she'd gone crazy. "I don't want to see you hurt, Suzi."

"And you want to marry me."

"Yes, I do." He should have known after reading her books all these years that she wasn't going to go from point A to point B in a straight line.

"Your divorce dragged on for ages."

"I wasn't planning on divorcing again. Once was enough."

She nodded. "I want to marry you, too."

"You do?"

"Yep." She grinned and nodded.

"Well, hallelujah. Now let's get out of here. The rocks are digging into my legs."

Epilogue

Suzi rearranged the mail on the hall table as an excuse to peek out the window, watching for Brian's car.

"Dad'll be home any second. Just go sit down already," Tess said. "It's not like he's going to hide from you."

"I know, but I want to know what Tessa tells him so we'll know if we can move ahead."

"Then why didn't you go with him?"

Suzi bit her lip.

"Oh, right. Morning sickness." Tess rolled her eyes. "I am never having kids if that's what you've got to go through. I'll do what Candy did and adopt a couple from China or something."

"You're sure you're okay with all this?" Their first logical step in changing the custody agreement with Bonnie was to ask the kids what they wanted. They were excited by the idea of a new sibling and living with their dad so if Tessa agreed, then it was off to Brian's divorce lawyer.

"Totally. What's not to be okay with?"

Hmm, moving in with their dad and his new wife and getting a brand new half sibling at the same time. Nothing to not be okay with there. "I'm just making sure."

"You worry too much. Dad's here."

Suzi turned to the window, and sure enough, Brian's car was pulling up the drive. She ran to the door and met him as he drove into the garage. Why did she still get so excited to see him? Back when they were friends, she smothered her eagerness because she shouldn't have been so happy to see a man who wasn't her boyfriend. Then when they first got together, she let herself be excited because he was excited, too. Now, over a year since they got together and after a lavish wedding and a wonderful family honeymoon, she still couldn't wait to throw her arms around him. "Well?"

"I talked to Tessa. She said we should look into getting you legal guardianship for Tess and Bri, and I need to consult with my divorce lawyer about support. Tessa thinks Bonnie would be happier with a onetime settlement. That'll make things tight for a while, but then it'll all be over except for visitations."

Suzi threw her arms around his shoulders. "Truly?"

"Yup, you and me and Tess and Bri and baby makes five." He lifted her off the floor, nuzzling her neck. "It's going to be just like we planned."

"Finally."

"I did have to tell her."

"Oh, Brian! I didn't want anybody to know." Suzi clenched her teeth. Now, if she lost the baby, she was going to get pitying looks from Tessa.

"It's only Tessa, and she guessed, so I had to tell her." Brian stroked her hair. "Just relax. I'm gonna take care of you. Everything will be fine."

Suzi squeezed her eyes closed and nodded. "I know."

Brian set her back on the floor. "I saw your buddy at the office."

"My buddy?"

"Brett Cherney."

"Brett? What was he doing there?"

"Dunno. He's either dating or not dating Tessa, depending on whose story you believe."

"What do you mean?" Suzi allowed Brian to guide her into the house. Candy had emailed her during the honeymoon to say that Tessa, Jody, Logan, and Brett all disappeared very early from the reception, but no one knew where any of them went. No surprise that Logan had left early. He'd only shown up to prove that he was growing as a person. At least he was still trying. "What happened?"

"I was talking to Tessa in her office with the door closed, and when I went to leave, Brett was standing outside all pissed off."

"I thought he was out in WVA with Jason."

"He's home getting his ears back in tune, and he told me he'd stopped by to see what Tessa was doing over the weekend."

"The weekend?"

"I thought he said weekend. Why? Is that important?"

Suzi groaned. "Men. What happened?"

"I asked if they were dating. He said yes, but she said no, and she looked pissed that he was at the office, too."

"What happened then?"

Brian dropped onto the couch, pulling Suzi into his lap. "I got the hell outta Dodge, that's what happened. I'm not stupid."

"She's not going to tell Brett about…you know."

"The baby?"

Suzi leaned her head on his shoulder. So sensitive. So intelligent. And at the same time such a dolt. A darling dolt.

"She won't say anything. Don't sweat it." Brian massaged the small of her back. "Everything will be fine, babe. I promise."

"Don't make promises you can't keep."

"I keep all my promises. Even the ones I make in my sleep."

Suzi let whatever tension remained in her to drain out. He would, and he did, and everything would be fine.

"Suzi, your phone is ringing!" Tess shouted.

"My phone is ringing." Suzi dragged herself off Brian's lap. "Where is my phone?"

"You lost it again?" Brian stood up. "I'm going to hang the damn thing from a lanyard around your neck."

"Has anybody seen my phone?" Suzi shouted up the stairs.

"No!" Tess shouted back.

No answer from Bri. Big surprise. Her phone chimed again. She had one more round before it stopped. Maybe she should let it go and catch it later.

Brian sifted through the newspaper on the coffee table. "Not here."

Suzi found her purse on the bottom of the stairs, but it wasn't making enough noise, and the ringing had stopped.

Bub shuffled into the living room and held out her phone that was playing the voicemail tune.

"Thanks, Bub. Where was it?"

"Kitchen counter." He shuffled out again.

"Where does he get the talkativeness from? You or Bonnie?"

Brian shrugged. "He's gearing up for his teens."

"He's got a couple of years to gear yet." Suzi navigated into her messages.

"Hey Suzi, it's Brett. I heard you were back in town, and I'm around, too. I wondered if you wanted to get together for lunch or something. If you have time. Anyway, give me a call. Bye."

"Aw, it was Brett. He sounds upset."

"No saving the world."

"I'm not saving the world. Just Brett." She hit the button to dial him back.

"Yeah."

"Brett! Hi, you just called, and by the time I found the phone, it had sent you to voicemail. Then it started playing that awful voicemail song. Bleh. So, you wanted to get together for lunch?"

"If you have time. I just happened to be in town."

Just happened to be in town. The Brett of a year and half ago would have been in town for fifteen minutes before he had a party going. She frowned at Brian who shook his head. "Brian said he bumped into you at the Touchstone offices."

"Yeah, I kinda wanted to talk to you about that. On the Q.T."

On the Q.T. Interestinger and interestinger. "Anything for you. I'm expecting a ton of work to hit me in about three days so it's got to be before then."

"Tomorrow?"

"Hang on, let me make sure Brian doesn't have plans for us." She pressed her thumb over the receiver. "Brett wants to have lunch with me tomorrow. That okay with you?"

"Like I could stop you."

"You make me sound like I run off on you all the time."

"No, you just dive into the bushes."

Suzi stuck out her tongue, and Brian grinned. "It's okay with you then?"

"Tell him he has to bring you back in the condition he borrowed you in." Brian smoothed his hand over her still flat belly, causing a warm flutter.

"Not a problem. I'm yours for the day, but Brian says you have to bring me back in the condition you borrowed me in."

"I will. I'll pick you up at noon."

"You're gonna get up early for me? I'm honored. You know where the house is?"

"Sure. Wear something pretty for me," he told her.

"Always. See ya tomorrow."

"I can't believe it. Just back from the honeymoon yesterday, and she's already running around with other men."

Suzi dropped her phone on the table so she could run her hands up her arms. He had great arms. So strong and flexible and supportive. "You know I'll come back."

"And why is that?"

Suzi rose up on her toes. "You want me to show you, we're going to have to go somewhere a little more private. We don't want to warp your kids anymore than they already are."

"Too late. Totally disgusted," Tess said from the stairs. "Seriously, I am doing what Candy did and adopting a couple of kids from Africa."

"China," Brian said.

"Maybe I'll adopt more than two." Tess put her hand on her hip.

"Take your time. I'm not ready to be a grandmother yet."

"Speaking of grandmothers," Brian said. "Did you call your mom?"

"My mom?" Suzi squirmed. Brian had insisted on meeting her parents before the wedding and on them being at the ceremony. Her father wasn't too sure about her choice of husband, but he had given her away. Her mother hadn't figured out how to transition from fan to mother-in-law yet.

"You don't want her finding out she's going to be a grandmother because there's a story on *Inside Edition*. Besides, you might want her help with the baby, and with the step-kids."

Suzi leaned her head on Brian's chest. Was she ready to be a mom? If she wasn't, Brian would be there to back her up. And wasn't that the best feeling?

Meet the Author

Christa Maurice has been obsessed with rock stars from early childhood when her older brother started randomly quizzing her on rock trivia. How many first graders knew who the headliners were on the Black and Blue Tour? Christa did. (Black Sabbath and Blue Oyster Cult.) When not listening to music and/or writing, she enjoys traveling, reading and science fiction. Let Me Be The One is the fourth book in her Drawn to the Rhythm Romance series. Readers can find Christa on Facebook or visit her website at christamaurice.wordpress.com.

Be sure not to miss Christa Maurice's Book 1 of the Arden FD series

Three Alarm Tenant

Three Alarm Tenant by Christa Maurice
Arden FD #1

Katherine lost one hero in the line of duty—can she risk loving another?

Katherine Pelham's fiancé was a police officer, shot and killed during a robbery. Left with a house she can't afford, she must rent out the first floor to solve her money woes. Before she can finishing putting up the For Rent sign, along comes a man who seems interested in more than just the apartment.

Fireman Jack Connelly is in a bind: he's rescued a dog, and his lease doesn't allow pets. The new apartment would be great. The new landlady, even better…

Three Alarm Tenant available now in digital and print.

Learn more about Christa at
http://www.kensingtonbooks.com/author.aspx/29516

Chapter 1

Katherine Pelham hefted the hammer and pounded the For Rent sign into the frozen ground.

"Happy Val-En-Tine's Day," she emphasized each syllable with a thwack. A truck slowed on the street, but she resisted the urge to look. She'd probably smash her thumb. Already this morning, she'd stubbed her toe, spilled hot coffee, and ripped a hole in her skirt getting it out of the dryer. Going back to bed sounded ideal.

She stepped back to admire her handiwork. The sign wasn't crooked and the post hadn't snapped. The perverse Ohio weather that transformed her yard to concrete had warmed the air until she only needed a sweatshirt. With the apartment done, she needed a reliable tenant. Then she could handle the mortgage, the credit cards and her leftover college loans. She started toward the front door and stopped. It wasn't her door anymore. Her apartment opened from the side.

The servants' entrance.

Oh, she could have taken the first floor, but it still would be half the house. And the half closer to the basement spiders. She walked around the side and up her new steps. As she reached for the door, a car pulled into the drive.

A truck actually. A green pick-up. A tall, broad-shouldered man climbed out. He looked as if he'd stepped out of an action adventure movie.

"Hi. You have a place for rent?"

His warm tenor voice worked its way through her ears and made straight for other parts of her body. She nodded.

"Do you take pets?"

"What kind of pets?" she asked.

"A dog."

A dog. She'd never had a dog and envied people who did. When other girls wanted ponies, she'd wanted a puppy. How wonderful would it be to have a dog romping in the back yard? How wonderful would it be to have this gorgeous man romping in the backyard with the dog? "What kind?"

"A big mutt." He held his hand two feet above the ground. Katherine wondered if that meant head height or shoulder height. Either one wasn't bad. Plenty to play with.

"Sure."

"How much is it?"

"Six hundred." Everybody said it was too low, but it sounded high to her. It covered the mortgage payment, freeing up her paycheck for other non-essentials like food.

"Plus utilities?"

She shook her head. "I cover utilities, but I control the thermostat."

He nodded. "What's the deposit?"

"One month's rent."

"And the pet deposit?"

Katherine bit her lip. Should she charge extra for pets? How much damage could it do? She supposed that depended on the animal, but the landlord book hadn't mentioned that, and she didn't want to take advantage. "Even for the dog."

He blinked. "Wow. Can I see the place?"

"Now?" Katherine's mind reeled. She'd just hammered the sign in the yard. She hadn't even put a notice in the paper yet. Everyone warned her it might take a month or, God forbid two, before anyone answered her ad. The book said she might show it dozens of times before an acceptable tenant came along. She'd braced herself to show the apartment until summer. This could be another annoyance in an already bad day, or a sign her luck was turning.

"If you've got time," he added.

"Of course." She walked back down the steps and tried to get a better look at him. Did he look crazy? No, he looked nice. Tall, well-proportioned, dark blond hair. His expression seemed to settle into bright-eyed amusement, as if life entertained him. He filled out his blue fleece jacket nicely. She caught her breath as she stepped past him to the door, wanting to run her hands over his fleece to see how soft and warm it was. What had gotten hold of her? His height? She didn't know many adult men anymore. Most of the males in her life were high school boys, or high school janitors who acted like juveniles.

"My name is Jack. Jack Conley," he announced, holding out his hand.

She caught his gaze sweeping up her body. He was checking her out. For a split second it annoyed her, but pleasure swamped that reaction.

She waited until his eyes met hers before shaking his hand. His eyes were extraordinary. Golden brown and smiling even when his face was serious. He had a good grip, firm, not crushing. His touch spread a liquid shiver up her arm.

"Katherine Pelham. Pleased to meet you," she said, struggling to keep the tremor out of her voice.

"Pleased to meet you, too." He raised one eyebrow.

She unlocked the front door. The foyer still looked strange with the stairs blocked off. It seemed cramped even though she'd painted the walls a pale tan to make it appear larger.

"The back door lets into the yard. This is the foyer, and there's the living room." She gestured through the archway as he pushed the door closed. She jumped away at the soft click. Her nerves hummed, but the sensation wasn't unpleasant, which confused her more.

"What?" he asked. His hand rested on the doorknob.

"Nothing." She stared at his hand. His fingers were long, graceful and ringless. She forced herself to meet his eyes.

He searched her face—his lips tightening to the closest thing she'd seen to a frown on him. "So. This is the foyer?"

Katherine forced herself to take a deep breath. She was acting like a fool. She couldn't deny a certain sense of tension around him, but it didn't feel like the tension of a scary situation. More like a warm ache she remembered feeling once or twice, a long time ago.

"It could be anything you want. It was the foyer before we divided the house. Through here is the kitchen." She started down the hall, pointing to another door. "This leads to the basement. This is the bathroom." She pushed open the bathroom door. "The shower's behind the door. It's very small."

He crowded behind her to peer into the narrow bathroom, which she'd painted mint green to brighten the windowless space.

Katherine found herself leaning toward him rather than away. He smelled good. His firm jaw came to the top of her head.

And he was looking down at her with those amused eyes.

She frowned, but didn't move. "It's very small," she repeated.

"It's fine."

She fled to the kitchen and waited for him, swearing she would gain control over this interview right now.

"This is the kitchen. The bathroom used to be part of the kitchen, so it was much larger. There's plenty of room in the nook for a table, but the floor gets cold in the wintertime. I don't think there's any insulation under there."

She'd loved the big kitchen when they bought the house. She considered it the heart of the house. Now it was the smallest room because she'd had to carve out space for the bathroom. "Through this door is—was, the dining room. I suppose it would make a wonderful bedroom." She blushed at the image of this room as a bedroom with him in it. She was developing some sort of obsession. Too many nights with a book and a bowl of soup. Nothing to do with the way he looked at her. Or the way she hoped he looked at her. She pushed open a door and stepped through it.

Jack crossed the room and peered at the inset china cabinet. He ran his finger along the dark mullion windows, studying the uneven glass. "Is this original?"

"As far as I know. The house was built in nineteen thirteen, and it was very fashionable back then to have built-in cabinets." Katherine tried to pull herself together. First time in a long time around an attractive man, and she started babbling like a schoolgirl in a chance encounter with the captain of the football team. So what if he was handsome? So what if she could almost feel his strong hands gliding down her spine?

She clenched her teeth and walked out of the dining room, acutely aware of him behind her. "There's another little room back here. We used it for storage. It's not insulated. Anything you put back here has to be able to take huge temperature fluctuations." She tugged open the French door leading to the storeroom. It popped open and she stepped through. "That's the back door. You could put in a doggie door, then your dog could get out if he needed to."

"Archer would like that."

Katherine found herself trapped between Jack and the door, struggling with the bolt. Blood rushed in her ears, and she couldn't remember when she'd last taken a decent breath. She seized the doorknob and yanked.

The door burst open. She stumbled backward. For an eternal moment, Jack's arms wrapped around her shoulders. Heat rushed to her face as she felt his hard chest through his coat. She wanted to sink into his embrace and stay there.

"Sticky door," he said, setting her on her feet. His hand trailed up her arm.

Katherine tried not to sound like a breathless fool. "It's worse in the summer when the wood swells." She pushed through the storm door and took a large step away to gain some room. Unfortunately, two feet of porch wasn't enough to slow her pulse or clear her mind. "This is the backyard. It's fenced and it goes all the way back to the alley." She pointed to the tree line.

"Big yard."

"We loved it when we bought the house, but we never got around to working on it. Our neighbor has a beautiful lawn. I have moss. Feel free to look around." She hurried inside and perched on what remained of the stairs.

Not long ago, these two steps had led to a landing and another nine steps to the upstairs. Now they led to a wall. On the other side was her front door, amputating her new home from what she'd always considered its heart. The symbolism was ironic. Katherine leaned back, trying not to think of Jack Conley, who she could hear walking around the kitchen and dining room.

It would be nice to have a tenant by the first of the month and to have a guy with a dog living downstairs for security purposes. That the potential tenant was gorgeous and that she'd been alone too long had nothing to do with the choice. This was business.

"Mrs. Pelham?"

Katherine looked up. He was admiring her legs. A giggle gathered in her throat. She stood, commanding those legs to hold her. "Ms."

His eyes swept up her body again. Low heat developed in her belly. "Ms. Pelham, then. It's a great place. Do you have an application?"

"Oh yes. Give me a minute, and I'll get it." She spun around to dart upstairs, checking herself before she ran into the wall. This chopped-up house would take getting used to. "I'll be back."

Katherine slowed to a walk as she stepped off the porch steps. Why was she running? It was business. Just because he looked at her like a woman and not like a teacher, or a friend, or a conquest didn't mean anything. She walked to her door and opened it. The applications lay on the steps. Without the wall, she could have handed him one through the banister. She heard Jack walking around, but knew she wouldn't be able to hear him upstairs. If she wanted to spy, she'd to have to sit at the bottom of the stairs. Or position herself at one of the heat vents.

Katherine shook her head. Why was she thinking of spying on her tenant? She didn't even have a tenant yet. She picked up one application, took a deep breath and went back around the house to the first floor. He waited in the foyer studying the cracks in the ceiling.

"Here you are," she said. "Drop it off in my mail box anytime."

"Thanks." Jack folded the paper and slipped it into his coat pocket. "You live upstairs?"

"Yes."

He nodded. "I'll have this back today."

"In a big hurry to move?" Katherine tensed.

"It's Archer. I just got him, and I can't have pets at my apartment. My landlord wants him out by the end of the month."

"I see. Well, you can drop the application off in the mailbox whenever."

"Thanks." He held out his hand. "Nice meeting you."

"Nice meeting you, too." She kept her composure when his hand enveloped hers, but it wasn't easy. "Good-bye."

He grinned. "See ya."

Katherine locked the front door as he backed his truck out of the drive. She'd forgotten to tell him about the garage and the basement, but it hadn't gone too badly. Chances were excellent he wouldn't bring the application back, and if he did, that he wouldn't be a good tenant. The book specifically discussed researching prospective tenants. Once they moved in, getting them out was impossible. She suspected evicting Mr. Conley would be the least of her troubles.

Living in half the house felt strange. Back in her own apartment, she turned toward her kitchen at the top of the stairs. This had been a four-bedroom house. Now, one was her bedroom, another her living room and the third room was her kitchen. Only her office stayed the same in the fourth bedroom. Her office didn't have bad memories attached to it, so she hadn't changed it.

She wandered back into the hall and studied the pictures on the wall. She didn't know why she hadn't taken them down. Photos of her 'happy' life with a hero. Getting engaged, college graduation, buying a home on a police force mortgage assistance program. All quite dandy until Gary was killed, leaving her with a mortgage she couldn't afford on her teacher's salary. And all Gary's cop buddies lost interest in his not-quite-widow. Four years later, she only rated an occasional drive by.

That mistake she wouldn't make again. The next time she married, if she married, she refused to marry a hero.